T0165970

The Adventures of Sally

The Adventures of Sally

P.G. Wodehouse

MINT EDITIONS

The Adventures of Sally was first published in 1923.

This edition published by Mint Editions 2021.

ISBN 9781513270739 | E-ISBN 9781513275734

Published by Mint Editions®

 MINT
EDITIONS

minteditionbooks.com

Publishing Director: Jennifer Newens
Design & Production: Rachel Lopez Metzger
Typesetting: Westchester Publishing Services

Contents

I

SALLY GIVES A PARTY

1

SALLY LOOKED CONTENTEDLY DOWN THE long table. She felt happy at last. Everybody was talking and laughing now, and her party, rallying after an uncertain start, was plainly the success she had hoped it would be. The first atmosphere of uncomfortable restraint, caused, she was only too well aware, by her brother Fillmore's white evening waistcoat, had worn off; and the male and female patrons of Mrs. Meecher's select boarding-house (transient and residential) were themselves again.

At her end of the table the conversation had turned once more to the great vital topic of Sally's legacy and what she ought to do with it. The next best thing to having money of one's own, is to dictate the spending of somebody else's, and Sally's guests were finding a good deal of satisfaction in arranging a Budget for her. Rumour having put the sum at their disposal at a high figure, their suggestions had certain spaciousness.

"Let me tell you," said Augustus Bartlett, briskly, "what I'd do, if I were you." Augustus Bartlett, who occupied an intensely subordinate position in the firm of Kahn, Morris and Brown, the Wall Street brokers, always affected a brisk, incisive style of speech, as befitted a man in close touch with the great ones of Finance. "I'd sink a couple of hundred thousand in some good, safe bond-issue—we've just put one out which you would do well to consider—and play about with the rest. When I say play about, I mean have a flutter in anything good that crops up. Multiple Steel's worth looking at. They tell me it'll be up to a hundred and fifty before next Saturday."

Elsa Doland, the pretty girl with the big eyes who sat on Mr. Bartlett's left, had other views.

"Buy a theatre, Sally, and put on good stuff."

"And lose every bean you've got," said a mild young man, with a deep voice across the table. "If I had a few hundred thousand," said the mild young man, "I'd put every cent of it on Benny Whistler for the heavyweight championship. I've private information that Battling Tuke has been got at and means to lie down in the seventh. . ."

"Say, listen," interrupted another voice, "lemme tell you what I'd do with four hundred thousand. . ."

"If I had four hundred thousand," said Elsa Doland, "I know what would be the first thing I'd do."

"What's that?" asked Sally.

"Pay my bill for last week, due this morning."

Sally got up quickly, and flitting down the table, put her arm round her friend's shoulder and whispered in her ear:

"Elsa darling, are you really broke? If you are, you know, I'll. . ."

Elsa Doland laughed.

"You're an angel, Sally. There's no one like you. You'd give your last cent to anyone. Of course I'm not broke. I've just come back from the road, and I've saved a fortune. I only said that to draw you."

Sally returned to her seat, relieved, and found that the company had now divided itself into two schools of thought. The conservative and prudent element, led by Augustus Bartlett, had definitely decided on three hundred thousand in Liberty Bonds and the rest in some safe real estate; while the smaller, more sporting section, impressed by the mild young man's inside information, had already placed Sally's money on Benny Whistler, doling it out cautiously in small sums so as not to spoil the market. And so solid, it seemed, was Mr. Tuke's reputation with those in the inner circle of knowledge that the mild young man was confident that, if you went about the matter cannily and without precipitation, three to one might be obtained. It seemed to Sally that the time had come to correct certain misapprehensions.

"I don't know where you get your figures," she said, "but I'm afraid they're wrong. I've just twenty-five thousand dollars."

The statement had a chilling effect. To these jugglers with half-millions the amount mentioned seemed for the moment almost too small to bother about. It was the sort of sum which they had been mentally setting aside for the heiress's car fare. Then they managed to adjust their minds to it. After all, one could do something even with a pittance like twenty-five thousand.

"If I'd twenty-five thousand," said Augustus Bartlett, the first to rally from the shock, "I'd buy Amalgamated. . ."

"If I had twenty-five thousand. . ." began Elsa Doland.

"If I'd had twenty-five thousand in the year nineteen hundred," observed a gloomy-looking man with spectacles, "I could have started a revolution in Paraguay."

P.G. WODEHOUSE

He brooded sombrely on what might have been.

"Well, I'll tell you exactly what I'm going to do," said Sally. "I'm going to start with a trip to Europe. . . France, specially. I've heard France well spoken of—as soon as I can get my passport; and after I've loafed there for a few weeks, I'm coming back to look about and find some nice cosy little business which will let me put money into it and keep me in luxury. Are there any complaints?"

"Even a couple of thousand on Benny Whistler. . ." said the mild young man.

"I don't want your Benny Whistler," said Sally. "I wouldn't have him if you gave him to me. If I want to lose money, I'll go to Monte Carlo and do it properly."

"Monte Carlo," said the gloomy man, brightening up at the magic name. "I was in Monte Carlo in the year '97, and if I'd had another fifty dollars. . . just fifty. . . I'd have. . ."

At the far end of the table there was a stir, a cough, and the grating of a chair on the floor; and slowly, with that easy grace which actors of the old school learned in the days when acting was acting, Mr. Maxwell Faucitt, the boarding-house's oldest inhabitant, rose to his feet.

"Ladies," said Mr. Faucitt, bowing courteously, "and. . ." ceasing to bow and casting from beneath his white and venerable eyebrows a quelling glance at certain male members of the boarding-house's younger set who were showing a disposition towards restiveness, ". . . gentlemen. I feel that I cannot allow this occasion to pass without saying a few words."

His audience did not seem surprised. It was possible that life, always prolific of incident in a great city like New York, might some day produce an occasion which Mr. Faucitt would feel that he could allow to pass without saying a few words; but nothing of the sort had happened as yet, and they had given up hope. Right from the start of the meal they had felt that it would be optimism run mad to expect the old gentleman to abstain from speech on the night of Sally Nicholas' farewell dinner party; and partly because they had braced themselves to it, but principally because Miss Nicholas' hospitality had left them with a genial feeling of repletion, they settled themselves to listen with something resembling equanimity. A movement on the part of the Marvellous Murphys—new arrivals, who had been playing the Bushwick with their equilibristic act during the preceding week—to form a party of the extreme left and heckle the speaker, broke down under a cold look from their hostess.

Brief though their acquaintance had been, both of these lissom young gentlemen admired Sally immensely.

And it should be set on record that this admiration of theirs was not misplaced. He would have been hard to please who had not been attracted by Sally. She was a small, trim, wisp of a girl with the tiniest hands and feet, the friendliest of smiles, and a dimple that came and went in the curve of her rounded chin. Her eyes, which disappeared when she laughed, which was often, were a bright hazel; her hair a soft mass of brown. She had, moreover, a manner, an air of distinction lacking in the majority of Mrs. Meecher's guests. And she carried youth like a banner. In approving of Sally, the Marvellous Murphys had been guilty of no lapse from their high critical standard.

"I have been asked," proceeded Mr. Faucitt, "though I am aware that there are others here far worthier of such a task—Brutuses compared with whom I, like Marc Antony, am no orator—I have been asked to propose the health. . ."

"Who asked you?" It was the smaller of the Marvellous Murphys who spoke. He was an unpleasant youth, snub-nosed and spotty. Still, he could balance himself with one hand on an inverted ginger-ale bottle while revolving a barrel on the soles of his feet. There is good in all of us.

"I have been asked," repeated Mr. Faucitt, ignoring the unmannerly interruption, which, indeed, he would have found it hard to answer, "to propose the health of our charming hostess (applause), coupled with the name of her brother, our old friend Fillmore Nicholas."

The gentleman referred to, who sat at the speaker's end of the table, acknowledged the tribute with a brief nod of the head. It was a nod of condescension; the nod of one who, conscious of being hedged about by social inferiors, nevertheless does his best to be not unkindly. And Sally, seeing it, debated in her mind for an instant the advisability of throwing an orange at her brother. There was one lying ready to her hand, and his glistening shirt-front offered an admirable mark; but she restrained herself. After all, if a hostess yields to her primitive impulses, what happens? Chaos. She had just frowned down the exuberance of the rebellious Murphys, and she felt that if, even with the highest motives, she began throwing fruit, her influence for good in that quarter would be weakened.

She leaned back with a sigh. The temptation had been hard to resist. A democratic girl, pomposity was a quality which she thoroughly disliked; and though she loved him, she could not disguise from herself that, ever since affluence had descended upon him some months ago, her brother Fillmore had become insufferably pompous. If there are any young men whom inherited wealth improves, Fillmore Nicholas was not one of them. He seemed to regard himself nowadays as a sort of Man of Destiny. To converse with him was for the ordinary human being like being received in audience by some more than stand-offish monarch. It had taken Sally over an hour to persuade him to leave his apartment on Riverside Drive and revisit the boarding-house for this special occasion; and, when he had come, he had entered wearing such faultless evening dress that he had made the rest of the party look like a gathering of tramp-cyclists. His white waistcoat alone was a silent reproach to honest poverty, and had caused an awkward constraint right through the soup and fish courses. Most of those present had known Fillmore Nicholas as an impecunious young man who could make a tweed suit last longer than one would have believed possible; they had called him "Fill" and helped him in more than usually lean times with small loans: but to-night they had eyed the waistcoat dumbly and shrank back abashed.

"Speaking," said Mr. Faucitt, "as an Englishman—for though I have long since taken out what are technically known as my 'papers' it was as a subject of the island kingdom that I first visited this great country—I may say that the two factors in American life which have always made the profoundest impression upon me have been the lavishness of American hospitality and the charm of the American girl. To-night we have been privileged to witness the American girl in the capacity of hostess, and I think I am right in saying, in asseverating, in committing myself to the statement that this has been a night which none of us present here will ever forget. Miss Nicholas has given us, ladies and gentlemen, a banquet. I repeat, a banquet. There has been alcoholic refreshment. I do not know where it came from: I do not ask how it was procured, but we have had it. Miss Nicholas. . ."

Mr. Faucitt paused to puff at his cigar. Sally's brother Fillmore suppressed a yawn and glanced at his watch. Sally continued to lean forward raptly. She knew how happy it made the old gentleman to deliver a formal speech; and though she wished the subject had been different, she was prepared to listen indefinitely.

"Miss Nicholas," resumed Mr. Faucitt, lowering his cigar, ". . . But why," he demanded abruptly, "do I call her Miss Nicholas?"

"Because it's her name," hazarded the taller Murphy.

Mr. Faucitt eyed him with disfavour. He disapproved of the marvellous brethren on general grounds because, himself a resident of years standing, he considered that these transients from the vaudeville stage lowered the tone of the boarding-house; but particularly because the one who had just spoken had, on his first evening in the place, addressed him as "grandpa."

"Yes, sir," he said severely, "it is her name. But she has another name, sweeter to those who love her, those who worship her, those who have watched her with the eye of sedulous affection through the three years she has spent beneath this roof, though that name," said Mr. Faucitt, lowering the tone of his address and descending to what might almost be termed personalities, "may not be familiar to a couple of dud acrobats who have only been in the place a week-end, thank heaven, and are off to-morrow to infest some other city. That name," said Mr. Faucitt, soaring once more to a loftier plane, "is Sally. Our Sally. For three years our Sally has flitted about this establishment like—I choose the simile advisedly—like a ray of sunshine. For three years she has made life for us a brighter, sweeter thing. And now a sudden access of worldly wealth, happily synchronizing with her twenty-first birthday, is to remove her from our midst. From our midst, ladies and gentlemen, but not from our hearts. And I think I may venture to hope, to prognosticate, that, whatever lofty sphere she may adorn in the future, to whatever heights in the social world she may soar, she will still continue to hold a corner in her own golden heart for the comrades of her Bohemian days. Ladies and gentlemen, I give you our hostess, Miss Sally Nicholas, coupled with the name of our old friend, her brother Fillmore."

Sally, watching her brother heave himself to his feet as the cheers died away, felt her heart beat a little faster with anticipation. Fillmore was a fluent young man, once a power in his college debating society, and it was for that reason that she had insisted on his coming here tonight.

She had guessed that Mr. Faucitt, the old dear, would say all sorts of delightful things about her, and she had mistrusted her ability to make a fitting reply. And it was imperative that a fitting reply should proceed from someone. She knew Mr. Faucitt so well. He looked on these occasions rather in the light of scenes from some play; and, sustaining his own part in them with such polished grace, was certain to be pained by anything in the nature of an anti-climax after he should have ceased to take the stage. Eloquent himself, he must be answered with eloquence, or his whole evening would be spoiled.

Fillmore Nicholas smoothed a wrinkle out of his white waistcoat; and having rested one podgy hand on the table-cloth and the thumb of the other in his pocket, glanced down the table with eyes so haughtily drooping that Sally's fingers closed automatically about her orange, as she wondered whether even now it might not be a good thing. . .

It seems to be one of Nature's laws that the most attractive girls should have the least attractive brothers. Fillmore Nicholas had not worn well. At the age of seven he had been an extraordinarily beautiful child, but after that he had gone all to pieces; and now, at the age of twenty-five, it would be idle to deny that he was something of a mess. For the three years preceding his twenty-fifth birthday, restricted means and hard work had kept his figure in check; but with money there had come an ever-increasing sleekness. He looked as if he fed too often and too well.

All this, however, Sally was prepared to forgive him, if he would only make a good speech. She could see Mr. Faucitt leaning back in his chair, all courteous attention. Rolling periods were meat and drink to the old gentleman.

Fillmore spoke.

"I'm sure," said Fillmore, "you don't want a speech. . . Very good of you to drink our health. Thank you."

He sat down.

The effect of these few simple words on the company was marked, but not in every case identical. To the majority the emotion which they brought was one of unmixed relief. There had been something so menacing, so easy and practised, in Fillmore's attitude as he had stood there that the gloomier-minded had given him at least twenty minutes, and even the optimists had reckoned that they would be lucky if they got off with ten. As far as the bulk of the guests were concerned, there was no grumbling. Fillmore's, to their thinking, had been the ideal after-dinner speech.

Far different was it with Mr. Maxwell Faucitt. The poor old man was wearing such an expression of surprise and dismay as he might have worn had somebody unexpectedly pulled the chair from under him. He was feeling the sick shock which comes to those who tread on a non-existent last stair. And Sally, catching sight of his face, uttered a sharp wordless exclamation as if she had seen a child fall down and hurt itself in the street. The next moment she had run round the table and was standing behind him with her arms round his neck. She spoke across him with a sob in her voice.

"My brother," she stammered, directing a malevolent look at the immaculate Fillmore, who, avoiding her gaze, glanced down his nose and smoothed another wrinkle out of his waistcoat, "has not said quite— quite all I hoped he was going to say. I can't make a speech, but. . ." Sally gulped, ". . . but, I love you all and of course I shall never forget you, and. . . and. . ."

Here Sally kissed Mr. Faucitt and burst into tears.

"There, there," said Mr. Faucitt, soothingly. The kindest critic could not have claimed that Sally had been eloquent: nevertheless Mr. Maxwell Faucitt was conscious of no sense of anti-climax.

2

SALLY HAD JUST FINISHED TELLING her brother Fillmore what a pig he was. The lecture had taken place in the street outside the boarding-house immediately on the conclusion of the festivities, when Fillmore, who had furtively collected his hat and overcoat, had stolen forth into the night, had been overtaken and brought to bay by his justly indignant sister. Her remarks, punctuated at intervals by bleating sounds from the accused, had lasted some ten minutes.

As she paused for breath, Fillmore seemed to expand, like an indiarubber ball which has been sat on. Dignified as he was to the world, he had never been able to prevent himself being intimidated by Sally when in one of these moods of hers. He regretted this, for it hurt his self-esteem, but he did not see how the fact could be altered. Sally had always been like that. Even the uncle, who after the deaths of their parents had become their guardian, had never, though a grim man, been able to cope successfully with Sally. In that last hectic scene three years ago, which had ended in their going out into the world, together like a second Adam and Eve, the verbal victory had been hers. And it had been Sally who had achieved triumph in the one battle which Mrs. Meecher, apparently as a matter of duty, always brought about with each of her patrons in the first week of their stay. A sweet-tempered girl, Sally, like most women of a generous spirit, had cyclonic potentialities.

As she seemed to have said her say, Fillmore kept on expanding till he had reached the normal, when he ventured upon a speech for the defence.

"What have I done?" demanded Fillmore plaintively.

"Do you want to hear all over again?"

"No, no," said Fillmore hastily. "But, listen, Sally, you don't understand my position. You don't seem to realize that all that sort of thing, all that boarding-house stuff, is a thing of the past. One's got beyond it. One wants to drop it. One wants to forget it, darn it! Be fair. Look at it from my viewpoint. I'm going to be a big man. . ."

"You're going to be a fat man," said Sally, coldly.

Fillmore refrained from discussing the point. He was sensitive.

"I'm going to do big things," he substituted. "I've got a deal on at this very moment which. . . well, I can't tell you about it, but it's going to be big. Well, what I'm driving at, is about all this sort of thing"—he indicated the lighted front of Mrs. Meecher's home-from-home with a wide gesture—"is that it's over. Finished and done with. These people were all very well when. . ."

". . . when you'd lost your week's salary at poker and wanted to borrow a few dollars for the rent."

"I always paid them back," protested Fillmore, defensively.

"I did."

"Well, we did," said Fillmore, accepting the amendment with the air of a man who has no time for chopping straws. "Anyway, what I mean is, I don't see why, just because one has known people at a certain period in one's life when one was practically down and out, one should have them round one's neck for ever. One can't prevent people forming an I-knew-him-when club, but, darn it, one needn't attend the meetings."

"One's friends. . ."

"Oh, friends," said Fillmore. "That's just where all this makes me so tired. One's in a position where all these people are entitled to call themselves one's friends, simply because father put it in his will that I wasn't to get the money till I was twenty-five, instead of letting me have it at twenty-one like anybody else. I wonder where I should have been by now if I could have got that money when I was twenty-one."

"In the poor-house, probably," said Sally.

Fillmore was wounded.

"Ah! you don't believe in me," he sighed.

"Oh, you would be all right if you had one thing," said Sally.

Fillmore passed his qualities in swift review before his mental eye. Brains? Dash? Spaciousness? Initiative? All present and correct. He wondered where Sally imagined the hiatus to exist.

"One thing?" he said. "What's that?"

"A nurse."

Fillmore's sense of injury deepened. He supposed that this was always the way, that those nearest to a man never believed in his ability till he had proved it so masterfully that it no longer required the assistance of faith. Still, it was trying; and there was not much consolation to be derived from the thought that Napoleon had had to go through this sort of thing in his day. "I shall find my place in the world," he said sulkily.

"Oh, you'll find your place all right," said Sally. "And I'll come round and bring you jelly and read to you on the days when visitors are allowed. . . Oh, hullo."

The last remark was addressed to a young man who had been swinging briskly along the sidewalk from the direction of Broadway and who now, coming abreast of them, stopped.

"Good evening, Mr. Foster."

"Good evening. Miss Nicholas."

"You don't know my brother, do you?"

"I don't believe I do."

"He left the underworld before you came to it," said Sally. "You wouldn't think it to look at him, but he was once a prune-eater among the proletariat, even as you and I. Mrs. Meecher looks on him as a son."

The two men shook hands. Fillmore was not short, but Gerald Foster with his lean, well-built figure seemed to tower over him. He was an Englishman, a man in the middle twenties, clean-shaven, keen-eyed, and very good to look at. Fillmore, who had recently been going in for one of those sum-up-your-fellow-man-at-a-glance courses, the better to fit himself for his career of greatness, was rather impressed. It seemed to him that this Mr. Foster, like himself, was one of those who Get There. If you are that kind yourself, you get into the knack of recognizing the others. It is a sort of gift.

There was a few moments of desultory conversation, of the kind that usually follows an introduction, and then Fillmore, by no means sorry to get the chance, took advantage of the coming of this new arrival to remove himself. He had not enjoyed his chat with Sally, and it seemed probable that he would enjoy a continuation of it even less. He was glad that Mr. Foster had happened along at this particular juncture. Excusing himself briefly, he hurried off down the street.

Sally stood for a minute, watching him till he had disappeared round the corner. She had a slightly regretful feeling that, now it was too late, she would think of a whole lot more good things which it would have been agreeable to say to him. And it had become obvious to her that

Fillmore was not getting nearly enough of that kind of thing said to him nowadays. Then she dismissed him from her mind and turning to Gerald Foster, slipped her arm through his.

"Well, Jerry, darling," she said. "What a shame you couldn't come to the party. Tell me all about everything."

3

IT WAS EXACTLY TWO MONTHS since Sally had become engaged to Gerald Foster; but so rigorously had they kept the secret that nobody at Mrs. Meecher's so much as suspected it. To Sally, who all her life had hated concealing things, secrecy of any kind was objectionable: but in this matter Gerald had shown an odd streak almost of furtiveness in his character. An announced engagement complicated life. People fussed about you and bothered you. People either watched you or avoided you. Such were his arguments, and Sally, who would have glossed over and found excuses for a disposition on his part towards homicide or arson, put them down to artistic sensitiveness. There is nobody so sensitive as your artist, particularly if he be unsuccessful: and when an artist has so little success that he cannot afford to make a home for the woman he loves, his sensitiveness presumably becomes great indeed. Putting herself in his place, Sally could see that a protracted engagement, known by everybody, would be a standing advertisement of Gerald's failure to make good: and she acquiesced in the policy of secrecy, hoping that it would not last long. It seemed absurd to think of Gerald as an unsuccessful man. He had in him, as the recent Fillmore had perceived, something dynamic. He was one of those men of whom one could predict that they would succeed very suddenly and rapidly—overnight, as it were.

"The party," said Sally, "went off splendidly." They had passed the boarding-house door, and were walking slowly down the street. "Everybody enjoyed themselves, I think, even though Fillmore did his best to spoil things by coming looking like an advertisement of What The Smart Men Will Wear This Season. You didn't see his waistcoat just now. He had covered it up. Conscience, I suppose. It was white and bulgy and gleaming and full up of pearl buttons and everything. I saw Augustus Bartlett curl up like a burnt feather when he caught sight of it. Still, time seemed to heal the wound, and everybody relaxed after a bit. Mr. Faucitt made a speech and I made a speech and cried, and. . . oh, it was all very festive. It only needed you."

"I wish I could have come. I had to go to that dinner, though. Sally. . ." Gerald paused, and Sally saw that he was electric with suppressed excitement. "Sally, the play's going to be put on!"

Sally gave a little gasp. She had lived this moment in anticipation for weeks. She had always known that sooner or later this would happen. She had read his plays over and over again, and was convinced that they were wonderful. Of course, hers was a biased view, but then Elsa Doland also admired them; and Elsa's opinion was one that carried weight. Elsa was another of those people who were bound to succeed suddenly. Even old Mr. Faucitt, who was a stern judge of acting and rather inclined to consider that nowadays there was no such thing, believed that she was a girl with a future who would do something big directly she got her chance.

"Jerry!" She gave his arm a hug. "How simply terrific! Then Goble and Kohn have changed their minds after all and want it? I knew they would."

A slight cloud seemed to dim the sunniness of the author's mood.

"No, not that one," he said reluctantly. "No hope there, I'm afraid. I saw Goble this morning about that, and he said it didn't add up right. The one that's going to be put on is 'The Primrose Way.' You remember? It's got a big part for a girl in it."

"Of course! The one Elsa liked so much. Well, that's just as good. Who's going to do it? I thought you hadn't sent it out again."

"Well, it happens. . ." Gerald hesitated once more. "It seems that this man I was dining with to-night—a man named Cracknell. . ."

"Cracknell? Not the Cracknell?"

"The Cracknell?"

"The one people are always talking about. The man they call the Millionaire Kid."

"Yes. Why, do you know him?"

"He was at Harvard with Fillmore. I never saw him, but he must be rather a painful person."

"Oh, he's all right. Not much brains, of course, but—well, he's all right. And, anyway, he wants to put the play on."

"Well, that's splendid," said Sally: but she could not get the right ring of enthusiasm into her voice. She had had ideals for Gerald. She had dreamed of him invading Broadway triumphantly under the banner of one of the big managers whose name carried a prestige, and there seemed something unworthy in this association with a man whose chief claim to eminence lay in the fact that he was credited by metropolitan gossip with possessing the largest private stock of alcohol in existence.

"I thought you would be pleased," said Gerald.

"Oh, I am," said Sally.

With the buoyant optimism which never deserted her for long, she had already begun to cast off her momentary depression. After all, did it matter who financed a play so long as it obtained a production? A manager was simply a piece of machinery for paying the bills; and if he had money for that purpose, why demand asceticism and the finer sensibilities from him? The real thing that mattered was the question of who was going to play the leading part, that deftly drawn character which had so excited the admiration of Elsa Doland. She sought information on this point.

"Who will play Ruth?" she asked. "You must have somebody wonderful. It needs a tremendously clever woman. Did Mr. Cracknell say anything about that?"

"Oh, yes, we discussed that, of course."

"Well?"

"Well, it seems. . ." Again Sally noticed that odd, almost stealthy embarrassment. Gerald appeared unable to begin a sentence to-night without feeling his way into it like a man creeping cautiously down a dark alley. She noticed it the more because it was so different from his usual direct method. Gerald, as a rule, was not one of those who apologize for themselves. He was forthright and masterful and inclined to talk to her from a height. To-night he seemed different.

He broke off, was silent for a moment, and began again with a question.

"Do you know Mabel Hobson?"

"Mabel Hobson? I've seen her in the 'Follies,' of course."

Sally started. A suspicion had stung her, so monstrous that its absurdity became manifest the moment it had formed. And yet was it absurd? Most Broadway gossip filtered eventually into the boarding-house, chiefly through the medium of that seasoned sport, the mild young man who thought so highly of the redoubtable Benny Whistler, and she was aware that the name of Reginald Cracknell, which was always getting itself linked with somebody, had been coupled with that of Miss Hobson. It seemed likely that in this instance rumour spoke truth, for the lady was of that compellingly blonde beauty which attracts the Cracknells of this world. But even so. . .

"It seems that Cracknell. . ." said Gerald. "Apparently this man Cracknell. . ." He was finding Sally's bright, horrified gaze somewhat trying. "Well, the fact is Cracknell believes in Mabel Hobson. . . and. . . well, he thinks this part would suit her."

"Oh, Jerry!"

Could infatuation go to such a length? Could even the spacious heart of a Reginald Cracknell so dominate that gentleman's small size in heads as to make him entrust a part like Ruth in "The Primrose Way" to one who, when desired by the producer of her last revue to carry a bowl of roses across the stage and place it on a table, had rebelled on the plea that she had not been engaged as a dancer? Surely even lovelorn Reginald could perceive that this was not the stuff of which great emotional actresses are made.

"Oh, Jerry!" she said again.

There was an uncomfortable silence. They turned and walked back in the direction of the boarding-house. Somehow Gerald's arm had managed to get itself detached from Sally's. She was conscious of a curious dull ache that was almost like a physical pain.

"Jerry! Is it worth it?" she burst out vehemently.

The question seemed to sting the young man into something like his usual decisive speech.

"Worth it? Of course it's worth it. It's a Broadway production. That's all that matters. Good heavens! I've been trying long enough to get a play on Broadway, and it isn't likely that I'm going to chuck away my chance when it comes along just because one might do better in the way of casting."

"But, Jerry! Mabel Hobson! It's. . . it's murder! Murder in the first degree."

"Nonsense. She'll be all right. The part will play itself. Besides, she has a personality and a following, and Cracknell will spend all the money in the world to make the thing a success. And it will be a start, whatever happens. Of course, it's worth it."

Fillmore would have been impressed by this speech. He would have recognized and respected in it the unmistakable ring which characterizes even the lightest utterances of those who get there. On Sally it had not immediately that effect. Nevertheless, her habit of making the best of things, working together with that primary article of her creed that the man she loved could do no wrong, succeeded finally in raising her spirits. Of course Jerry was right. It would have been foolish to refuse a contract because all its clauses were not ideal.

"You old darling," she said affectionately attaching herself to the vacant arm once more and giving it a penitent squeeze, "you're quite right. Of course you are. I can see it now. I was only a little startled at first. Everything's going to be wonderful. Let's get all our chickens out and count 'em. How are you going to spend the money?"

"I know how I'm going to spend a dollar of it," said Gerald completely restored.

"I mean the big money. What's a dollar?"

"It pays for a marriage-licence."

Sally gave his arm another squeeze.

"Ladies and gentlemen," she said. "Look at this man. Observe him. My partner!"

II

Enter Ginger

1

SALLY WAS SITTING WITH HER back against a hillock of golden sand, watching with half-closed eyes the denizens of Roville-sur-Mer at their familiar morning occupations. At Roville, as at most French seashore resorts, the morning is the time when the visiting population assembles in force on the beach. Whiskered fathers of families made cheerful patches of colour in the foreground. Their female friends and relatives clustered in groups under gay parasols. Dogs roamed to and fro, and children dug industriously with spades, ever and anon suspending their labours in order to smite one another with these handy implements. One of the dogs, a poodle of military aspect, wandered up to Sally: and discovering that she was in possession of a box of sweets, decided to remain and await developments.

Few things are so pleasant as the anticipation of them, but Sally's vacation had proved an exception to this rule. It had been a magic month of lazy happiness. She had drifted luxuriously from one French town to another, till the charm of Roville, with its blue sky, its Casino, its snow-white hotels along the Promenade, and its general glitter and gaiety, had brought her to a halt. Here she could have stayed indefinitely, but the voice of America was calling her back. Gerald had written to say that "The Primrose Way" was to be produced in Detroit, preliminary to its New York run, so soon that, if she wished to see the opening, she must return at once. A scrappy, hurried, unsatisfactory letter, the letter of a busy man: but one that Sally could not ignore. She was leaving Roville to-morrow.

To-day, however, was to-day: and she sat and watched the bathers with a familiar feeling of peace, revelling as usual in the still novel sensation of having nothing to do but bask in the warm sunshine and listen to the faint murmur of the little waves.

But, if there was one drawback, she had discovered, to a morning on the Roville plage, it was that you had a tendency to fall asleep: and this is a degrading thing to do so soon after breakfast, even if you are on a holiday. Usually, Sally fought stoutly against the temptation, but to-day the sun was so warm and the whisper of the waves so insinuating that she had almost dozed off, when she was aroused by voices close at hand. There were many voices on the beach, both near and distant, but these were talking English, a novelty in Roville, and the sound of the familiar tongue jerked Sally back from the borders of sleep. A few feet away, two men had seated themselves on the sand.

From the first moment she had set out on her travels, it had been one of Sally's principal amusements to examine the strangers whom chance threw in her way and to try by the light of her intuition to fit them out with characters and occupations: nor had she been discouraged by an almost consistent failure to guess right. Out of the corner of her eye she inspected these two men.

The first of the pair did not attract her. He was a tall, dark man whose tight, precise mouth and rather high cheeks bones gave him an appearance vaguely sinister. He had the dusky look of the clean-shaven man whose life is a perpetual struggle with a determined beard. He certainly shaved twice a day, and just as certainly had the self-control not to swear when he cut himself. She could picture him smiling nastily when this happened.

"Hard," diagnosed Sally. "I shouldn't like him. A lawyer or something, I think."

She turned to the other and found herself looking into his eyes. This was because he had been staring at Sally with the utmost intentness ever since his arrival. His mouth had opened slightly. He had the air of a man who, after many disappointments, has at last found something worth looking at.

"Rather a dear," decided Sally.

He was a sturdy, thick-set young man with an amiable, freckled face and the reddest hair Sally had ever seen. He had a square chin, and at one angle of the chin a slight cut. And Sally was convinced that, however he had behaved on receipt of that wound, it had not been with superior self-control.

"A temper, I should think," she meditated. "Very quick, but soon over. Not very clever, I should say, but nice."

She looked away, finding his fascinated gaze a little embarrassing.

The dark man, who in the objectionably competent fashion which, one felt, characterized all his actions, had just succeeded in lighting a cigarette in the teeth of a strong breeze, threw away the match and resumed the conversation, which had presumably been interrupted by the process of sitting down.

"And how is Scrymgeour?" he inquired.

"Oh, all right," replied the young man with red hair absently. Sally was looking straight in front of her, but she felt that his eyes were still busy.

"I was surprised at his being here. He told me he meant to stay in Paris."

There was a slight pause. Sally gave the attentive poodle a piece of nougat.

"I say," observed the red-haired young man in clear, penetrating tones that vibrated with intense feeling, "that's the prettiest girl I've seen in my life!"

2

AT THIS FRANK REVELATION OF the red-haired young man's personal opinions, Sally, though considerably startled, was not displeased. A broad-minded girl, the outburst seemed to her a legitimate comment on a matter of public interest. The young man's companion, on the other hand, was unmixedly shocked.

"My dear fellow!" he exclaimed.

"Oh, it's all right," said the red-haired young man, unmoved. "She can't understand. There isn't a bally soul in this dashed place that can speak a word of English. If I didn't happen to remember a few odd bits of French, I should have starved by this time. That girl," he went on, returning to the subject most imperatively occupying his mind, "is an absolute topper! I give you my solemn word I've never seen anybody to touch her. Look at those hands and feet. You don't get them outside France. Of course, her mouth is a bit wide," he said reluctantly.

Sally's immobility, added to the other's assurance concerning the linguistic deficiencies of the inhabitants of Roville, seemed to reassure the dark man. He breathed again. At no period of his life had he ever behaved with anything but the most scrupulous correctness himself, but he had quailed at the idea of being associated even remotely with incorrectness in another. It had been a black moment for him when the red-haired young man had uttered those few kind words.

"Still you ought to be careful," he said austerely.

He looked at Sally, who was now dividing her attention between the poodle and a raffish-looking mongrel, who had joined the party, and returned to the topic of the mysterious Scrymgeour.

"How is Scrymgeour's dyspepsia?"

The red-haired young man seemed but faintly interested in the vicissitudes of Scrymgeour's interior.

"Do you notice the way her hair sort of curls over her ears?" he said. "Eh? Oh, pretty much the same, I think."

"What hotel are you staying at?"

"The Normandie."

Sally, dipping into the box for another chocolate cream, gave an imperceptible start. She, too, was staying at the Normandie. She presumed that her admirer was a recent arrival, for she had seen nothing of him at the hotel.

"The Normandie?" The dark man looked puzzled. "I know Roville pretty well by report, but I've never heard of any Hotel Normandie. Where is it?"

"It's a little shanty down near the station. Not much of a place. Still, it's cheap, and the cooking's all right."

His companion's bewilderment increased.

"What on earth is a man like Scrymgeour doing there?" he said. Sally was conscious of an urgent desire to know more and more about the absent Scrymgeour. Constant repetition of his name had made him seem almost like an old friend. "If there's one thing he's fussy about. . ."

"There are at least eleven thousand things he's fussy about," interrupted the red-haired young man disapprovingly. "Jumpy old blighter!"

"If there's one thing he's particular about, it's the sort of hotel he goes to. Ever since I've known him he has always wanted the best. I should have thought he would have gone to the Splendide." He mused on this problem in a dissatisfied sort of way for a moment, then seemed to reconcile himself to the fact that a rich man's eccentricities must be humoured. "I'd like to see him again. Ask him if he will dine with me at the Splendide to-night. Say eight sharp."

Sally, occupied with her dogs, whose numbers had now been augmented by a white terrier with a black patch over its left eye, could not see the young man's face: but his voice, when he replied, told her that something was wrong. There was a false airiness in it.

"Oh, Scrymgeour isn't in Roville."

"No? Where is he?"

"Paris, I believe."

"What!" The dark man's voice sharpened. He sounded as though he were cross-examining a reluctant witness. "Then why aren't you there? What are you doing here? Did he give you a holiday?"

"Yes, he did."

"When do you rejoin him?"

"I don't."

"What!"

The red-haired young man's manner was not unmistakably dogged.

"Well, if you want to know," he said, "the old blighter fired me the day before yesterday."

3

THERE WAS A SHUFFLING OF sand as the dark man sprang up. Sally, intent on the drama which was unfolding itself beside her, absent-mindedly gave the poodle a piece of nougat which should by rights have gone to the terrier. She shot a swift glance sideways, and saw the dark man standing in an attitude rather reminiscent of the stern father of melodrama about to drive his erring daughter out into the snow. The red-haired young man, outwardly stolid, was gazing before him down the beach at a fat bather in an orange suit who, after six false starts, was now actually in the water, floating with the dignity of a wrecked balloon.

"Do you mean to tell me," demanded the dark man, "that, after all the trouble the family took to get you what was practically a sinecure with endless possibilities if you only behaved yourself, you have deliberately thrown away. . ." A despairing gesture completed the sentence. "Good God, you're hopeless!"

The red-haired young man made no reply. He continued to gaze down the beach. Of all outdoor sports, few are more stimulating than watching middle-aged Frenchmen bathe. Drama, action, suspense, all are here. From the first stealthy testing of the water with an apprehensive toe to the final seal-like plunge, there is never a dull moment. And apart from the excitement of the thing, judging it from a purely aesthetic standpoint, his must be a dull soul who can fail to be uplifted by the spectacle of a series of very stout men with whiskers, seen in tight bathing suits against a background of brightest blue. Yet the young man with red hair, recently in the employment of Mr. Scrymgeour, eyed this free circus without any enjoyment whatever.

"It's maddening! What are you going to do? What do you expect us to do? Are we to spend our whole lives getting you positions which you won't keep? I can tell you we're. . . it's monstrous! It's sickening! Good God!"

And with these words the dark man, apparently feeling, as Sally had sometimes felt in the society of her brother Fillmore, the futility of mere language, turned sharply and stalked away up the beach, the dignity of his exit somewhat marred a moment later by the fact of his straw hat blowing off and being trodden on by a passing child.

He left behind him the sort of electric calm which follows the falling of a thunderbolt; that stunned calm through which the air seems still to quiver protestingly. How long this would have lasted one cannot say: for towards the end of the first minute it was shattered by a purely terrestrial uproar. With an abruptness heralded only by one short, low gurgling snarl, there sprang into being the prettiest dog fight that Roville had seen that season.

It was the terrier with the black patch who began it. That was Sally's opinion: and such, one feels, will be the verdict of history. His best friend, anxious to make out a case for him, could not have denied that he fired the first gun of the campaign. But we must be just. The fault was really Sally's. Absorbed in the scene which had just concluded and acutely inquisitive as to why the shadowy Scrymgeour had seen fit to dispense with the red-haired young man's services, she had thrice in succession helped the poodle out of his turn. The third occasion was too much for the terrier.

There is about any dog fight a wild, gusty fury which affects the average mortal with something of the helplessness induced by some vast clashing of the elements. It seems so outside one's jurisdiction. One is oppressed with a sense of the futility of interference. And this was no ordinary dog fight. It was a stunning mêlée, which would have excited favourable comment even among the blasé residents of a negro quarter or the not easily-pleased critics of a Lancashire mining-village. From all over the beach dogs of every size, breed, and colour were racing to the scene: and while some of these merely remained in the ringside seats and barked, a considerable proportion immediately started fighting one another on general principles, well content to be in action without bothering about first causes. The terrier had got the poodle by the left hind-leg and was restating his war-aims. The raffish mongrel was apparently endeavouring to fletcherize a complete stranger of the Sealyham family.

Sally was frankly unequal to the situation, as were the entire crowd of spectators who had come galloping up from the water's edge. She had been paralysed from the start. Snarling bundles bumped against her legs and bounced away again, but she made no move. Advice in fluent French rent the air. Arms waved, and well-filled bathing suits leaped up and down. But nobody did anything practical until in the centre of the theatre of war there suddenly appeared the red-haired young man.

The only reason why dog fights do not go on for ever is that Providence has decided that on each such occasion there shall always be among those present one Master Mind; one wizard who, whatever his shortcomings in other battles of life, is in this single particular sphere competent and dominating. At Roville-sur-Mer it was the red-haired young man. His dark companion might have turned from him in disgust: his services might not have seemed worth retaining by the haughty Scrymgeour: he might be a pain in the neck to "the family"; but he did know how to stop a dog fight. From the first moment of his intervention calm began to steal over the scene. He had the same effect on the almost inextricably entwined belligerents as, in mediaeval legend, the Holy Grail, sliding down the sunbeam, used to have on battling knights. He did not look like a dove of peace, but the most captious could not have denied that he brought home the goods. There was a magic in his soothing hands, a spell in his voice: and in a shorter time than one would have believed possible dog after dog had been sorted out and calmed down; until presently all that was left of Armageddon was one solitary small Scotch terrier, thoughtfully licking a chewed leg. The rest of the combatants, once more in their right mind and wondering what all the fuss was about, had been captured and haled away in a whirl of recrimination by voluble owners.

Having achieved this miracle, the young man turned to Sally. Gallant, one might say reckless, as he had been a moment before, he now gave indications of a rather pleasing shyness. He braced himself with that painful air of effort which announces to the world that an Englishman is about to speak a language other than his own.

"J'espère," he said, having swallowed once or twice to brace himself up for the journey through the jungle of a foreign tongue, "J'espère que vous n'êtes pas—oh, dammit, what's the word—J'espère que vous n'êtes pas blessée?"

"Blessée?"

"Yes, blessée. Wounded. Hurt, don't you know. Bitten. Oh, dash it. J'espère. . ."

"Oh, bitten!" said Sally, dimpling. "Oh, no, thanks very much. I wasn't bitten. And I think it was awfully brave of you to save all our lives."

The compliment seemed to pass over the young man's head. He stared at Sally with horrified eyes. Over his amiable face there swept a vivid blush. His jaw dropped.

"Oh, my sainted aunt!" he exclaimed.

Then, as if the situation was too much for him and flight the only possible solution, he spun round and disappeared at a walk so rapid that it was almost a run. Sally watched him go and was sorry that he had torn himself away. She still wanted to know why Scrymgeour had fired him.

4

BEDTIME AT ROVILLE IS AN hour that seems to vary according to one's proximity to the sea. The gilded palaces along the front keep deplorable hours, polluting the night air till dawn with indefatigable jazz: but at the pensions of the economical like the Normandie, early to bed is the rule. True, Jules, the stout young native who combined the offices of night-clerk and lift attendant at that establishment, was on duty in the hall throughout the night, but few of the Normandie's patrons made use of his services.

Sally, entering shortly before twelve o'clock on the night of the day on which the dark man, the red-haired young man, and their friend Scrymgeour had come into her life, found the little hall dim and silent. Through the iron cage of the lift a single faint bulb glowed: another, over the desk in the far corner, illuminated the upper half of Jules, slumbering in a chair. Jules seemed to Sally to be on duty in some capacity or other all the time. His work, like women's, was never done. He was now restoring his tissues with a few winks of much-needed beauty sleep. Sally, who had been to the Casino to hear the band and afterwards had strolled on the moonlit promenade, had a guilty sense of intrusion.

As she stood there, reluctant to break in on Jules' rest—for her sympathetic heart, always at the disposal of the oppressed, had long ached for this overworked peon—she was relieved to hear footsteps in the street outside, followed by the opening of the front door. If Jules would have had to wake up anyway, she felt her sense of responsibility lessened. The door, having opened, closed again with a bang. Jules stirred, gurgled, blinked, and sat up, and Sally, turning, perceived that the new arrival was the red-haired young man.

"Oh, good evening," said Sally welcomingly.

The young man stopped, and shuffled uncomfortably. The morning's happenings were obviously still green in his memory. He had either not ceased blushing since their last meeting or he was celebrating their reunion by beginning to blush again: for his face was a familiar scarlet.

"Er—good evening," he said, disentangling his feet, which, in the embarrassment of the moment, had somehow got coiled up together.

"Or bon soir, I suppose you would say," murmured Sally.

The young man acknowledged receipt of this thrust by dropping his hat and tripping over it as he stooped to pick it up.

Jules, meanwhile, who had been navigating in a sort of somnambulistic trance in the neighbourhood of the lift, now threw back the cage with a rattle.

"It's a shame to have woken you up," said Sally, commiseratingly, stepping in.

Jules did not reply, for the excellent reason that he had not been woken up. Constant practice enabled him to do this sort of work without breaking his slumber. His brain, if you could call it that, was working automatically. He had shut up the gate with a clang and was tugging sluggishly at the correct rope, so that the lift was going slowly up instead of retiring down into the basement, but he was not awake.

Sally and the red-haired young man sat side by side on the small seat, watching their conductor's efforts. After the first spurt, conversation had languished. Sally had nothing of immediate interest to say, and her companion seemed to be one of these strong, silent men you read about. Only a slight snore from Jules broke the silence.

At the third floor Sally leaned forward and prodded Jules in the lower ribs. All through her stay at Roville, she had found in dealing with the native population that actions spoke louder than words. If she wanted anything in a restaurant or at a shop, she pointed; and, when she wished the lift to stop, she prodded the man in charge. It was a system worth a dozen French conversation books.

Jules brought the machine to a halt: and it was at this point that he should have done the one thing connected with his professional activities which he did really well—the opening, to wit, of the iron cage. There are ways of doing this. Jules' was the right way. He was accustomed to do it with a flourish, and generally remarked "V'la!" in a modest but self-congratulatory voice as though he would have liked to see another man who could have put through a job like that. Jules' opinion was that he might not be much to look at, but that he could open a lift door.

To-night, however, it seemed as if even this not very exacting feat was beyond his powers. Instead of inserting his key in the lock, he stood staring in an attitude of frozen horror. He was a man who took most things in life pretty seriously, and whatever was the little difficulty just now seemed to have broken him all up.

"There appears," said Sally, turning to her companion, "to be a hitch. Would you mind asking what's the matter? I don't know any French myself except 'oo la la!'"

The young man, thus appealed to, nerved himself to the task. He eyed the melancholy Jules doubtfully, and coughed in a strangled sort of way.

"Oh, esker. . . esker vous. . ."

"Don't weaken," said Sally. "I think you've got him going."

"Esker vous. . . Pourquoi vous ne. . . I mean ne vous. . . that is to say, quel est le raison. . ."

He broke off here, because at this point Jules began to explain. He explained very rapidly and at considerable length. The fact that neither of his hearers understood a word of what he was saying appeared not to have impressed itself upon him. Or, if he gave a thought to it, he dismissed the objection as trifling. He wanted to explain, and he explained. Words rushed from him like water from a geyser. Sounds which you felt you would have been able to put a meaning to if he had detached them from the main body and repeated them slowly, went swirling down the stream and were lost for ever.

"Stop him!" said Sally firmly.

The red-haired young man looked as a native of Johnstown might have looked on being requested to stop that city's celebrated flood.

"Stop him?"

"Yes. Blow a whistle or something."

Out of the depths of the young man's memory there swam to the surface a single word—a word which he must have heard somewhere or read somewhere: a legacy, perhaps, from long-vanished school-days.

"Zut!" he barked, and instantaneously Jules turned himself off at the main. There was a moment of dazed silence, such as might occur in a boiler-factory if the works suddenly shut down.

"Quick! Now you've got him!" cried Sally. "Ask him what he's talking about—if he knows, which I doubt—and tell him to speak slowly. Then we shall get somewhere."

The young man nodded intelligently. The advice was good.

"Lentement," he said. "Parlez lentement. Pas si—you know what I mean—pas si dashed vite!"

"Ah-a-ah!" cried Jules, catching the idea on the fly. "Lentement. Ah, oui, lentement."

There followed a lengthy conversation which, while conveying nothing to Sally, seemed intelligible to the red-haired linguist.

"The silly ass," he was able to announce some few minutes later, "has made a bloomer. Apparently he was half asleep when we came in, and he shoved us into the lift and slammed the door, forgetting that he had left the keys on the desk."

"I see," said Sally. "So we're shut in?"

"I'm afraid so. I wish to goodness," said the young man, "I knew French well. I'd curse him with some vim and not a little animation, the chump! I wonder what 'blighter' is in French," he said, meditating.

"It's the merest suggestion," said Sally, "but oughtn't we to do something?"

"What could we do?"

"Well, for one thing, we might all utter a loud yell. It would scare most of the people in the hotel to death, but there might be a survivor or two who would come and investigate and let us out."

"What a ripping idea!" said the young man, impressed.

"I'm glad you like it. Now tell him the main out-line, or he'll think we've gone mad."

The young man searched for words, and eventually found some which expressed his meaning lamely but well enough to cause Jules to nod in a depressed sort of way.

"Fine!" said Sally. "Now, all together at the word 'three.' One—two—Oh, poor darling!" she broke off. "Look at him!"

In the far corner of the lift, the emotional Jules was sobbing silently into the bunch of cotton-waste which served him in the office of a pocket-handkerchief. His broken-hearted gulps echoed hollowly down the shaft.

5

IN THESE DAYS OF CHEAP books of instruction on every subject under the sun, we most of us know how to behave in the majority of life's little crises. We have only ourselves to blame if we are ignorant of what to do before the doctor comes, of how to make a dainty winter coat for baby out of father's last year's under-vest and of the best method of coping with the cold mutton. But nobody yet has come forward with practical advice as to the correct method of behaviour to be adopted when a lift-attendant starts crying. And Sally and her companion, as a consequence, for a few moments merely stared at each other helplessly.

"Poor darling!" said Sally, finding speech. "Ask him what's the matter."

The young man looked at her doubtfully.

"You know," he said, "I don't enjoy chatting with this blighter. I mean to say, it's a bit of an effort. I don't know why it is, but talking French always makes me feel as if my nose were coming off. Couldn't we just leave him to have his cry out by himself?"

"The idea!" said Sally. "Have you no heart? Are you one of those fiends in human shape?"

He turned reluctantly to Jules, and paused to overhaul his vocabulary.

"You ought to be thankful for this chance," said Sally. "It's the only real way of learning French, and you're getting a lesson for nothing. What did he say then?"

"Something about losing something, it seemed to me. I thought I caught the word perdu."

"But that means a partridge, doesn't it? I'm sure I've seen it on the menus."

"Would he talk about partridges at a time like this?"

"He might. The French are extraordinary people."

"Well, I'll have another go at him. But he's a difficult chap to chat with. If you give him the least encouragement, he sort of goes off like a rocket." He addressed another question to the sufferer, and listened attentively to the voluble reply.

"Oh!" he said with sudden enlightenment. "Your job?" He turned to Sally. "I got it that time," he said. "The trouble is, he says, that if we yell and rouse the house, we'll get out all right, but he will lose his job, because this is the second time this sort of thing has happened, and they warned him last time that once more would mean the push."

"Then we mustn't dream of yelling," said Sally, decidedly. "It means a pretty long wait, you know. As far as I can gather, there's just a chance of somebody else coming in later, in which case he could let us out. But it's doubtful. He rather thinks that everybody has gone to roost."

"Well, we must try it. I wouldn't think of losing the poor man his job. Tell him to take the car down to the ground-floor, and then we'll just sit and amuse ourselves till something happens. We've lots to talk about. We can tell each other the story of our lives."

Jules, cheered by his victims' kindly forbearance, lowered the car to the ground floor, where, after a glance of infinite longing at the keys on the distant desk, the sort of glance which Moses must have cast at the Promised Land from the summit of Mount Pisgah, he sagged down in a heap and resumed his slumbers. Sally settled herself as comfortably as possible in her corner.

"You'd better smoke," she said. "It will be something to do."

"Thanks awfully."

"And now," said Sally, "tell me why Scrymgeour fired you."

Little by little, under the stimulating influence of this nocturnal adventure, the red-haired young man had lost that shy confusion which had rendered him so ill at ease when he had encountered Sally in the hall of the hotel; but at this question embarrassment gripped him once more. Another of those comprehensive blushes of his raced over his face, and he stammered.

"I say, I'm glad. . . I'm fearfully sorry about that, you know!"

"About Scrymgeour?"

"You know what I mean. I mean, about making such a most ghastly ass of myself this morning. I. . . I never dreamed you understood English."

"Why, I didn't object. I thought you were very nice and complimentary. Of course, I don't know how many girls you've seen in your life, but. . ."

"No, I say, don't! It makes me feel such a chump."

"And I'm sorry about my mouth. It is wide. But I know you're a fair-minded man and realize that it isn't my fault."

"Don't rub it in," pleaded the young man. "As a matter of fact, if you want to know, I think your mouth is absolutely perfect. I think," he proceeded, a little feverishly, "that you are the most indescribable topper that ever. . ."

"You were going to tell me about Scrymgeour," said Sally.

The young man blinked as if he had collided with some hard object while sleep-walking. Eloquence had carried him away.

"Scrymgeour?" he said. "Oh, that would bore you."

"Don't be silly," said Sally reprovingly. "Can't you realize that we're practically castaways on a desert island? There's nothing to do till to-morrow but talk about ourselves. I want to hear all about you, and then I'll tell you all about myself. If you feel diffident about starting the revelations, I'll begin. Better start with names. Mine is Sally Nicholas. What's yours?"

"Mine? Oh, ah, yes, I see what you mean."

"I thought you would. I put it as clearly as I could. Well, what is it?"

"Kemp."

"And the first name?"

"Well, as a matter of fact," said the young man, "I've always rather hushed up my first name, because when I was christened they worked a low-down trick on me!"

"You can't shock me," said Sally, encouragingly. "My father's name was Ezekiel, and I've a brother who was christened Fillmore."

Mr. Kemp brightened. "Well, mine isn't as bad as that. . . No, I don't mean that," he broke off apologetically. "Both awfully jolly names, of course. . ."

"Get on," said Sally.

"Well, they called me Lancelot. And, of course, the thing is that I don't look like a Lancelot and never shall. My pals," he added in a more cheerful strain, "call me Ginger."

"I don't blame them," said Sally.

"Perhaps you wouldn't mind thinking of me as Ginger?" suggested the young man diffidently.

"Certainly."

"That's awfully good of you."

"Not at all."

Jules stirred in his sleep and grunted. No other sound came to disturb the stillness of the night.

"You were going to tell me about yourself?" said Mr. Lancelot (Ginger) Kemp.

"I'm going to tell you all about myself," said Sally, "not because I think it will interest you. . ."

"Oh, it will!"

"Not, I say, because I think it will interest you. . ."

"It will, really."

Sally looked at him coldly.

"Is this a duet?" she inquired, "or have I the floor?"

"I'm awfully sorry."

"Not, I repeat for the third time, because I think It will interest you, but because if I do you won't have any excuse for not telling me your life-history, and you wouldn't believe how inquisitive I am. Well, in the first place, I live in America. I'm over here on a holiday. And it's the first real holiday I've had in three years—since I left home, in fact." Sally paused. "I ran away from home," she said.

"Good egg!" said Ginger Kemp.

"I beg your pardon?"

"I mean, quite right. I bet you were quite right."

"When I say home," Sally went on, "it was only a sort of imitation home, you know. One of those just-as-good homes which are never as satisfactory as the real kind. My father and mother both died a good many years ago. My brother and I were dumped down on the reluctant doorstep of an uncle."

"Uncles," said Ginger Kemp, feelingly, "are the devil. I've got an. . . but I'm interrupting you."

"My uncle was our trustee. He had control of all my brother's money and mine till I was twenty-one. My brother was to get his when he was twenty-five. My poor father trusted him blindly, and what do you think happened?"

"Good Lord! The blighter embezzled the lot?"

"No, not a cent. Wasn't it extraordinary! Have you ever heard of a blindly trusted uncle who was perfectly honest? Well, mine was. But the trouble was that, while an excellent man to have looking after one's money, he wasn't a very lovable character. He was very hard. Hard! He was as hard as—well, nearly as hard as this seat. He hated poor Fill. . ."

"Phil?"

"I broke it to you just now that my brother's name was Fillmore."

"Oh, your brother. Oh, ah, yes."

"He was always picking on poor Fill. And I'm bound to say that Fill rather laid himself out as what you might call a pickee. He was always getting into trouble. One day, about three years ago, he was expelled from Harvard, and my uncle vowed he would have nothing more to do with him. So I said, if Fill left, I would leave. And, as this seemed to be my uncle's idea of a large evening, no objection was raised, and Fill and I departed. We went to New York, and there we've been ever since. About six months' ago Fill passed the twenty-five mark and collected his money, and last month I marched past the given point and got mine. So it all ends happily, you see. Now tell me about yourself."

"But, I say, you know, dash it, you've skipped a lot. I mean to say, you must have had an awful time in New York, didn't you? How on earth did you get along?"

"Oh, we found work. My brother tried one or two things, and finally became an assistant stage-manager with some theatre people. The only thing I could do, having been raised in enervating luxury, was ballroom dancing, so I ball-room danced. I got a job at a place in Broadway called 'The Flower Garden' as what is humorously called an 'instructress,' as if anybody could 'instruct' the men who came there. One was lucky if one saved one's life and wasn't quashed to death."

"How perfectly foul!"

"Oh, I don't know. It was rather fun for a while. Still," said Sally, meditatively, "I'm not saying I could have held out much longer: I was beginning to give. I suppose I've been trampled underfoot by more fat men than any other girl of my age in America. I don't know why it was, but every man who came in who was a bit overweight seemed to make for me by instinct. That's why I like to sit on the sands here and watch these Frenchmen bathing. It's just heavenly to lie back and watch a two hundred and fifty pound man, coming along and feel that he isn't going to dance with me."

"But, I say! How absolutely rotten it must have been for you!"

"Well, I'll tell you one thing. It's going to make me a very domesticated wife one of these days. You won't find me gadding about in gilded jazz-palaces! For me, a little place in the country somewhere, with my knitting and an Elsie book, and bed at half-past nine! And now tell me the story of your life. And make it long because I'm perfectly certain there's going to be no relief-expedition. I'm sure the last dweller under this roof came in years ago. We shall be here till morning."

"I really think we had better shout, you know."

"And lose Jules his job? Never!"

"Well, of course, I'm sorry for poor old Jules' troubles, but I hate to think of you having to. . ."

"Now get on with the story," said Sally.

6

GINGER KEMP EXHIBITED SOME OF the symptoms of a young bridegroom called upon at a wedding-breakfast to respond to the toast. He moved his feet restlessly and twisted his fingers.

"I hate talking about myself, you know," he said.

"So I supposed," said Sally. "That's why I gave you my autobiography first, to give you no chance of backing out. Don't be such a shrinking violet. We're all shipwrecked mariners here. I am intensely interested in your narrative. And, even if I wasn't, I'd much rather listen to it than to Jules' snoring."

"He is snoring a bit, what? Does it annoy you? Shall I stir him?"

"You seem to have an extraordinary brutal streak in your nature," said Sally. "You appear to think of nothing else but schemes for harassing poor Jules. Leave him alone for a second, and start telling me about yourself."

"Where shall I start?"

"Well, not with your childhood, I think. We'll skip that."

"Well. . ." Ginger Kemp knitted his brow, searching for a dramatic opening. "Well, I'm more or less what you might call an orphan, like you. I mean to say, both my people are dead and all that sort of thing."

"Thanks for explaining. That has made it quite clear."

"I can't remember my mother. My father died when I was in my last year at Cambridge. I'd been having a most awfully good time at the 'varsity,'" said Ginger, warming to his theme. "Not thick, you know, but good. I'd got my rugger and boxing blues and I'd just been picked for scrum-half for England against the North in the first trial match, and between ourselves it really did look as if I was more or less of a snip for my international."

Sally gazed at him wide eyed.

"Is that good or bad?" she asked.

"Eh?"

"Are you reciting a catalogue of your crimes, or do you expect me to get up and cheer? What is a rugger blue, to start with?"

"Well, it's. . . it's a rugger blue, you know."

"Oh, I see," said Sally. "You mean a rugger blue."

"I mean to say, I played rugger—footer—that's to say, football—Rugby football—for Cambridge, against Oxford. I was scrum-half."

"And what is a scrum-half?" asked Sally, patiently. "Yes, I know you're going to say it's a scrum-half, but can't you make it easier?"

"The scrum-half," said Ginger, "is the half who works the scrum. He slings the pill out to the fly-half, who starts the three-quarters going. I don't know if you understand?"

"I don't."

"It's dashed hard to explain," said Ginger Kemp, unhappily. "I mean, I don't think I've ever met anyone before who didn't know what a scrum-half was."

"Well, I can see that it has something to do with football, so we'll leave it at that. I suppose it's something like our quarter-back. And what's an international?"

"It's called getting your international when you play for England, you know. England plays Wales, France, Ireland, and Scotland. If it hadn't been for the smash, I think I should have played for England against Wales."

"I see at last. What you're trying to tell me is that you were very good at football."

Ginger Kemp blushed warmly.

"Oh, I don't say that. England was pretty short of scrum-halves that year."

"What a horrible thing to happen to a country! Still, you were likely to be picked on the All-England team when the smash came? What was the smash?"

"Well, it turned out that the poor old pater hadn't left a penny. I never understood the process exactly, but I'd always supposed that we were pretty well off; and then it turned out that I hadn't anything at all. I'm bound to say it was a bit of a jar. I had to come down from Cambridge and go to work in my uncle's office. Of course, I made an absolute hash of it."

"Why, of course?"

"Well, I'm not a very clever sort of chap, you see. I somehow didn't seem able to grasp the workings. After about a year, my uncle, getting a bit fed-up, hoofed me out and got me a mastership at a school, and I made a hash of that. He got me one or two other jobs, and I made a hash of those."

"You certainly do seem to be one of our most prominent young hashers!" gasped Sally.

"I am," said Ginger, modestly.

There was a silence.

"And what about Scrymgeour?" Sally asked.

"That was the last of the jobs," said Ginger. "Scrymgeour is a pompous old ass who thinks he's going to be Prime Minister some day. He's a big bug at the Bar and has just got into Parliament. My cousin used to devil for him. That's how I got mixed up with the blighter."

"Your cousin used. . . ? I wish you would talk English."

"That was my cousin who was with me on the beach this morning."

"And what did you say he used to do for Mr. Scrymgeour?"

"Oh, it's called devilling. My cousin's at the Bar, too—one of our rising nibs, as a matter of fact. . ."

"I thought he was a lawyer of some kind."

"He's got a long way beyond it now, but when he started he used to devil for Scrymgeour—assist him, don't you know. His name's Carmyle, you know. Perhaps you've heard of him? He's rather a prominent johnny in his way. Bruce Carmyle, you know."

"I haven't."

"Well, he got me this job of secretary to Scrymgeour."

"And why did Mr. Scrymgeour fire you?"

Ginger Kemp's face darkened. He frowned. Sally, watching him, felt that she had been right when she had guessed that he had a temper. She liked him none the worse for it. Mild men did not appeal to her.

"I don't know if you're fond of dogs?" said Ginger.

"I used to be before this morning," said Sally. "And I suppose I shall be again in time. For the moment I've had what you might call rather a surfeit of dogs. But aren't you straying from the point? I asked you why Mr. Scrymgeour dismissed you."

"I'm telling you."

"I'm glad of that. I didn't know."

"The old brute," said Ginger, frowning again, "has a dog. A very jolly little spaniel. Great pal of mine. And Scrymgeour is the sort of fool who oughtn't to be allowed to own a dog. He's one of those asses who isn't fit to own a dog. As a matter of fact, of all the blighted, pompous, bullying, shrivelled-souled old devils. . ."

"One moment," said Sally. "I'm getting an impression that you don't like Mr. Scrymgeour. Am I right?"

"Yes!"

"I thought so. Womanly intuition! Go on."

"He used to insist on the poor animal doing tricks. I hate seeing a dog do tricks. Dogs loathe it, you know. They're frightfully sensitive. Well, Scrymgeour used to make this spaniel of his do tricks—fool-things that no self-respecting dogs would do: and eventually poor old Billy got fed up and jibbed. He was too polite to bite, but he sort of shook his head and crawled under a chair. You'd have thought anyone would have let it go at that, but would old Scrymgeour? Not a bit of it! Of all the poisonous. . ."

"Yes, I know. Go on."

"Well, the thing ended in the blighter hauling him out from under the chair and getting more and more shirty, until finally he laid into him with a stick. That is to say," said Ginger, coldly accurate, "he started laying into him with a stick." He brooded for a moment with knit brows.

P.G. WODEHOUSE

"A spaniel, mind you! Can you imagine anyone beating a spaniel? It's like hitting a little girl. Well, he's a fairly oldish man, you know, and that hampered me a bit: but I got hold of the stick and broke it into about eleven pieces, and by great good luck it was a stick he happened to value rather highly. It had a gold knob and had been presented to him by his constituents or something. I minced it up a goodish bit, and then I told him a fair amount about himself. And then—well, after that he shot me out, and I came here."

Sally did not speak for a moment.

"You were quite right," she said at last, in a sober voice that had nothing in it of her customary flippancy. She paused again. "And what are you going to do now?" she said.

"I don't know."

"You'll get something?"

"Oh, yes, I shall get something, I suppose. The family will be pretty sick, of course."

"For goodness' sake! Why do you bother about the family?" Sally burst out. She could not reconcile this young man's flabby dependence on his family with the enterprise and vigour which he had shown in his dealings with the unspeakable Scrymgeour. Of course, he had been brought up to look on himself as a rich man's son and appeared to have drifted as such young men are wont to do; but even so. . . "The whole trouble with you," she said, embarking on a subject on which she held strong views, "is that. . ."

Her harangue was interrupted by what—at the Normandie, at one o'clock in the morning—practically amounted to a miracle. The front door of the hotel opened, and there entered a young man in evening dress. Such persons were sufficiently rare at the Normandie, which catered principally for the staid and middle-aged, and this youth's presence was due, if one must pause to explain it, to the fact that, in the middle of his stay at Roville, a disastrous evening at the Casino had so diminished his funds that he had been obliged to make a hurried shift from the Hotel Splendide to the humbler Normandie. His late appearance to-night was caused by the fact that he had been attending a dance at the Splendide, principally in the hope of finding there some kind-hearted friend of his prosperity from whom he might borrow.

A rapid-fire dialogue having taken place between Jules and the newcomer, the keys were handed through the cage, the door opened and the lift was set once more in motion. And a few minutes later, Sally, suddenly aware of an overpowering sleepiness, had switched off her light and jumped into bed. Her last waking thought was a regret that she had not been able to speak at length to Mr. Ginger Kemp on the subject of enterprise, and resolve that the address should be delivered at the earliest opportunity.

III

The Dignified Mr. Carmyle

1

By six o'clock on the following evening, however, Sally had been forced to the conclusion that Ginger would have to struggle through life as best he could without the assistance of her contemplated remarks: for she had seen nothing of him all day and in another hour she would have left Roville on the seven-fifteen express which was to take her to Paris, en route for Cherbourg and the liner whereon she had booked her passage for New York.

It was in the faint hope of finding him even now that, at half-past six, having conveyed her baggage to the station and left it in charge of an amiable porter, she paid a last visit to the Casino Municipale. She disliked the thought of leaving Ginger without having uplifted him. Like so many alert and active-minded girls, she possessed in a great degree the quality of interesting herself in—or, as her brother Fillmore preferred to put it, messing about with—the private affairs of others. Ginger had impressed her as a man to whom it was worth while to give a friendly shove on the right path; and it was with much gratification, therefore, that, having entered the Casino, she perceived a flaming head shining through the crowd which had gathered at one of the roulette-tables.

There are two Casinos at Roville-sur-Mer. The one on the Promenade goes in mostly for sea-air and a mild game called boule. It is the big Casino Municipale down in the Palace Massena near the railway station which is the haunt of the earnest gambler who means business; and it was plain to Sally directly she arrived that Ginger Kemp not only meant business but was getting results. Ginger was going extremely strong. He was entrenched behind an opulent-looking mound of square counters: and, even as Sally looked, a wooden-faced croupier shoved a further instalment across the table to him at the end of his long rake.

"Epatant!" murmured a wistful man at Sally's side, removing an elbow from her ribs in order the better to gesticulate. Sally, though no French scholar, gathered that he was startled and gratified. The entire crowd seemed to be startled and gratified. There is undoubtedly a certain altruism in the make-up of the spectators at a Continental roulette-table. They seem to derive a spiritual pleasure from seeing somebody else win.

The croupier gave his moustache a twist with his left hand and the wheel a twist with his right, and silence fell again. Sally, who had shifted to a spot where the pressure of the crowd was less acute, was now able to see Ginger's face, and as she saw it she gave an involuntary laugh. He looked exactly like a dog at a rat-hole. His hair seemed to bristle with excitement. One could almost fancy that his ears were pricked up.

In the tense hush which had fallen on the crowd at the restarting of the wheel, Sally's laugh rang out with an embarrassing clearness. It had a marked effect on all those within hearing. There is something almost of religious ecstasy in the deportment of the spectators at a table where anyone is having a run of luck at roulette, and if she had guffawed in a cathedral she could not have caused a more pained consternation. The earnest worshippers gazed at her with shocked eyes, and Ginger, turning with a start, saw her and jumped up. As he did so, the ball fell with a rattling click into a red compartment of the wheel; and, as it ceased to revolve and it was seen that at last the big winner had picked the wrong colour, a shuddering groan ran through the congregation like that which convulses the penitents' bench at a negro revival meeting. More glances of reproach were cast at Sally. It was generally felt that her injudicious behaviour had changed Ginger's luck.

The only person who did not appear to be concerned was Ginger himself. He gathered up his loot, thrust it into his pocket, and elbowed his way to where Sally stood, now definitely established in the eyes of the crowd as a pariah. There was universal regret that he had decided to call it a day. It was to the spectators as though a star had suddenly walked off the stage in the middle of his big scene; and not even a loud and violent quarrel which sprang up at this moment between two excitable gamblers over a disputed five-franc counter could wholly console them.

"I say," said Ginger, dexterously plucking Sally out of the crowd, "this is topping, meeting you like this. I've been looking for you everywhere."

"It's funny you didn't find me, then, for that's where I've been. I was looking for you."

"No, really?" Ginger seemed pleased. He led the way to the quiet ante-room outside the gambling-hall, and they sat down in a corner. It was pleasant here, with nobody near except the gorgeously uniformed attendant over by the door. "That was awfully good of you."

"I felt I must have a talk with you before my train went."

Ginger started violently.

"Your train? What do you mean?"

"The puff-puff," explained Sally. "I'm leaving to-night, you know."

"Leaving?" Ginger looked as horrified as the devoutest of the congregation of which Sally had just ceased to be a member. "You don't mean leaving? You're not going away from Roville?"

"I'm afraid so."

"But why? Where are you going?"

"Back to America. My boat sails from Cherbourg tomorrow."

"Oh, my aunt!"

"I'm sorry," said Sally, touched by his concern. She was a warm-hearted girl and liked being appreciated. "But. . ."

"I say. . ." Ginger Kemp turned bright scarlet and glared before him at the uniformed official, who was regarding their tête-à-tête with the indulgent eye of one who has been through this sort of thing himself. "I say, look here, will you marry me?"

2

SALLY STARED AT HIS VERMILION profile in frank amazement. Ginger, she had realized by this time, was in many ways a surprising young man, but she had not expected him to be as surprising as this.

"Marry you!"

"You know what I mean."

"Well, yes, I suppose I do. You allude to the holy state. Yes, I know what you mean."

"Then how about it?"

Sally began to regain her composure. Her sense of humour was tickled. She looked at Ginger gravely. He did not meet her eye, but continued to drink in the uniformed official, who was by now so carried away by the romance of it all that he had begun to hum a love-ballad under his breath. The official could not hear what they were saying, and would not have been able to understand it even if he could have heard; but he was an expert in the language of the eyes.

"But isn't this—don't think I am trying to make difficulties—isn't this a little sudden?"

"It's got to be sudden," said Ginger Kemp, complainingly. "I thought you were going to be here for weeks."

"But, my infant, my babe, has it occurred to you that we are practically strangers?" She patted his hand tolerantly, causing the uniformed official to heave a tender sigh. "I see what has happened," she said. "You're mistaking me for some other girl, some girl you know really well, and were properly introduced to. Take a good look at me, and you'll see."

"If I take a good look at you," said Ginger, feverishly, "I'm dashed if I'll answer for the consequences."

"And this is the man I was going to lecture on 'Enterprise.'"

"You're the most wonderful girl I've ever met, dash it!" said Ginger, his gaze still riveted on the official by the door "I dare say it is sudden. I can't help that. I fell in love with you the moment I saw you, and there you are!"

"But. . ."

"Now, look here, I know I'm not much of a chap and all that, but. . . well, I've just won the deuce of a lot of money in there. . ."

"Would you buy me with your gold?"

"I mean to say, we should have enough to start on, and. . . of course I've made an infernal hash of everything I've tried up till now, but there must be something I can do, and you can jolly well bet I'd have a goodish stab at it. I mean to say, with you to buck me up and so forth, don't you know. Well, I mean. . ."

"Has it struck you that I may already be engaged to someone else?"

"Oh, golly! Are you?"

For the first time he turned and faced her, and there was a look in his eyes which touched Sally and drove all sense of the ludicrous out of her. Absurd as it was, this man was really serious.

"Well, yes, as a matter of fact I am," she said soberly.

Ginger Kemp bit his lip and for a moment was silent.

"Oh, well, that's torn it!" he said at last.

Sally was aware of an emotion too complex to analyse. There was pity in it, but amusement too. The emotion, though she did not recognize it, was maternal. Mothers, listening to their children pleading with engaging absurdity for something wholly out of their power to bestow, feel that same wavering between tears and laughter. Sally wanted to pick Ginger up and kiss him. The one thing she could not do was to look on him, sorry as she was for him, as a reasonable, grown-up man.

"You don't really mean it, you know."

"Don't I!" said Ginger, hollowly. "Oh, don't I!"

"You can't! There isn't such a thing in real life as love at first sight. Love's a thing that comes when you know a person well and. . ." She paused. It had just occurred to her that she was hardly the girl to lecture in this strain. Her love for Gerald Foster had been sufficiently sudden, even instantaneous. What did she know of Gerald except that she loved him? They had become engaged within two weeks of their first meeting. She found this recollection damping to her eloquence, and ended by saying tamely:

"It's ridiculous."

Ginger had simmered down to a mood of melancholy resignation.

"I couldn't have expected you to care for me, I suppose, anyway," he said, sombrely. "I'm not much of a chap."

It was just the diversion from the theme under discussion which Sally had been longing to find. She welcomed the chance of continuing the conversation on a less intimate and sentimental note.

"That's exactly what I wanted to talk to you about," she said, seizing the opportunity offered by this display of humility. "I've been looking for you all day to go on with what I was starting to say in the lift last night when we were interrupted. Do you mind if I talk to you like an aunt—or a sister, suppose we say? Really, the best plan would be for you to adopt me as an honorary sister. What do you think?"

Ginger did not appear noticeably elated at the suggested relationship.

"Because I really do take a tremendous interest in you."

Ginger brightened. "That's awfully good of you."

"I'm going to speak words of wisdom. Ginger, why don't you brace up?"

"Brace up?"

"Yes, stiffen your backbone and stick out your chin, and square your elbows, and really amount to something. Why do you simply flop about and do nothing and leave everything to what you call 'the family'? Why do you have to be helped all the time? Why don't you help yourself? Why do you have to have jobs found for you? Why don't you rush out and get one? Why do you have to worry about what, 'the family' thinks of you? Why don't you make yourself independent of them? I know you had hard luck, suddenly finding yourself without money and all that, but, good heavens, everybody else in the world who has ever done anything has been broke at one time or another. It's part of the fun. You'll never get anywhere by letting yourself be picked up by the family like. . . like a floppy Newfoundland puppy and dumped down in any old place that happens to suit them. A job's a thing you've got to choose for yourself and get for yourself. Think what you can do—there must be something—and then go at it with a snort and grab it and hold it down and teach it to take a joke. You've managed to collect some money. It will give you time to look round. And, when you've had a look round, do something! Try to realize you're alive, and try to imagine the family isn't!"

Sally stopped and drew a deep breath. Ginger Kemp did not reply for a moment. He seemed greatly impressed.

"When you talk quick," he said at length, in a serious meditative voice, "your nose sort of goes all squiggly. Ripping, it looks!"

Sally uttered an indignant cry.

"Do you mean to say you haven't been listening to a word I've been saying," she demanded.

"Oh, rather! Oh, by Jove, yes."

"Well, what did I say?"

"You. . . er. . . And your eyes sort of shine, too."

"Never mind my eyes. What did I say?"

"You told me," said Ginger, on reflection, "to get a job."

"Well, yes. I put it much better than that, but that's what it amounted to, I suppose. All right, then. I'm glad you. . ."

Ginger was eyeing her with mournful devotion. "I say," he interrupted, "I wish you'd let me write to you. Letters, I mean, and all that. I have an idea it would kind of buck me up."

"You won't have time for writing letters."

"I'll have time to write them to you. You haven't an address or anything of that sort in America, have you, by any chance? I mean, so that I'd know where to write to."

"I can give you an address which will always find me." She told him the number and street of Mrs. Meecher's boarding-house, and he wrote them down reverently on his shirt-cuff. "Yes, on second thoughts, do write," she said. "Of course, I shall want to know how you've got on. I. . . oh, my goodness! That clock's not right?"

"Just about. What time does your train go?"

"Go! It's gone! Or, at least, it goes in about two seconds." She made a rush for the swing-door, to the confusion of the uniformed official who had not been expecting this sudden activity. "Good-bye, Ginger. Write to me, and remember what I said."

Ginger, alert after his unexpected fashion when it became a question of physical action, had followed her through the swing-door, and they emerged together and started running down the square.

"Stick it!" said Ginger, encouragingly. He was running easily and well, as becomes a man who, in his day, had been a snip for his international at scrum-half.

Sally saved her breath. The train was beginning to move slowly out of the station as they sprinted abreast on to the platform. Ginger dived for the nearest door, wrenched it open, gathered Sally neatly in his arms, and flung her in. She landed squarely on the toes of a man who occupied the corner seat, and, bounding off again, made for the window. Ginger, faithful to the last, was trotting beside the train as it gathered speed.

"Ginger! My poor porter! Tip him. I forgot."

"Right ho!"

"And don't forget what I've been saying."

"Right ho!"

"Look after yourself and 'Death to the Family!'"

"Right ho!"

The train passed smoothly out of the station. Sally cast one last look back at her red-haired friend, who had now halted and was waving a handkerchief. Then she turned to apologize to the other occupant of the carriage.

"I'm so sorry," she said, breathlessly. "I hope I didn't hurt you."

She found herself facing Ginger's cousin, the dark man of yesterday's episode on the beach, Bruce Carmyle.

3

MR. CARMYLE WAS NOT A MAN who readily allowed himself to be disturbed by life's little surprises, but at the present moment he could not help feeling slightly dazed. He recognized Sally now as the French girl who had attracted his cousin Lancelot's notice on the beach. At least he had assumed that she was French, and it was startling to be addressed by her now in fluent English. How had she suddenly acquired this gift of tongues? And how on earth had she had time since yesterday, when he had been a total stranger to her, to become sufficiently intimate with Cousin Lancelot to be sprinting with him down station platforms and addressing him out of railway-carriage windows as Ginger? Bruce Carmyle was aware that most members of that sub-species of humanity, his cousin's personal friends, called him by that familiar—and, so Carmyle held, vulgar—nickname: but how had this girl got hold of it?

If Sally had been less pretty, Mr. Carmyle would undoubtedly have looked disapprovingly at her, for she had given his rather rigid sense of the proprieties a nasty jar. But as, panting and flushed from her run, she was prettier than any girl he had yet met, he contrived to smile.

"Not at all," he said in answer to her question, though it was far from the truth. His left big toe was aching confoundedly. Even a girl with a foot as small as Sally's can make her presence felt on a man's toe if the scrum-half who is handling her aims well and uses plenty of vigour.

"If you don't mind," said Sally, sitting down, "I think I'll breathe a little."

She breathed. The train sped on.

"Quite a close thing," said Bruce Carmyle, affably. The pain in his toe was diminishing. "You nearly missed it."

"Yes. It was lucky Mr. Kemp was with me. He throws very straight, doesn't he."

"Tell me," said Carmyle, "how do you come to know my Cousin? On the beach yesterday morning. . ."

"Oh, we didn't know each other then. But we were staying at the same hotel, and we spent an hour or so shut up in an elevator together. That was when we really got acquainted."

A waiter entered the compartment, announcing in unexpected English that dinner was served in the restaurant car. "Would you care for dinner?"

"I'm starving," said Sally.

She reproved herself, as they made their way down the corridor, for being so foolish as to judge anyone by his appearance. This man was perfectly pleasant in spite of his grim exterior. She had decided by the time they had seated themselves at the table she liked him.

At the table, however, Mr. Carmyle's manner changed for the worse. He lost his amiability. He was evidently a man who took his meals seriously and believed in treating waiters with severity. He shuddered austerely at a stain on the table-cloth, and then concentrated himself frowningly on the bill of fare. Sally, meanwhile, was establishing cosy relations with the much too friendly waiter, a cheerful old man who from the start seemed to have made up his mind to regard her as a favourite daughter. The waiter talked no English and Sally no French, but they were getting along capitally, when Mr. Carmyle, who had been irritably waving aside the servitor's light-hearted advice—at the Hotel Splendide the waiters never bent over you and breathed cordial suggestions down the side of your face—gave his order crisply in the Anglo-Gallic dialect of the travelling Briton. The waiter remarked, "Boum!" in a pleased sort of way, and vanished.

P.G. WODEHOUSE

"Nice old man!" said Sally.

"Infernally familiar!" said Mr. Carmyle.

Sally perceived that on the topic of the waiter she and her host did not see eye to eye and that little pleasure or profit could be derived from any discussion centring about him. She changed the subject. She was not liking Mr. Carmyle quite so much as she had done a few minutes ago, but it was courteous of him to give her dinner, and she tried to like him as much as she could.

"By the way," she said, "my name is Nicholas. I always think it's a good thing to start with names, don't you?"

"Mine. . ."

"Oh, I know yours. Ginger—Mr. Kemp told me."

Mr. Carmyle, who since the waiter's departure, had been thawing, stiffened again at the mention of Ginger.

"Indeed?" he said, coldly. "Apparently you got intimate."

Sally did not like his tone. He seemed to be criticizing her, and she resented criticism from a stranger. Her eyes opened wide and she looked dangerously across the table.

"Why 'apparently'? I told you that we had got intimate, and I explained how. You can't stay shut up in an elevator half the night with anybody without getting to know him. I found Mr. Kemp very pleasant."

"Really?"

"And very interesting."

Mr. Carmyle raised his eyebrows.

"Would you call him interesting?"

"I did call him interesting." Sally was beginning to feel the exhilaration of battle. Men usually made themselves extremely agreeable to her, and she reacted belligerently under the stiff unfriendliness which had come over her companion in the last few minutes.

"He told me all about himself."

"And you found that interesting?"

"Why not?"

"Well. . ." A frigid half-smile came and went on Bruce Carmyle's dark face. "My cousin has many excellent qualities, no doubt—he used to play football well, and I understand that he is a capable amateur pugilist—but I should not have supposed him entertaining. We find him a little dull."

"I thought it was only royalty that called themselves 'we.'"

"I meant myself—and the rest of the family."

The mention of the family was too much for Sally. She had to stop talking in order to allow her mind to clear itself of rude thoughts.

"Mr. Kemp was telling me about Mr. Scrymgeour," she went on at length.

Bruce Carmyle stared for a moment at the yard or so of French bread which the waiter had placed on the table.

"Indeed?" he said. "He has an engaging lack of reticence."

The waiter returned bearing soup and dumped it down.

"V'la!" he observed, with the satisfied air of a man who has successfully performed a difficult conjuring trick. He smiled at Sally expectantly, as though confident of applause from this section of his audience at least. But Sally's face was set and rigid. She had been snubbed, and the sensation was as pleasant as it was novel.

"I think Mr. Kemp had hard luck," she said.

"If you will excuse me, I would prefer not to discuss the matter."

Mr. Carmyle's attitude was that Sally might be a pretty girl, but she was a stranger, and the intimate affairs of the Family were not to be discussed with strangers, however prepossessing.

"He was quite in the right. Mr. Scrymgeour was beating a dog. . ."

"I've heard the details."

"Oh, I didn't know that. Well, don't you agree with me, then?"

"I do not. A man who would throw away an excellent position simply because. . ."

"Oh, well, if that's your view, I suppose it is useless to talk about it."

"Quite."

"Still, there's no harm in asking what you propose to do about Gin—about Mr. Kemp."

Mr. Carmyle became more glacial.

"I'm afraid I cannot discuss. . ."

Sally's quick impatience, nobly restrained till now, finally got the better of her.

"Oh, for goodness' sake," she snapped, "do try to be human, and don't always be snubbing people. You remind me of one of those portraits of men in the eighteenth century, with wooden faces, who look out of heavy gold frames at you with fishy eyes as if you were a regrettable incident."

"Rosbif," said the waiter genially, manifesting himself suddenly beside them as if he had popped up out of a trap.

Bruce Carmyle attacked his roast beef morosely. Sally who was in the mood when she knew that she would be ashamed of herself later on, but was full of battle at the moment, sat in silence.

"I am sorry," said Mr. Carmyle ponderously, "if my eyes are fishy. The fact has not been called to my attention before."

"I suppose you never had any sisters," said Sally. "They would have told you."

Mr. Carmyle relapsed into an offended dumbness, which lasted till the waiter had brought the coffee.

"I think," said Sally, getting up, "I'll be going now. I don't seem to want any coffee, and, if I stay on, I may say something rude. I thought I might be able to put in a good word for Mr. Kemp and save him from being massacred, but apparently it's no use. Good-bye, Mr. Carmyle, and thank you for giving me dinner."

She made her way down the car, followed by Bruce Carmyle's indignant, yet fascinated, gaze. Strange emotions were stirring in Mr. Carmyle's bosom.

IV

GINGER IN DANGEROUS MOOD

Some few days later, owing to the fact that the latter, being preoccupied, did not see him first, Bruce Carmyle met his cousin Lancelot in Piccadilly. They had returned by different routes from Roville, and Ginger would have preferred the separation to continue. He was hurrying on with a nod, when Carmyle stopped him.

"Just the man I wanted to see," he observed.

"Oh, hullo!" said Ginger, without joy.

"I was thinking of calling at your club."

"Yes?"

"Yes. Cigarette?"

Ginger peered at the proffered case with the vague suspicion of the man who has allowed himself to be lured on to the platform and is accepting a card from the conjurer. He felt bewildered. In all the years of their acquaintance he could not recall another such exhibition of geniality on his cousin's part. He was surprised, indeed, at Mr. Carmyle's speaking to him at all, for the affaire Scrymgeour remained an un-healed wound, and the Family, Ginger knew, were even now in session upon it.

"Been back in London long?"

"Day or two."

"I heard quite by accident that you had returned and that you were staying at the club. By the way, thank you for introducing me to Miss Nicholas."

Ginger started violently.

"What!"

"I was in that compartment, you know, at Roville Station. You threw her right on top of me. We agreed to consider that an introduction. An attractive girl."

Bruce Carmyle had not entirely made up his mind regarding Sally, but on one point he was clear, that she should not, if he could help it, pass out of his life. Her abrupt departure had left him with that baffled and dissatisfied feeling which, though it has little in common with love at first sight, frequently produces the same effects. She had had, he could not disguise it from himself, the better of their late encounter and he was conscious of a desire to meet her again and show her that there was more in him than she apparently supposed. Bruce Carmyle, in a word, was piqued: and, though he could not quite decide whether he liked or disliked Sally, he was very sure that a future without her would have an element of flatness.

"A very attractive girl. We had a very pleasant talk."

"I bet you did," said Ginger enviously.

"By the way, she did not give you her address by any chance?"

"Why?" said Ginger suspiciously. His attitude towards Sally's address resembled somewhat that of a connoisseur who has acquired a unique work of art. He wanted to keep it to himself and gloat over it.

"Well, I—er—I promised to send her some books she was anxious to read. . ."

"I shouldn't think she gets much time for reading."

"Books which are not published in America."

"Oh, pretty nearly everything is published in America, what? Bound to be, I mean."

"Well, these particular books are not," said Mr. Carmyle shortly. He was finding Ginger's reserve a little trying, and wished that he had been more inventive.

"Give them to me and I'll send them to her," suggested Ginger.

"Good Lord, man!" snapped Mr. Carmyle. "I'm capable of sending a few books to America. Where does she live?"

Ginger revealed the sacred number of the holy street which had the luck to be Sally's headquarters. He did it because with a persistent devil like his cousin there seemed no way of getting out of it: but he did it grudgingly.

"Thanks." Bruce Carmyle wrote the information down with a gold pencil in a dapper little morocco-bound note-book. He was the sort of man who always has a pencil, and the backs of old envelopes never enter into his life.

There was a pause. Bruce Carmyle coughed.

"I saw Uncle Donald this morning," he said.

His manner had lost its geniality. There was no need for it now, and he was a man who objected to waste. He spoke coldly, and in his voice there was a familiar sub-tingle of reproof.

"Yes?" said Ginger moodily. This was the uncle in whose office he had made his debut as a hasher: a worthy man, highly respected in the National Liberal Club, but never a favourite of Ginger's. There were other minor uncles and a few subsidiary aunts who went to make up the Family, but Uncle Donald was unquestionably the managing director of that body and it was Ginger's considered opinion that in this capacity he approximated to a human blister.

"He wants you to dine with him to-night at Bleke's."

Ginger's depression deepened. A dinner with Uncle Donald would hardly have been a cheerful function, even in the surroundings of a banquet in the Arabian Nights. There was that about Uncle Donald's personality which would have cast a sobering influence over the orgies of the Emperor Tiberius at Capri. To dine with him at a morgue like that relic of Old London, Bleke's Coffee House, which confined its custom principally to regular patrons who had not missed an evening there for half a century, was to touch something very near bed-rock. Ginger was extremely doubtful whether flesh and blood were equal to it.

"To-night?" he said. "Oh, you mean to-night? Well. . ."

"Don't be a fool. You know as well as I do that you've got to go." Uncle Donald's invitations were royal commands in the Family. "If you've another engagement you must put it off."

"Oh, all right."

"Seven-thirty sharp."

"All right," said Ginger gloomily.

The two men went their ways, Bruce Carmyle eastwards because he had clients to see in his chambers at the Temple; Ginger westwards because Mr. Carmyle had gone east. There was little sympathy between these cousins: yet, oddly enough, their thoughts as they walked centred on the same object. Bruce Carmyle, threading his way briskly through the crowds of Piccadilly Circus, was thinking of Sally: and so was Ginger as he loafed aimlessly towards Hyde Park Corner, bumping in a sort of coma from pedestrian to pedestrian.

Since his return to London Ginger had been in bad shape. He mooned through the days and slept poorly at night. If there is one thing rottener than another in a pretty blighted world, one thing which gives a fellow the pip and reduces him to the condition of an absolute onion, it is hopeless love. Hopeless love had got Ginger all stirred up. His had been hitherto a placid soul. Even the financial crash which had so altered his life had not bruised him very deeply. His temperament had enabled him to bear the slings and arrows of outrageous fortune with a philosophic "Right ho!" But now everything seemed different. Things irritated him acutely, which before he had accepted as inevitable—

his Uncle Donald's moustache, for instance, and its owner's habit of employing it during meals as a sort of zareba or earthwork against the assaults of soup.

"By gad!" thought Ginger, stopping suddenly opposite Devonshire House. "If he uses that damned shrubbery as soup-strainer to-night, I'll slosh him with a fork!"

Hard thoughts. . . hard thoughts! And getting harder all the time, for nothing grows more quickly than a mood of rebellion. Rebellion is a forest fire that flames across the soul. The spark had been lighted in Ginger, and long before he reached Hyde Park Corner he was ablaze and crackling. By the time he returned to his club he was practically a menace to society—to that section of it, at any rate, which embraced his Uncle Donald, his minor uncles George and William, and his aunts Mary, Geraldine, and Louise.

Nor had the mood passed when he began to dress for the dismal festivities of Bleke's Coffee House. He scowled as he struggled morosely with an obstinate tie. One cannot disguise the fact—Ginger was warming up. And it was just at this moment that Fate, as though it had been waiting for the psychological instant, applied the finishing touch. There was a knock at the door, and a waiter came in with a telegram.

Ginger looked at the envelope. It had been readdressed and forwarded on from the Hotel Normandie. It was a wireless, handed in on board the White Star liner Olympic, and it ran as follows:

Remember. Death to the Family. S.

Ginger sat down heavily on the bed.

The driver of the taxi-cab which at twenty-five minutes past seven drew up at the dingy door of Bleke's Coffee House in the Strand was rather struck by his fare's manner and appearance. A determined-looking sort of young bloke, was the taxi-driver's verdict.

V

Sally Hears News

It had been Sally's intention, on arriving in New York, to take a room at the St. Regis and revel in the gilded luxury to which her wealth entitled her before moving into the small but comfortable apartment which, as soon as she had the time, she intended to find and make her permanent abode. But when the moment came and she was giving directions to the taxi-driver at the dock, there seemed to her something revoltingly Fillmorian about the scheme. It would be time enough to sever herself from the boarding-house which had been her home for three years when she had found the apartment. Meanwhile, the decent thing to do, if she did not want to brand herself in the sight of her conscience as a female Fillmore, was to go back temporarily to Mrs. Meecher's admirable establishment and foregather with her old friends. After all, home is where the heart is, even if there are more prunes there than the gourmet would consider judicious.

Perhaps it was the unavoidable complacency induced by the thought that she was doing the right thing, or possibly it was the tingling expectation of meeting Gerald Foster again after all these weeks of separation, that made the familiar streets seem wonderfully bright as she drove through them. It was a perfect, crisp New York morning, all blue sky and amber sunshine, and even the ash-cans had a stimulating look about them. The street cars were full of happy people rollicking off to work: policemen directed the traffic with jaunty affability: and the white-clad street-cleaners went about their poetic tasks with a quiet but none the less noticeable relish. It was improbable that any of these people knew that she was back, but somehow they all seemed to be behaving as though this were a special day.

The first discordant note in this overture of happiness was struck by Mrs. Meecher, who informed Sally, after expressing her gratification at the news that she required her old room, that Gerald Foster had left town that morning.

"Gone to Detroit, he has," said Mrs. Meecher. "Miss Doland, too." She broke off to speak a caustic word to the boarding-house handyman, who, with Sally's trunk as a weapon, was depreciating the value of the wall-paper in the hall. "There's that play of his being tried out there, you know, Monday," resumed Mrs. Meecher, after the handyman had bumped his way up the staircase. "They been rehearsing ever since you left."

Sally was disappointed, but it was such a beautiful morning, and New York was so wonderful after the dull voyage in the liner that she was not going to allow herself to be depressed without good reason. After all, she could go on to Detroit tomorrow. It was nice to have something to which she could look forward.

"Oh, is Elsa in the company?" she said.

"Sure. And very good too, I hear." Mrs. Meecher kept abreast of theatrical gossip. She was an ex-member of the profession herself, having been in the first production of "Florodora," though, unlike everybody else, not one of the original Sextette. "Mr. Faucitt was down to see a rehearsal, and he said Miss Doland was fine. And he's not easy to please, as you know."

"How is Mr. Faucitt?"

Mrs. Meecher, not unwillingly, for she was a woman who enjoyed the tragedies of life, made her second essay in the direction of lowering Sally's uplifted mood.

"Poor old gentleman, he ain't over and above well. Went to bed early last night with a headache, and this morning I been to see him and he don't look well. There's a lot of this Spanish influenza about. It might be that. Lots o' people have been dying of it, if you believe what you see in the papers," said Mrs. Meecher buoyantly.

"Good gracious! You don't think. . . ?"

"Well, he ain't turned black," admitted Mrs. Meecher with regret. "They say they turn black. If you believe what you see in the papers, that is. Of course, that may come later," she added with the air of one confident that all will come right in the future. "The doctor'll be in to see him pretty soon. He's quite happy. Toto's sitting with him."

Sally's concern increased. Like everyone who had ever spent any length of time in the house, she had strong views on Toto. This quadruped, who stained the fame of the entire canine race by posing as a dog, was a small woolly animal with a persistent and penetrating yap, hard to bear with equanimity in health and certainly quite outside the range of a sick man. Her heart bled for Mr. Faucitt. Mrs. Meecher, on the other hand, who held a faith in her little pet's amiability and power to soothe which seven years' close association had been unable to shake, seemed to feel that, with Toto on the spot, all that could be done had been done as far as pampering the invalid was concerned.

"I must go up and see him," cried Sally. "Poor old dear."

"Sure. You know his room. You can hear Toto talking to him now," said Mrs. Meecher complacently. "He wants a cracker, that's what he wants. Toto likes a cracker after breakfast."

The invalid's eyes, as Sally entered the room, turned wearily to the door. At the sight of Sally they lit up with an incredulous rapture. Almost any intervention would have pleased Mr. Faucitt at that moment, for his little playmate had long outstayed any welcome that might originally have been his: but that the caller should be his beloved Sally seemed to the old man something in the nature of a return of the age of miracles.

"Sally!"

"One moment. Here, Toto!"

Toto, struck momentarily dumb by the sight of food, had jumped off the bed and was standing with his head on one side, peering questioningly at the cracker. He was a suspicious dog, but he allowed himself to be lured into the passage, upon which Sally threw the cracker down and slipped in and shut the door. Toto, after a couple of yaps, which may have been gratitude or baffled fury, trotted off downstairs, and Mr. Faucitt drew a deep breath.

"Sally, you come, as ever, as an angel of mercy. Our worthy Mrs. Meecher means well, and I yield to no man in my respect for her innate kindness of heart: but she errs in supposing that that thrice-damned whelp of hers is a combination of sick-nurse, soothing medicine, and a week at the seaside. She insisted on bringing him here. He was yapping then, as he was yapping when, with womanly resource which I cannot sufficiently praise, you decoyed him hence. And each yap went through me like hammer-strokes on sheeted tin. Sally, you stand alone among womankind. You shine like a good deed in a naughty world. When did you get back?"

"I've only just arrived in my hired barouche from the pier."

"And you came to see your old friend without delay? I am grateful and flattered. Sally, my dear."

"Of course I came to see you. Do you suppose that, when Mrs. Meecher told me you were sick, I just said 'Is that so?' and went on talking about the weather? Well, what do you mean by it? Frightening everybody. Poor old darling, do you feel very bad?"

"One thousand individual mice are nibbling the base of my spine, and I am conscious of a constant need of cooling refreshment. But what of that? Your presence is a tonic. Tell me, how did our Sally enjoy foreign travel?"

"Our Sally had the time of her life."

"Did you visit England?"

"Only passing through."

"How did it look?" asked Mr. Faucitt eagerly.

"Moist. Very moist."

"It would," said Mr. Faucitt indulgently. "I confess that, happy as I have been in this country, there are times when I miss those wonderful London days, when a sort of cosy brown mist hangs over the streets and the pavements ooze with a perspiration of mud and water, and you see through the haze the yellow glow of the Bodega lamps shining in the distance like harbour-lights. Not," said Mr. Faucitt, "that I specify the Bodega to the exclusion of other and equally worthy hostelries. I have passed just as pleasant hours in Rule's and Short's. You missed something by not lingering in England, Sally."

"I know I did—pneumonia."

Mr. Faucitt shook his head reproachfully.

"You are prejudiced, my dear. You would have enjoyed London if you had had the courage to brave its superficial gloom. Where did you spend your holiday? Paris?"

"Part of the time. And the rest of the while I was down by the sea. It was glorious. I don't think I would ever have come back if I hadn't had to. But, of course, I wanted to see you all again. And I wanted to be at the opening of Mr. Foster's play. Mrs. Meecher tells me you went to one of the rehearsals."

"I attended a dog-fight which I was informed was a rehearsal," said Mr. Faucitt severely. "There is no rehearsing nowadays."

"Oh dear! Was it as bad as all that?"

"The play is good. The play—I will go further—is excellent. It has fat. But the acting. . ."

"Mrs. Meecher said you told her that Elsa was good."

"Our worthy hostess did not misreport me. Miss Doland has great possibilities. She reminds me somewhat of Matilda Devine, under whose banner I played a season at the Old Royalty in London many years ago. She has the seeds of greatness in her, but she is wasted in the present case on an insignificant part. There is only one part in the play. I allude to the one murdered by Miss Mabel Hobson."

"Murdered!" Sally's heart sank. She had been afraid of this, and it was no satisfaction to feel that she had warned Gerald. "Is she very terrible?"

"She has the face of an angel and the histrionic ability of that curious suet pudding which our estimable Mrs. Meecher is apt to give us on Fridays. In my professional career I have seen many cases of what I may term the Lady Friend in the role of star, but Miss Hobson eclipses them all. I remember in the year '94 a certain scion of the plutocracy took it into his head to present a female for whom he had conceived an admiration in a part which would have taxed the resources of the ablest. I was engaged in her support, and at the first rehearsal I recollect saying to my dear old friend, Arthur Moseby—dead, alas, these many years. An excellent juvenile, but, like so many good fellows, cursed with a tendency to lift the elbow—I recollect saying to him 'Arthur, dear boy, I give it two weeks.' 'Max,' was his reply, 'you are an incurable optimist. One consecutive night, laddie, one consecutive night.' We had, I recall, an even half-crown upon it. He won. We opened at Wigan, our leading lady got the bird, and the show closed next day. I was forcibly reminded of this incident as I watched Miss Hobson rehearsing."

"Oh, poor Ger—poor Mr. Foster!"

"I do not share your commiseration for that young man," said Mr. Faucitt austerely. "You probably are almost a stranger to him, but he and I have been thrown together a good deal of late. A young man upon whom, mark my words, success, if it ever comes, will have the worst effects. I dislike him. Sally. He is, I think, without exception, the most selfish and self-centred young man of my acquaintance. He reminds me very much of old Billy Fothergill, with whom I toured a good deal in the later eighties. Did I ever tell you the story of Billy and the amateur who. . . ?"

Sally was in no mood to listen to the adventures of Mr. Fothergill. The old man's innocent criticism of Gerald had stabbed her deeply. A momentary impulse to speak hotly in his defence died away as she saw Mr. Faucitt's pale, worn old face. He had meant no harm, after all. How could he know what Gerald was to her?

She changed the conversation abruptly.

"Have you seen anything of Fillmore while I've been away?"

"Fillmore? Why yes, my dear, curiously enough I happened to run into him on Broadway only a few days ago. He seemed changed—less stiff and aloof than he had been for some time past. I may be wronging

P.G. WODEHOUSE

him, but there have been times of late when one might almost have fancied him a trifle up-stage. All that was gone at our last encounter. He appeared glad to see me and was most cordial."

Sally found her composure restored. Her lecture on the night of the party had evidently, she thought, not been wasted. Mr. Faucitt, however, advanced another theory to account for the change in the Man of Destiny.

"I rather fancy," he said, "that the softening influence has been the young man's fiancée."

"What? Fillmore's not engaged?"

"Did he not write and tell you? I suppose he was waiting to inform you when you returned. Yes, Fillmore is betrothed. The lady was with him when we met. A Miss Winch. In the profession, I understand. He introduced me. A very charming and sensible young lady, I thought."

Sally shook her head.

"She can't be. Fillmore would never have got engaged to anyone like that. Was her hair crimson?"

"Brown, if I recollect rightly."

"Very loud, I suppose, and overdressed?"

"On the contrary, neat and quiet."

"You've made a mistake," said Sally decidedly. "She can't have been like that. I shall have to look into this. It does seem hard that I can't go away for a few weeks without all my friends taking to beds of sickness and all my brothers getting ensnared by vampires."

A knock at the door interrupted her complaint. Mrs. Meecher entered, ushering in a pleasant little man with spectacles and black bag.

"The doctor to see you, Mr. Faucitt." Mrs. Meecher cast an appraising eye at the invalid, as if to detect symptoms of approaching discoloration. "I've been telling him that what I think you've gotten is this here new Spanish influenza. Two more deaths there were in the paper this morning, if you can believe what you see. . ."

"I wonder," said the doctor, "if you would mind going and bringing me a small glass of water?"

"Why, sure."

"Not a large glass—a small glass. Just let the tap run for a few moments and take care not to spill any as you come up the stairs. I always ask ladies, like our friend who has just gone," he added as the door closed, "to bring me a glass of water. It keeps them amused and interested and gets them out of the way, and they think I am going to do a conjuring trick with it. As a matter of fact, I'm going to drink it. Now let's have a look at you."

The examination did not take long. At the end of it the doctor seemed somewhat chagrined.

"Our good friend's diagnosis was correct. I'd give a leg to say it wasn't, but it was. It is this here new Spanish influenza. Not a bad attack. You want to stay in bed and keep warm, and I'll write you out a prescription. You ought to be nursed. Is this young lady a nurse?"

"No, no, merely. . ."

"Of course I'm a nurse," said Sally decidedly. "It isn't difficult, is it, doctor? I know nurses smooth pillows. I can do that. Is there anything else?"

"Their principal duty is to sit here and prevent the excellent and garrulous lady who has just left us from getting in. They must also be able to aim straight with a book or an old shoe, if that small woolly dog I met downstairs tries to force an entrance. If you are equal to these tasks, I can leave the case in your hands with every confidence."

"But, Sally, my dear," said Mr. Faucitt, concerned, "you must not waste your time looking after me. You have a thousand things to occupy you."

"There's nothing I want to do more than help you to get better. I'll just go out and send a wire, and then I'll be right back."

Five minutes later, Sally was in a Western Union office, telegraphing to Gerald that she would be unable to reach Detroit in time for the opening.

VI

First Aid for Fillmore

1

IT WAS NOT TILL THE following Friday that Sally was able to start for Detroit. She arrived on the Saturday morning and drove to the Hotel Statler. Having ascertained that Gerald was stopping in the hotel and having 'phoned up to his room to tell him to join her, she went into the dining-room and ordered breakfast.

She felt low-spirited as she waited for the food to arrive. The nursing of Mr. Faucitt had left her tired, and she had not slept well on the train. But the real cause of her depression was the fact that there had been a lack of enthusiasm in Gerald's greeting over the telephone just now. He had spoken listlessly, as though the fact of her returning after all these weeks was a matter of no account, and she felt hurt and perplexed.

A cup of coffee had a stimulating effect. Men, of course, were always like this in the early morning. It would, no doubt, be a very different Gerald who would presently bound into the dining-room, quickened and restored by a cold shower-bath. In the meantime, here was food, and she needed it.

She was pouring out her second cup of coffee when a stout young man, of whom she had caught a glimpse as he moved about that section of the hotel lobby which was visible through the open door of the dining-room, came in and stood peering about as though in search of someone. The momentary sight she had had of this young man had interested Sally. She had thought how extraordinarily like he was to her brother Fillmore. Now she perceived that it was Fillmore himself.

Sally was puzzled. What could Fillmore be doing so far west? She had supposed him to be a permanent resident of New York. But, of course, your man of affairs and vast interests flits about all over the place. At any rate, here he was, and she called him. And, after he had stood in the doorway looking in every direction except the right one for another minute, he saw her and came over to her table.

"Why, Sally?" His manner, she thought, was nervous—one might almost have said embarrassed. She attributed this to a guilty conscience.

Presently he would have to break to her the news that he had become engaged to be married without her sisterly sanction, and no doubt he was wondering how to begin. "What are you doing here? I thought you were in Europe."

"I got back a week ago, but I've been nursing poor old Mr. Faucitt ever since then. He's been ill, poor old dear. I've come here to see Mr. Foster's play, 'The Primrose Way,' you know. Is it a success?"

"It hasn't opened yet."

"Don't be silly, Fill. Do pull yourself together. It opened last Monday."

"No, it didn't. Haven't you heard? They've closed all the theatres because of this infernal Spanish influenza. Nothing has been playing this week. You must have seen it in the papers."

"I haven't had time to read the papers. Oh, Fill, what an awful shame!"

"Yes, it's pretty tough. Makes the company all on edge. I've had the darndest time, I can tell you."

"Why, what have you got to do with it?"

Fillmore coughed.

"I—er—oh, I didn't tell you that. I'm sort of—er—mixed up in the show. Cracknell—you remember he was at college with me—suggested that I should come down and look at it. Shouldn't wonder if he wants me to put money into it and so on."

"I thought he had all the money in the world."

"Yes, he has a lot, but these fellows like to let a pal in on a good thing."

"Is it a good thing?"

"The play's fine."

"That's what Mr. Faucitt said. But Mabel Hobson. . ."

Fillmore's ample face registered emotion.

"She's an awful woman, Sally! She can't act, and she throws her weight about all the time. The other day there was a fuss about a paper-knife. . ."

"How do you mean, a fuss about a paper-knife?"

"One of the props, you know. It got mislaid. I'm certain it wasn't my fault. . ."

"How could it have been your fault?" asked Sally wonderingly. Love seemed to have the worst effects on Fillmore's mentality.

"Well—er—you know how it is. Angry woman. . . blames the first person she sees. . . This paper-knife. . ."

Fillmore's voice trailed off into pained silence.

"Mr. Faucitt said Elsa Doland was good."

"Oh, she's all right," said Fillmore indifferently. "But—" His face brightened and animation crept into his voice. "But the girl you want to watch is Miss Winch. Gladys Winch. She plays the maid. She's only in the first act, and hasn't much to say, except 'Did you ring, madam?' and things like that. But it's the way she says 'em! Sally, that girl's a genius! The greatest character actress in a dozen years! You mark my words, in a darned little while you'll see her name up on Broadway in electric light. Personality? Ask me! Charm? She wrote the words and music! Looks? . . ."

"All right! All right! I know all about it, Fill. And will you kindly inform me how you dared to get engaged without consulting me?"

Fillmore blushed richly.

"Oh, do you know?"

"Yes. Mr. Faucitt told me."

"Well. . ."

"Well?"

"Well, I'm only human," argued Fillmore.

"I call that a very handsome admission. You've got quite modest, Fill."

He had certainly changed for the better since their last meeting. It was as if someone had punctured him and let out all the pomposity. If this was due, as Mr. Faucitt had suggested, to the influence of Miss Winch, Sally felt that she could not but approve of the romance.

"I'll introduce you sometime,' said Fillmore.

"I want to meet her very much."

"I'll have to be going now. I've got to see Bunbury. I thought he might be in here."

"Who's Bunbury?"

"The producer. I suppose he is breakfasting in his room. I'd better go up."

"You are busy, aren't you. Little marvel! It's lucky they've got you to look after them."

Fillmore retired and Sally settled down to wait for Gerald, no longer hurt by his manner over the telephone. Poor Gerald! No wonder he had seemed upset.

A few minutes later he came in.

"Oh, Jerry darling," said Sally, as he reached the table, "I'm so sorry. I've just been hearing about it."

Gerald sat down. His appearance fulfilled the promise of his voice over the telephone. A sort of nervous dullness wrapped him about like a garment.

"It's just my luck," he said gloomily. "It's the kind of thing that couldn't happen to anyone but me. Damned fools! Where's the sense in shutting the theatres, even if there is influenza about? They let people jam against one another all day in the stores. If that doesn't hurt them why should it hurt them to go to theatres? Besides, it's all infernal nonsense about this thing. I don't believe there is such a thing as Spanish influenza. People get colds in their heads and think they're dying. It's all a fake scare."

"I don't think it's that," said Sally. "Poor Mr. Faucitt had it quite badly. That's why I couldn't come earlier."

Gerald did not seem interested either by the news of Mr. Faucitt's illness or by the fact that Sally, after delay, had at last arrived. He dug a spoon sombrely into his grape-fruit.

"We've been hanging about here day after day, getting bored to death all the time. . . The company's going all to pieces. They're sick of rehearsing and rehearsing when nobody knows if we'll ever open. They were all keyed up a week ago, and they've been sagging ever since. It will ruin the play, of course. My first chance! Just chucked away."

Sally was listening with a growing feeling of desolation. She tried to be fair, to remember that he had had a terrible disappointment and was under a great strain. And yet. . . it was unfortunate that self-pity was a thing she particularly disliked in a man. Her vanity, too, was hurt. It was obvious that her arrival, so far from acting as a magic restorative, had effected nothing. She could not help remembering, though it made her feel disloyal, what Mr. Faucitt had said about Gerald. She had never noticed before that he was remarkably self-centred, but he was thrusting the fact upon her attention now.

"That Hobson woman is beginning to make trouble," went on Gerald, prodding in a despairing sort of way at scrambled eggs. "She ought never to have had the part, never. She can't handle it. Elsa Doland could play it a thousand times better. I wrote Elsa in a few lines the other day, and the Hobson woman went right up in the air. You don't know what a star is till you've seen one of these promoted clothes-props from the Follies trying to be one. It took me an hour to talk her round and keep her from throwing up her part."

"Why not let her throw up her part?"

"For heaven's sake talk sense," said Gerald querulously. "Do you suppose that man Cracknell would keep the play on if she wasn't in it? He would close the show in a second, and where would I be then?

You don't seem to realize that this is a big chance for me. I'd look a fool throwing it away."

"I see," said Sally, shortly. She had never felt so wretched in her life. Foreign travel, she decided, was a mistake. It might be pleasant and broadening to the mind, but it seemed to put you so out of touch with people when you got back. She analysed her sensations, and arrived at the conclusion that what she was resenting was the fact that Gerald was trying to get the advantages of two attitudes simultaneously. A man in trouble may either be the captain of his soul and superior to pity, or he may be a broken thing for a woman to pet and comfort. Gerald, it seemed to her, was advertising himself as an object for her commiseration, and at the same time raising a barrier against it. He appeared to demand her sympathy while holding himself aloof from it. She had the uncomfortable sensation of feeling herself shut out and useless.

"By the way," said Gerald, "there's one thing. I have to keep her jollying along all the time, so for goodness' sake don't go letting it out that we're engaged."

Sally's chin went up with a jerk. This was too much.

"If you find it a handicap being engaged to me. . ."

"Don't be silly." Gerald took refuge in pathos. "Good God! It's tough! Here am I, worried to death, and you. . ."

Before he could finish the sentence, Sally's mood had undergone one of those swift changes which sometimes made her feel that she must be lacking in character. A simple, comforting thought had come to her, altering her entire outlook. She had come off the train tired and gritty, and what seemed the general out-of-jointness of the world was entirely due, she decided, to the fact that she had not had a bath and that her hair was all anyhow. She felt suddenly tranquil. If it was merely her grubby and dishevelled condition that made Gerald seem to her so different, all was well. She put her hand on his with a quick gesture of penitence.

"I'm so sorry," she said. "I've been a brute, but I do sympathize, really."

"I've had an awful time," mumbled Gerald.

"I know, I know. But you never told me you were glad to see me."

"Of course I'm glad to see you."

"Why didn't you say so, then, you poor fish? And why didn't you ask me if I had enjoyed myself in Europe?"

"Did you enjoy yourself?"

"Yes, except that I missed you so much. There! Now we can consider my lecture on foreign travel finished, and you can go on telling me your troubles."

Gerald accepted the invitation. He spoke at considerable length, though with little variety. It appeared definitely established in his mind that Providence had invented Spanish influenza purely with a view to wrecking his future. But now he seemed less aloof, more open to sympathy. The brief thunderstorm had cleared the air. Sally lost that sense of detachment and exclusion which had weighed upon her.

"Well," said Gerald, at length, looking at his watch, "I suppose I had better be off."

"Rehearsal?"

"Yes, confound it. It's the only way of getting through the day. Are you coming along?"

"I'll come directly I've unpacked and tidied myself up."

"See you at the theatre, then."

Sally went out and rang for the lift to take her up to her room.

2

THE REHEARSAL HAD STARTED WHEN she reached the theatre. As she entered the dark auditorium, voices came to her with that thin and reedy effect which is produced by people talking in an empty building. She sat down at the back of the house, and, as her eyes grew accustomed to the gloom, was able to see Gerald sitting in the front row beside a man with a bald head fringed with orange hair whom she took correctly to be Mr. Bunbury, the producer. Dotted about the house in ones and twos were members of the company whose presence was not required in the first act. On the stage, Elsa Doland, looking very attractive, was playing a scene with a man in a bowler hat. She was speaking a line, as Sally came in.

"Why, what do you mean, father?"

"Tiddly-omty-om," was the bowler-hatted one's surprising reply. "Tiddly-omty-om. . . long speech ending in 'find me in the library.' And exit," said the man in the bowler hat, starting to do so.

For the first time Sally became aware of the atmosphere of nerves. Mr. Bunbury, who seemed to be a man of temperament, picked up his walking-stick, which was leaning against the next seat, and flung it with some violence across the house.

"For God's sake!" said Mr. Bunbury.

"Now what?" inquired the bowler hat, interested, pausing hallway across the stage.

"Do speak the lines, Teddy," exclaimed Gerald. "Don't skip them in that sloppy fashion."

"You don't want me to go over the whole thing?" asked the bowler hat, amazed.

"Yes!"

"Not the whole damn thing?" queried the bowler hat, fighting with incredulity.

"This is a rehearsal," snapped Mr. Bunbury. "If we are not going to do it properly, what's the use of doing it at all?"

This seemed to strike the erring Teddy, if not as reasonable, at any rate as one way of looking at it. He delivered the speech in an injured tone and shuffled off. The atmosphere of tenseness was unmistakable now. Sally could feel it. The world of the theatre is simply a large nursery and its inhabitants children who readily become fretful if anything goes wrong. The waiting and the uncertainty, the loafing about in strange hotels in a strange city, the dreary rehearsing of lines which had been polished to the last syllable more than a week ago—these things had sapped the nerve of the Primrose Way company and demoralization had set in. It would require only a trifle to produce an explosion.

Elsa Doland now moved to the door, pressed a bell, and, taking a magazine from the table, sat down in a chair near the footlights. A moment later, in answer to the ring, a young woman entered, to be greeted instantly by an impassioned bellow from Mr. Bunbury.

"Miss Winch!"

The new arrival stopped and looked out over the footlights, not in the pained manner of the man in the bowler hat, but with the sort of genial indulgence of one who has come to a juvenile party to amuse the children. She was a square, wholesome, good-humoured looking girl with a serious face, the gravity of which was contradicted by the faint smile that seemed to lurk about the corner of her mouth. She was certainly not pretty, and Sally, watching her with keen interest, was surprised that Fillmore had had the sense to disregard surface homeliness and recognize her charm. Deep down in Fillmore, Sally decided, there must lurk an unsuspected vein of intelligence.

"Hello?" said Miss Winch, amiably.

Mr. Bunbury seemed profoundly moved.

"Miss Winch, did I or did I not ask you to refrain from chewing gum during rehearsal?"

"That's right, so you did," admitted Miss Winch, chummily.

"Then why are you doing it?"

Fillmore's fiancée revolved the criticized refreshment about her tongue for a moment before replying.

"Bit o' business," she announced, at length.

"What do you mean, a bit of business?"

"Character stuff," explained Miss Winch in her pleasant, drawling voice. "Thought it out myself. Maids chew gum, you know."

Mr. Bunbury ruffled his orange hair in an over-wrought manner with the palm of his right hand.

"Have you ever seen a maid?" he asked, despairingly.

"Yes, sir. And they chew gum."

"I mean a parlour-maid in a smart house," moaned Mr. Bunbury. "Do you imagine for a moment that in a house such as this is supposed to be the parlour-maid would be allowed to come into the drawing-room champing that disgusting, beastly stuff?"

Miss Winch considered the point.

"Maybe you're right." She brightened. "Listen! Great idea! Mr. Foster can write in a line for Elsa, calling me down, and another giving me a good come-back, and then another for Elsa saying something else, and then something really funny for me, and so on. We can work it up into a big comic scene. Five or six minutes, all laughs."

This ingenious suggestion had the effect of depriving the producer momentarily of speech, and while he was struggling for utterance, there dashed out from the wings a gorgeous being in blue velvet and a hat of such unimpeachable smartness that Sally ached at the sight of it with a spasm of pure envy.

"Say!"

Miss Mabel Hobson had practically every personal advantage which nature can bestow with the exception of a musical voice. Her figure was perfect, her face beautiful, and her hair a mass of spun gold; but her voice in moments of emotion was the voice of a peacock.

"Say, listen to me for just one moment!"

Mr. Bunbury recovered from his trance.

"Miss Hobson! Please!"

"Yes, that's all very well. . ."

"You are interrupting the rehearsal."

"You bet your sorrowful existence I'm interrupting the rehearsal," agreed Miss Hobson, with emphasis. "And, if you want to make a little easy money, you go and bet somebody ten seeds that I'm going to interrupt it again every time there's any talk of writing up any darned part in the show except mine. Write up other people's parts? Not while I have my strength!"

A young man with butter-coloured hair, who had entered from the wings in close attendance on the injured lady, attempted to calm the storm.

"Now, sweetie!"

"Oh, can it, Reggie!" said Miss Hobson, curtly.

Mr. Cracknell obediently canned it. He was not one of your brutal cave-men. He subsided into the recesses of a high collar and began to chew the knob of his stick.

"I'm the star," resumed Miss Hobson, vehemently, "and, if you think anybody else's part's going to be written up. . . well, pardon me while I choke with laughter! If so much as a syllable is written into anybody's part, I walk straight out on my two feet. You won't see me go, I'll be so quick."

Mr. Bunbury sprang to his feet and waved his hands.

"For heaven's sake! Are we rehearsing, or is this a debating society? Miss Hobson, nothing is going to be written into anybody's part. Now are you satisfied?"

"She said. . ."

"Oh, never mind," observed Miss Winch, equably. "It was only a random thought. Working for the good of the show all the time. That's me."

"Now, sweetie!" pleaded Mr. Cracknell, emerging from the collar like a tortoise.

Miss Hobson reluctantly allowed herself to be reassured.

"Oh, well, that's all right, then. But don't forget I know how to look after myself," she said, stating a fact which was abundantly obvious to all who had had the privilege of listening to her. "Any raw work, and out I walk so quick it'll make you giddy."

She retired, followed by Mr. Cracknell, and the wings swallowed her up.

"Shall I say my big speech now?" inquired Miss Winch, over the footlights.

"Yes, yes! Get on with the rehearsal. We've wasted half the morning."

"Did you ring, madam?" said Miss Winch to Elsa, who had been reading her magazine placidly through the late scene.

The rehearsal proceeded, and Sally watched it with a sinking heart. It was all wrong. Novice as she was in things theatrical, she could see that. There was no doubt that Miss Hobson was superbly beautiful and would have shed lustre on any part which involved the minimum of words and the maximum of clothes: but in the pivotal role of a serious play, her very physical attributes only served to emphasize and point her hopeless incapacity. Sally remembered Mr. Faucitt's story of the lady who got the bird at Wigan. She did not see how history could fail to repeat itself. The theatrical public of America will endure much from youth and beauty, but there is a limit.

A shrill, passionate cry from the front row, and Mr. Bunbury was on his feet again. Sally could not help wondering whether things were going particularly wrong to-day, or whether this was one of Mr. Bunbury's ordinary mornings.

"Miss Hobson!"

The action of the drama had just brought that emotional lady on left centre and had taken her across to the desk which stood on the other side of the stage. The desk was an important feature of the play, for it symbolized the absorption in business which, exhibited by her husband, was rapidly breaking Miss Hobson's heart. He loved his desk better than his young wife, that was what it amounted to, and no wife can stand that sort of thing.

"Oh, gee!" said Miss Hobson, ceasing to be the distressed wife and becoming the offended star. "What's it this time?"

"I suggested at the last rehearsal and at the rehearsal before and the rehearsal before that, that, on that line, you, should pick up the paper-knife and toy negligently with it. You did it yesterday, and to-day you've forgotten it again."

"My God!" cried Miss Hobson, wounded to the quick. "If this don't beat everything! How the heck can I toy negligently with a paper-knife when there's no paper-knife for me to toy negligently with?"

"The paper-knife is on the desk."

"It's not on the desk."

"No paper-knife?"

"No paper-knife. And it's no good picking on me. I'm the star, not the assistant stage manager. If you're going to pick on anybody, pick on him."

P.G. WODEHOUSE

The advice appeared to strike Mr. Bunbury as good. He threw back his head and bayed like a bloodhound.

There was a momentary pause, and then from the wings on the prompt side there shambled out a stout and shrinking figure, in whose hand was a script of the play and on whose face, lit up by the footlights, there shone a look of apprehension. It was Fillmore, the Man of Destiny.

3

ALAS, POOR FILLMORE! HE STOOD in the middle of the stage with the lightning of Mr. Bunbury's wrath playing about his defenceless head, and Sally, recovering from her first astonishment, sent a wave of sisterly commiseration floating across the theatre to him. She did not often pity Fillmore. His was a nature which in the sunshine of prosperity had a tendency to grow a trifle lush; and such of the minor ills of life as had afflicted him during the past three years, had, she considered, been wholesome and educative and a matter not for concern but for congratulation. Unmoved, she had watched him through that lean period lunching on coffee and buckwheat cakes, and curbing from motives of economy a somewhat florid taste in dress. But this was different. This was tragedy. Somehow or other, blasting disaster must have smitten the Fillmore bank-roll, and he was back where he had started. His presence here this morning could mean nothing else.

She recalled his words at the breakfast-table about financing the play. How like Fillmore to try to save his face for the moment with an outrageous bluff, though well aware that he would have to reveal the truth sooner or later. She realized how he must have felt when he had seen her at the hotel. Yes, she was sorry for Fillmore.

And, as she listened to the fervent eloquence of Mr. Bunbury, she perceived that she had every reason to be. Fillmore was having a bad time. One of the chief articles of faith in the creed of all theatrical producers is that if anything goes wrong it must be the fault of the assistant stage manager and Mr. Bunbury was evidently orthodox in his views. He was showing oratorical gifts of no mean order. The paper-knife seemed to inspire him. Gradually, Sally began to get the feeling that this harmless, necessary stage-property was the source from which sprang most, if not all, of the trouble in the world. It had disappeared before. Now it had disappeared again. Could Mr. Bunbury go on struggling in a universe where this sort of thing happened? He seemed to doubt it. Being a red-blooded, one-hundred-per-cent American man, he would try hard, but it was a hundred to one shot that he would get through. He had asked for a paper-knife. There was no paper-knife. Why was there no paper-knife? Where was the paper-knife anyway?

"I assure you, Mr. Bunbury," bleated the unhappy Fillmore, obsequiously. "I placed it with the rest of the properties after the last rehearsal."

"You couldn't have done."

"I assure you I did."

"And it walked away, I suppose," said Miss Hobson with cold scorn, pausing in the operation of brightening up her lower lip with a lip-stick.

A calm, clear voice spoke.

"It was taken away," said the calm, clear voice.

Miss Winch had added herself to the symposium. She stood beside Fillmore, chewing placidly. It took more than raised voices and gesticulating hands to disturb Miss Winch.

"Miss Hobson took it," she went on in her cosy, drawling voice. "I saw her."

Sensation in court. The prisoner, who seemed to feel his position deeply, cast a pop-eyed glance full of gratitude at his advocate. Mr. Bunbury, in his capacity of prosecuting attorney, ran his fingers through his hair in some embarrassment, for he was regretting now that he had made such a fuss. Miss Hobson thus assailed by an underling, spun round and dropped the lip-stick, which was neatly retrieved by the assiduous Mr. Cracknell. Mr. Cracknell had his limitations, but he was rather good at picking up lip-sticks.

"What's that? I took it? I never did anything of the sort."

"Miss Hobson took it after the rehearsal yesterday," drawled Gladys Winch, addressing the world in general, "and threw it negligently at the theatre cat."

Miss Hobson seemed taken aback. Her composure was not restored by Mr. Bunbury's next remark. The producer, like his company, had been feeling the strain of the past few days, and, though as a rule he avoided anything in the nature of a clash with the temperamental star, this matter of the missing paper-knife had bitten so deeply into his soul that he felt compelled to speak his mind.

"In future, Miss Hobson, I should be glad if, when you wish to throw anything at the cat, you would not select a missile from the property box. Good heavens!" he cried, stung by the way fate was maltreating him, "I have never experienced anything like this before. I have been producing plays all my life, and this is the first time this has happened. I have produced Nazimova. Nazimova never threw paper-knives at cats."

"Well, I hate cats," said Miss Hobson, as though that settled it.

"I," murmured Miss Winch, "love little pussy, her fur is so warm, and if I don't hurt her she'll do me no. . ."

"Oh, my heavens!" shouted Gerald Foster, bounding from his seat and for the first time taking a share in the debate. "Are we going to spend the whole day arguing about cats and paper-knives? For goodness' sake, clear the stage and stop wasting time."

Miss Hobson chose to regard this intervention as an affront.

"Don't shout at me, Mr. Foster!"

"I wasn't shouting at you."

"If you have anything to say to me, lower your voice."

"He can't," observed Miss Winch. "He's a tenor."

"Nazimova never. . ." began Mr. Bunbury.

Miss Hobson was not to be diverted from her theme by reminiscences of Nazimova. She had not finished dealing with Gerald.

"In the shows I've been in," she said, mordantly, "the author wasn't allowed to go about the place getting fresh with the leading lady. In the shows I've been in the author sat at the back and spoke when he was spoken to. In the shows I've been in. . ."

Sally was tingling all over. This reminded her of the dog-fight on the Roville sands. She wanted to be in it, and only the recognition that it was a private fight and that she would be intruding kept her silent. The lure of the fray, however, was too strong for her wholly to resist it. Almost unconsciously, she had risen from her place and drifted down the aisle so as to be nearer the white-hot centre of things. She was now standing in the lighted space by the orchestra-pit, and her presence attracted the roving attention of Miss Hobson, who, having concluded her remarks on authors and their legitimate sphere of activity, was looking about for some other object of attack.

"Who the devil," inquired Miss Hobson, "is that?"

Sally found herself an object of universal scrutiny and wished that she had remained in the obscurity of the back rows.

"I am Mr. Nicholas' sister," was the best method of identification that she could find.

"Who's Mr. Nicholas?"

Fillmore timidly admitted that he was Mr. Nicholas. He did it in the manner of one in the dock pleading guilty to a major charge, and at least half of those present seemed surprised. To them, till now, Fillmore had been a nameless thing, answering to the shout of "Hi!"

Miss Hobson received the information with a laugh of such exceeding bitterness that strong men blanched and Mr. Cracknell started so convulsively that he nearly jerked his collar off its stud.

"Now, sweetie!" urged Mr. Cracknell.

Miss Hobson said that Mr. Cracknell gave her a pain in the gizzard. She recommended his fading away, and he did so—into his collar. He seemed to feel that once well inside his collar he was "home" and safe from attack.

"I'm through!" announced Miss Hobson. It appeared that Sally's presence had in some mysterious fashion fulfilled the function of the last straw. "This is the by-Goddest show I was ever in! I can stand for a whole lot, but when it comes to the assistant stage manager being allowed to fill the theatre with his sisters and his cousins and his aunts it's time to quit."

"But, sweetie!" pleaded Mr. Cracknell, coming to the surface.

"Oh, go and choke yourself!" said Miss Hobson, crisply. And, swinging round like a blue panther, she strode off. A door banged, and the sound of it seemed to restore Mr. Cracknell's power of movement. He, too, shot up stage and disappeared.

"Hello, Sally," said Elsa Doland, looking up from her magazine. The battle, raging all round her, had failed to disturb her detachment. "When did you get back?"

Sally trotted up the steps which had been propped against the stage to form a bridge over the orchestra pit.

"Hello, Elsa."

The late debaters had split into groups. Mr. Bunbury and Gerald were pacing up and down the central aisle, talking earnestly. Fillmore had subsided into a chair.

"Do you know Gladys Winch?" asked Elsa.

Sally shook hands with the placid lodestar of her brother's affections. Miss Winch, on closer inspection, proved to have deep grey eyes and freckles. Sally's liking for her increased.

"Thank you for saving Fillmore from the wolves," she said. "They would have torn him in pieces but for you."

"Oh, I don't know," said Miss Winch.

"It was noble."

"Oh, well!"

"I think," said Sally, "I'll go and have a talk with Fillmore. He looks as though he wanted consoling."

She made her way to that picturesque ruin.

4

FILLMORE HAD THE AIR OF a man who thought it wasn't loaded. A wild, startled expression had settled itself upon his face and he was breathing heavily.

"Cheer up!" said Sally. Fillmore jumped like a stricken jelly. "Tell me all," said Sally, sitting down beside him. "I leave you a gentleman of large and independent means, and I come back and find you one of the wage-slaves again. How did it all happen?"

"Sally," said Fillmore, "I will be frank with you. Can you lend me ten dollars?"

"I don't see how you make that out an answer to my question, but here you are."

"Thanks." Fillmore pocketed the bill. "I'll let you have it back next week. I want to take Miss Winch out to lunch."

"If that's what you want it for, don't look on it as a loan, take it as a gift with my blessing thrown in." She looked over her shoulder at Miss Winch, who, the cares of rehearsal being temporarily suspended, was practising golf-shots with an umbrella at the other side of the stage. "However did you have the sense to fall in love with her, Fill?"

"Do you like her?" asked Fillmore, brightening.

"I love her."

"I knew you would. She's just the right girl for me, isn't she?"

"She certainly is."

"So sympathetic."

"Yes."

"So kind."

"Yes."

"And she's got brains enough for two, which is the exact quantity the girl who marries you will need."

Fillmore drew himself up with as much hauteur as a stout man sitting in a low chair can achieve.

"Some day I will make you believe in me, Sally."

"Less of the Merchant Prince, my lad," said Sally, firmly. "You just confine yourself to explaining how you got this way, instead of taking up my valuable time telling me what you mean to do in the future. You've lost all your money?"

"I have suffered certain reverses," said Fillmore, with dignity, "which have left me temporarily. . . Yes, every bean," he concluded simply.

"How?"

"Well. . ." Fillmore hesitated. "I've had bad luck, you know. First I bought Consolidated Rails for the rise, and they fell. So that went wrong."

"Yes?"

"And then I bought Russian Roubles for the fall, and they rose. So that went wrong."

"Good gracious! Why, I've heard all this before."

"Who told you?"

"No, I remember now. It's just that you remind me of a man I met at Roville. He was telling me the story of his life, and how he had made a hash of everything. Well, that took all you had, I suppose?"

"Not quite. I had a few thousand left, and I went into a deal that really did look cast-iron."

"And that went wrong!"

"It wasn't my fault," said Fillmore querulously. "It was just my poisonous luck. A man I knew got me to join a syndicate which had bought up a lot of whisky. The idea was to ship it into Chicago in herring-barrels. We should have cleaned up big, only a mutt of a detective took it into his darned head to go fooling about with a crowbar. Officious ass! It wasn't as if the barrels weren't labelled 'Herrings' as plainly as they could be," said Fillmore with honest indignation. He shuddered. "I nearly got arrested."

"But that went wrong? Well, that's something to be thankful for. Stripes wouldn't suit your figure." Sally gave his arm a squeeze. She was very fond of Fillmore, though for the good of his soul she generally concealed her affection beneath a manner which he had once compared, not without some reason, to that of a governess who had afflicted their mutual childhood. "Never mind, you poor ill-used martyr. Things are sure to come right. We shall see you a millionaire some day. And, oh heavens, brother Fillmore, what a bore you'll be when you are! I can just see you being interviewed and giving hints to young men on how to make good. 'Mr. Nicholas attributes his success to sheer hard work. He can lay his hand on his bulging waistcoat and say that he has never once indulged in those rash get-rich-quick speculations, where you buy for the rise and watch things fall and then rush out and buy for the fall and watch 'em rise.' Fill. . . I'll tell you what I'll do. They all say it's the first bit of money that counts in building a vast fortune. I'll lend you some of mine."

"You will? Sally, I always said you were an ace."

"I never heard you. You oughtn't to mumble so."

"Will you lend me twenty thousand dollars?"

Sally patted his hand soothingly.

"Come slowly down to earth," she said. "Two hundred was the sum I had in mind."

"I want twenty thousand."

"You'd better rob a bank. Any policeman will direct you to a good bank."

"I'll tell you why I want twenty thousand."

"You might just mention it."

"If I had twenty thousand, I'd buy this production from Cracknell. He'll be back in a few minutes to tell us that the Hobson woman has quit: and, if she really has, you take it from me that he will close the show. And, even if he manages to jolly her along this time and she comes back, it's going to happen sooner or later. It's a shame to let a show like this close. I believe in it, Sally. It's a darn good play. With Elsa Doland in the big part, it couldn't fail."

Sally started. Her money was too recent for her to have grown fully accustomed to it, and she had never realized that she was in a position to wave a wand and make things happen on any big scale. The financing of a theatrical production had always been to her something mysterious and out of the reach of ordinary persons like herself. Fillmore, that spacious thinker, had brought it into the sphere of the possible.

"He'd sell for less than that, of course, but one would need a bit in hand. You have to face a loss on the road before coming into New York. I'd give you ten per cent on your money, Sally."

Sally found herself wavering. The prudent side of her nature, which hitherto had steered her safely through most of life's rapids, seemed oddly dormant. Sub-consciously she was aware that on past performances Fillmore was decidedly not the man to be allowed control of anybody's little fortune, but somehow the thought did not seem to grip her. He had touched her imagination.

"It's a gold-mine!"

Sally's prudent side stirred in its sleep. Fillmore had chosen an unfortunate expression. To the novice in finance the word gold-mine had repellent associations. If there was one thing in which Sally had proposed not to invest her legacy, it was a gold-mine; what she had had in view, as a matter of fact, had been one of those little fancy shops which are called Ye Blue Bird or Ye Corner Shoppe, or something like that, where you sell exotic bric-a-brac to the wealthy at extortionate prices. She knew two girls who were doing splendidly in that line. As Fillmore spoke those words, Ye Corner Shoppe suddenly looked very good to her.

At this moment, however, two things happened. Gerald and Mr. Bunbury, in the course of their perambulations, came into the glow of the footlights, and she was able to see Gerald's face: and at the same time Mr. Reginald Cracknell hurried on to the stage, his whole demeanour that of the bearer of evil tidings.

The sight of Gerald's face annihilated Sally's prudence at a single stroke. Ye Corner Shoppe, which a moment before had been shining brightly before her mental eye, flickered and melted out. The whole issue became clear and simple. Gerald was miserable and she had it in her power to make him happy. He was sullenly awaiting disaster and she with a word could avert it. She wondered that she had ever hesitated.

"All right," she said simply.

Fillmore quivered from head to foot. A powerful electric shock could not have produced a stronger convulsion. He knew Sally of old as cautious and clear-headed, by no means to be stampeded by a brother's eloquence; and he had never looked on this thing as anything better than a hundred to one shot.

"You'll do it?" he whispered, and held his breath. After all he might not have heard correctly.

"Yes."

All the complex emotion in Fillmore's soul found expression in one vast whoop. It rang through the empty theatre like the last trump, beating against the back wall and rising in hollow echoes to the very gallery. Mr. Bunbury, conversing in low undertones with Mr. Cracknell across the footlights, shied like a startled mule. There was reproach and menace in the look he cast at Fillmore, and a minute earlier it would have reduced that financial magnate to apologetic pulp. But Fillmore was not to be intimidated now by a look. He strode down to the group at the footlights,

"Cracknell," he said importantly, "one moment, I should like a word with you."

VII

Some Meditations on Success

If actors and actresses are like children in that they are readily depressed by disaster, they have the child's compensating gift of being easily uplifted by good fortune. It amazed Sally that any one mortal should have been able to spread such universal happiness as she had done by the simple act of lending her brother Fillmore twenty thousand dollars. If the Millennium had arrived, the members of the Primrose Way Company could not have been on better terms with themselves. The lethargy and dispiritedness, caused by their week of inaction, fell from them like a cloak. The sudden elevation of that creature of the abyss, the assistant stage manager, to the dizzy height of proprietor of the show appealed to their sense of drama. Most of them had played in pieces where much the same thing had happened to the persecuted heroine round about eleven o'clock, and the situation struck them as theatrically sound. Also, now that she had gone, the extent to which Miss Hobson had acted as a blight was universally recognized.

A spirit of optimism reigned, and cheerful rumours became current. The bowler-hatted Teddy had it straight from the lift-boy at his hotel that the ban on the theatres was to be lifted on Tuesday at the latest; while no less an authority than the cigar-stand girl at the Pontchatrain had informed the man who played the butler that Toledo and Cleveland were opening to-morrow. It was generally felt that the sun was bursting through the clouds and that Fate would soon despair of the hopeless task of trying to keep good men down.

Fillmore was himself again. We all have our particular mode of self-expression in moments of elation. Fillmore's took the shape of buying a new waistcoat and a hundred half-dollar cigars and being very fussy about what he had for lunch. It may have been an optical illusion, but he appeared to Sally to put on at least six pounds in weight on the first day of the new regime. As a serf looking after paper-knives and other properties, he had been—for him—almost slim. As a manager he blossomed out into soft billowy curves, and when he stood on the sidewalk in front of the theatre, gloating over the new posters which bore the legend, the populace had to make a detour to get round him.

In this era of bubbling joy, it was hard that Sally, the fairy godmother responsible for it all, should not have been completely happy too; and it puzzled her why she was not. But whatever it was that cast the faint shadow refused obstinately to come out from the back of her mind and show itself and be challenged. It was not till she was out driving in a hired car with Gerald one afternoon on Belle Isle that enlightenment came.

Gerald, since the departure of Miss Hobson, had been at his best. Like Fillmore, he was a man who responded to the sunshine of prosperity. His moodiness had vanished, and all his old charm had returned. And yet. . . it seemed to Sally, as the car slid smoothly through the pleasant woods and fields by the river, that there was something that jarred.

Gerald was cheerful and talkative. He, at any rate, found nothing wrong with life. He held forth spaciously on the big things he intended to do.

"If this play get over—and it's going to—I'll show 'em!" His jaw was squared, and his eyes glowed as they stared into the inviting future. "One success—that's all I need—then watch me! I haven't had a chance yet, but. . ."

His voice rolled on, but Sally had ceased to listen. It was the time of year when the chill of evening follows swiftly on the mellow warmth of afternoon. The sun had gone behind the trees, and a cold wind was blowing up from the river. And quite suddenly, as though it was the wind that had cleared her mind, she understood what it was that had been lurking at the back of her thoughts. For an instant it stood out nakedly without concealment, and the world became a forlorn place. She had realized the fundamental difference between man's outlook on life and woman's.

Success! How men worshipped it, and how little of themselves they had to spare for anything else. Ironically, it was the theme of this very play of Gerald's which she had saved from destruction. Of all the men she knew, how many had any view of life except as a race which they must strain every nerve to win, regardless of what they missed by the wayside in their haste? Fillmore—Gerald—all of them. There might be a woman in each of their lives, but she came second—an afterthought—a thing for their spare time. Gerald was everything to her. His success would never be more than a side-issue as far as she was concerned. He himself, without any of the trappings of success, was enough for her. But she was not enough for him. A spasm of futile jealousy shook her. She shivered.

"Cold?" said Gerald. "I'll tell the man to drive back. . . I don't see any reason why this play shouldn't run a year in New York. Everybody says it's good. . . if it does get over, they'll all be after me. I. . ."

Sally stared out into a bleak world. The sky was a leaden grey, and the wind from the river blew with a dismal chill.

VIII

Reappearance of Mr. Carmyle— and Ginger

1

When Sally left Detroit on the following Saturday, accompanied by Fillmore, who was returning to the metropolis for a few days in order to secure offices and generally make his presence felt along Broadway, her spirits had completely recovered. She felt guiltily that she had been fanciful, even morbid. Naturally men wanted to get on in the world. It was their job. She told herself that she was bound up with Gerald's success, and that the last thing of which she ought to complain was the energy he put into efforts of which she as well as he would reap the reward.

To this happier frame of mind the excitement of the last few days had contributed. Detroit, that city of amiable audiences, had liked "The Primrose Way." The theatre, in fulfilment of Teddy's prophecy, had been allowed to open on the Tuesday, and a full house, hungry for entertainment after its enforced abstinence, had welcomed the play wholeheartedly. The papers, not always in agreement with the applause of a first-night audience, had on this occasion endorsed the verdict, with agreeable unanimity hailing Gerald as the coming author and Elsa Doland as the coming star. There had even been a brief mention of Fillmore as the coming manager. But there is always some trifle that jars in our greatest moments, and Fillmore's triumph had been almost spoilt by the fact that the only notice taken of Gladys Winch was by the critic who printed her name—spelt Wunch—in the list of those whom the cast "also included."

"One of the greatest character actresses on the stage," said Fillmore bitterly, talking over this outrage with Sally on the morning after the production.

From this blow, however, his buoyant nature had soon enabled him to rally. Life contained so much that was bright that it would have been churlish to concentrate the attention on the one dark spot. Business had been excellent all through the week. Elsa Doland had got better at every performance. The receipt of a long and agitated telegram from Mr. Cracknell, pleading to be allowed to buy the piece back, the passage of time having apparently softened Miss Hobson, was a pleasant incident. And, best of all, the great Ike Schumann, who owned half the theatres in New York and had been in Detroit superintending one of his musical productions, had looked in one evening and stamped "The Primrose Way" with the seal of his approval. As Fillmore sat opposite Sally on the train, he radiated contentment and importance.

"Yes, do," said Sally, breaking a long silence.

Fillmore awoke from happy dreams.

"Eh?"

"I said 'Yes, do.' I think you owe it to your position."

"Do what?"

"Buy a fur coat. Wasn't that what you were meditating about?"

"Don't be a chump," said Fillmore, blushing nevertheless. It was true that once or twice during the past week he had toyed negligently, as Mr. Bunbury would have said, with the notion, and why not? A fellow must keep warm.

"With an astrakhan collar," insisted Sally.

"As a matter of fact," said Fillmore loftily, his great soul ill-attuned to this badinage, "what I was really thinking about at the moment was something Ike said."

"Ike?"

"Ike Schumann. He's on the train. I met him just now."

"We call him Ike!"

"Of course I call him Ike," said Fillmore heatedly. "Everyone calls him Ike."

"He wears a fur coat," Sally murmured.

Fillmore registered annoyance.

"I wish you wouldn't keep on harping on that damned coat. And, anyway, why shouldn't I have a fur coat?"

"Fill. . . ! How can you be so brutal as to suggest that I ever said you shouldn't? Why, I'm one of the strongest supporters of the fur coat. With big cuffs. And you must roll up Fifth Avenue in your car, and I'll point and say 'That's my brother!' 'Your brother? No!' 'He is, really.' 'You're joking. Why, that's the great Fillmore Nicholas.' 'I know. But he really is my brother. And I was with him when he bought that coat.'"

"Do leave off about the coat!"

"'And it isn't only the coat,' I shall say. 'It's what's underneath. Tucked away inside that mass of fur, dodging about behind that dollar cigar, is one to whom we point with pride. . .'"

Fillmore looked coldly at his watch.

"I've got to go and see Ike Schumann."

"We are in hourly consultation with Ike."

"He wants to see me about the show. He suggests putting it into Chicago before opening in New York."

"Oh no," cried Sally, dismayed.

"Why not?"

Sally recovered herself. Identifying Gerald so closely with his play, she had supposed for a moment that if the piece opened in Chicago it would mean a further prolonged separation from him. But of course there would be no need, she realized, for him to stay with the company after the first day or two.

"You're thinking that we ought to have a New York reputation before tackling Chicago. There's a lot to be said for that. Still, it works both ways. A Chicago run would help us in New York. Well, I'll have to think it over," said Fillmore, importantly, "I'll have to think it over."

He mused with drawn brows.

"All wrong," said Sally.

"Eh?"

"Not a bit like it. The lips should be compressed and the forefinger of the right hand laid in a careworn way against the right temple. You've a lot to learn. Fill."

"Oh, stop it!"

"Fillmore Nicholas," said Sally, "if you knew what pain it gives me to josh my only brother, you'd be sorry for me. But you know it's for your good. Now run along and put Ike out of his misery. I know he's waiting for you with his watch out. 'You do think he'll come, Miss Nicholas?' were his last words to me as he stepped on the train, and oh, Fill, the yearning in his voice. 'Why, of course he will, Mr. Schumann,' I said. 'For all his exalted position, my brother is kindliness itself. Of course he'll come.' 'If I could only think so!' he said with a gulp. 'If I could only think so. But you know what these managers are. A thousand calls on their time. They get brooding on their fur coats and forget everything else.' 'Have no fear, Mr. Schumann,' I said. 'Fillmore Nicholas is a man of his word.'"

She would have been willing, for she was a girl who never believed in sparing herself where it was a question of entertaining her nearest and dearest, to continue the dialogue, but Fillmore was already moving down the car, his rigid back a silent protest against sisterly levity. Sally watched him disappear, then picked up a magazine and began to read.

She had just finished tracking a story of gripping interest through a jungle of advertisements, only to find that it was in two parts, of which the one she was reading was the first, when a voice spoke.

"How do you do, Miss Nicholas?"

Into the seat before her, recently released from the weight of the coming manager, Bruce Carmyle of all people in the world insinuated himself with that well-bred air of deferential restraint which never left him.

2

SALLY WAS CONSIDERABLY STARTLED. EVERYBODY travels nowadays, of course, and there is nothing really remarkable in finding a man in America whom you had supposed to be in Europe: but nevertheless she was conscious of a dream-like sensation, as though the clock had been turned back and a chapter of her life reopened which she had thought closed for ever.

"Mr. Carmyle!" she cried.

If Sally had been constantly in Bruce Carmyle's thoughts since they had parted on the Paris express, Mr. Carmyle had been very little in Sally's—so little, indeed, that she had had to search her memory for a moment before she identified him.

"We're always meeting on trains, aren't we?" she went on, her composure returning. "I never expected to see you in America."

"I came over."

Sally was tempted to reply that she gathered that, but a sudden embarrassment curbed her tongue. She had just remembered that at their last meeting she had been abominably rude to this man. She was never rude to anyone, without subsequent remorse. She contented herself with a tame "Yes."

"Yes," said Mr. Carmyle, "it is a good many years since I have taken a real holiday. My doctor seemed to think I was a trifle run down. It seemed a good opportunity to visit America. Everybody," said Mr. Carmyle oracularly, endeavouring, as he had often done since his ship had left England, to persuade himself that his object in making the trip had not been merely to renew his acquaintance with Sally, "everybody ought to visit America at least once. It is part of one's education."

"And what are your impressions of our glorious country?" said Sally rallying.

Mr. Carmyle seemed glad of the opportunity of lecturing on an impersonal subject. He, too, though his face had shown no trace of it, had been embarrassed in the opening stages of the conversation. The sound of his voice restored him.

"I have been visiting Chicago," he said after a brief travelogue.

"Oh!"

"A wonderful city."

"I've never seen it. I've come from Detroit."

"Yes, I heard you were in Detroit."

Sally's eyes opened.

"You heard I was in Detroit? Good gracious! How?"

"I—ah—called at your New York address and made inquiries," said Mr. Carmyle a little awkwardly.

"But how did you know where I lived?"

"My cousin—er—Lancelot told me."

Sally was silent for a moment. She had much the same feeling that comes to the man in the detective story who realizes that he is being shadowed. Even if this almost complete stranger had not actually come to America in direct pursuit of her, there was no disguising the fact that he evidently found her an object of considerable interest. It was a compliment, but Sally was not at all sure that she liked it. Bruce Carmyle meant nothing to her, and it was rather disturbing to find that she was apparently of great importance to him. She seized on the mention of Ginger as a lever for diverting the conversation from its present too intimate course.

"How is Mr. Kemp?" she asked.

Mr. Carmyle's dark face seemed to become a trifle darker.

"We have had no news of him," he said shortly.

"No news? How do you mean? You speak as though he had disappeared."

"He has disappeared!"

"Good heavens! When?"

"Shortly after I saw you last."

"Disappeared!"

Mr. Carmyle frowned. Sally, watching him, found her antipathy stirring again. There was something about this man which she had disliked instinctively from the first, a sort of hardness.

"But where has he gone to?"

"I don't know." Mr. Carmyle frowned again. The subject of Ginger was plainly a sore one. "And I don't want to know," he went on heatedly, a dull flush rising in the cheeks which Sally was sure he had to shave twice a day. "I don't care to know. The Family have washed their hands of him. For the future he may look after himself as best he can. I believe he is off his head."

Sally's rebellious temper was well ablaze now, but she fought it down. She would dearly have loved to give battle to Mr. Carmyle—it was odd, she felt, how she seemed to have constituted herself Ginger's champion and protector—but she perceived that, if she wished, as she did, to hear more of her red-headed friend, he must be humoured and conciliated.

"But what happened? What was all the trouble about?"

Mr. Carmyle's eyebrows met.

"He—insulted his uncle. His uncle Donald. He insulted him—grossly. The one man in the world he should have made a point of—er—"

"Keeping in with?"

"Yes. His future depended upon him."

"But what did he do?" cried Sally, trying hard to keep a thoroughly reprehensible joy out of her voice.

"I have heard no details. My uncle is reticent as to what actually took place. He invited Lancelot to dinner to discuss his plans, and it appears that Lancelot—defied him. Defied him! He was rude and insulting. My uncle refuses to have anything more to do with him. Apparently the young fool managed to win some money at the tables at Roville, and this seems to have turned his head completely. My uncle insists that he is mad. I agree with him. Since the night of that dinner nothing has been heard of Lancelot."

Mr. Carmyle broke off to brood once more, and before Sally could speak the impressive bulk of Fillmore loomed up in the aisle beside them. Explanations seemed to Fillmore to be in order. He cast a questioning glance at the mysterious stranger, who, in addition to being in conversation with his sister, had collared his seat.

"Oh, hullo, Fill," said Sally. "Fillmore, this is Mr. Carmyle. We met abroad. My brother Fillmore, Mr. Carmyle."

Proper introduction having been thus effected, Fillmore approved of Mr. Carmyle. His air of being someone in particular appealed to him.

"Strange you meeting again like this," he said affably.

The porter, who had been making up berths along the car, was now hovering expectantly in the offing.

"You two had better go into the smoking room," suggested Sally. "I'm going to bed."

She wanted to be alone, to think. Mr. Carmyle's tale of a roused and revolting Ginger had stirred her.

The two men went off to the smoking-room, and Sally found an empty seat and sat down to wait for her berth to be made up. She was aglow with a curious exhilaration. So Ginger had taken her advice! Excellent Ginger! She felt proud of him. She also had that feeling of complacency, amounting almost to sinful pride, which comes to those who give advice and find it acted upon. She had the emotions of a creator. After all, had she not created this new Ginger? It was she who had stirred him up. It was she who had unleashed him. She had changed him from a meek dependent of the Family to a ravening creature, who went about the place insulting uncles.

It was a feat, there was no denying it. It was something attempted, something done: and by all the rules laid down by the poet it should, therefore, have earned a night's repose. Yet, Sally, jolted by the train, which towards the small hours seemed to be trying out some new buck-and-wing steps of its own invention, slept ill, and presently, as she lay awake, there came to her bedside the Spectre of Doubt, gaunt and questioning. Had she, after all, wrought so well? Had she been wise in tampering with this young man's life?

"What about it?" said the Spectre of Doubt.

3

DAYLIGHT BROUGHT NO COMFORTING ANSWER to the question. Breakfast failed to manufacture an easy mind. Sally got off the train, at the Grand Central station in a state of remorseful concern. She declined the offer of Mr. Carmyle to drive her to the boarding-house, and started to walk there, hoping that the crisp morning air would effect a cure.

She wondered now how she could ever have looked with approval on her rash act. She wondered what demon of interference and meddling had possessed her, to make her blunder into people's lives, upsetting them. She wondered that she was allowed to go around loose. She was nothing more nor less than a menace to society. Here was an estimable young man, obviously the sort of young man who would always have to be assisted through life by his relatives, and she had deliberately egged him on to wreck his prospects. She blushed hotly as she remembered that mad wireless she had sent him from the boat.

Miserable Ginger! She pictured him, his little stock of money gone, wandering foot-sore about London, seeking in vain for work; forcing himself to call on Uncle Donald; being thrown down the front steps by haughty footmen; sleeping on the Embankment; gazing into the dark waters of the Thames with the stare of hopelessness; climbing to the parapet and. . .

"Ugh!" said Sally.

She had arrived at the door of the boarding-house, and Mrs. Meecher was regarding her with welcoming eyes, little knowing that to all practical intents and purposes she had slain in his prime a red-headed young man of amiable manners and—when not ill-advised by meddling, muddling females—of excellent behaviour.

Mrs. Meecher was friendly and garrulous. Variety, the journal which, next to the dog Toto, was the thing she loved best in the world, had informed her on the Friday morning that Mr. Foster's play had got over big in Detroit, and that Miss Doland had made every kind of hit. It was not often that the old alumni of the boarding-house forced their way after this fashion into the Hall of Fame, and, according to Mrs. Meecher, the establishment was ringing with the news. That blue ribbon round Toto's neck was worn in honour of the triumph. There was also, though you could not see it, a chicken dinner in Toto's interior, by way of further celebration.

And was it true that Mr. Fillmore had bought the piece? A great man, was Mrs. Meecher's verdict. Mr. Faucitt had always said so. . .

"Oh, how is Mr. Faucitt?" Sally asked, reproaching herself for having allowed the pressure of other matters to drive all thoughts of her late patient from her mind.

"He's gone," said Mrs. Meecher with such relish that to Sally, in her morbid condition, the words had only one meaning. She turned white and clutched at the banisters.

"Gone!"

"To England," added Mrs. Meecher. Sally was vastly relieved.

"Oh, I thought you meant. . ."

"Oh no, not that." Mrs. Meecher sighed, for she had been a little disappointed in the old gentleman, who started out as such a promising invalid, only to fall away into the dullness of robust health once more. "He's well enough. I never seen anybody better. You'd think," said

Mrs. Meecher, bearing up with difficulty under her grievance, "you'd think this here new Spanish influenza was a sort of a tonic or somep'n, the way he looks now. Of course," she added, trying to find justification for a respected lodger, "he's had good news. His brother's dead."

"What!"

"Not, I don't mean, that that was good news, far from it, though, come to think of it, all flesh is as grass and we all got to be prepared for somep'n of the sort breaking loose. . . but it seems this here new brother of his—I didn't know he'd a brother, and I don't suppose you knew he had a brother. Men are secretive, ain't they!—this brother of his has left him a parcel of money, and Mr. Faucitt he had to get on the Wednesday boat quick as he could and go right over to the other side to look after things. Wind up the estate, I believe they call it. Left in a awful hurry, he did. Sent his love to you and said he'd write. Funny him having a brother, now, wasn't it? Not," said Mrs. Meecher, at heart a reasonable woman, "that folks don't have brothers. I got two myself, one in Portland, Oregon, and the other goodness knows where he is. But what I'm trying to say. . ."

Sally disengaged herself, and went up to her room. For a brief while the excitement which comes of hearing good news about those of whom we are fond acted as a stimulant, and she felt almost cheerful. Dear old Mr. Faucitt. She was sorry for his brother, of course, though she had never had the pleasure of his acquaintance and had only just heard that he had ever existed; but it was nice to think that her old friend's remaining years would be years of affluence.

Presently, however, she found her thoughts wandering back into their melancholy groove. She threw herself wearily on the bed. She was tired after her bad night.

But she could not sleep. Remorse kept her awake. Besides, she could hear Mrs. Meecher prowling disturbingly about the house, apparently in search of someone, her progress indicated by creaking boards and the strenuous yapping of Toto.

Sally turned restlessly, and, having turned remained for a long instant transfixed and rigid. She had seen something, and what she had seen was enough to surprise any girl in the privacy of her bedroom. From underneath the bed there peeped coyly forth an undeniably masculine shoe and six inches of a grey trouser-leg.

Sally bounded to the floor. She was a girl of courage, and she meant to probe this matter thoroughly.

"What are you doing under my bed?"

The question was a reasonable one, and evidently seemed to the intruder to deserve an answer. There was a muffled sneeze, and he began to crawl out.

The shoe came first. Then the legs. Then a sturdy body in a dusty coat. And finally there flashed on Sally's fascinated gaze a head of so nearly the maximum redness that it could only belong to one person in the world.

"Ginger!"

Mr. Lancelot Kemp, on all fours, blinked up at her.

"Oh, hullo!" he said.

IX

GINGER BECOMES A RIGHT-HAND MAN

It was not till she saw him actually standing there before her with his hair rumpled and a large smut on the tip of his nose, that Sally really understood how profoundly troubled she had been about this young man, and how vivid had been that vision of him bobbing about on the waters of the Thames, a cold and unappreciated corpse. She was a girl of keen imagination, and she had allowed her imagination to riot unchecked. Astonishment, therefore, at the extraordinary fact of his being there was for the moment thrust aside by relief. Never before in her life had she experienced such an overwhelming rush of exhilaration. She flung herself into a chair and burst into a screech of laughter which even to her own ears sounded strange. It struck Ginger as hysterical.

"I say, you know!" said Ginger, as the merriment showed no signs of abating. Ginger was concerned. Nasty shock for a girl, finding blighters under her bed.

Sally sat up, gurgling, and wiped her eyes.

"Oh, I am glad to see you," she gasped.

"No, really?" said Ginger, gratified. "That's fine." It occurred to him that some sort of apology would be a graceful act. "I say, you know, awfully sorry. About barging in here, I mean. Never dreamed it was your room. Unoccupied, I thought."

"Don't mention it. I ought not to have disturbed you. You were having a nice sleep, of course. Do you always sleep on the floor?"

"It was like this. . ."

"Of course, if you're wearing it for ornament, as a sort of beauty-spot," said Sally, "all right. But in case you don't know, you've a smut on your nose."

"Oh, my aunt! Not really?"

"Now would I deceive you on an important point like that?"

"Do you mind if I have a look in the glass?"

"Certainly, if you can stand it."

Ginger moved hurriedly to the dressing-table.

"You're perfectly right," he announced, applying his handkerchief.

"I thought I was. I'm very quick at noticing things."

"My hair's a bit rumpled, too."

"Very much so."

"You take my tip," said Ginger, earnestly, "and never lie about under beds. There's nothing in it."

"That reminds me. You won't be offended if I asked you something?"

"No, no. Go ahead."

"It's rather an impertinent question. You may resent it."

"No, no."

"Well, then, what were you doing under my bed?"

"Oh, under your bed?"

"Yes. Under my bed. This. It's a bed, you know. Mine. My bed. You were under it. Why? Or putting it another way, why were you under my bed?"

"I was hiding."

"Playing hide-and-seek? That explains it."

"Mrs. What's-her-name—Beecher—Meecher—was after me."

Sally shook her head disapprovingly.

"You mustn't encourage Mrs. Meecher in these childish pastimes. It unsettles her."

Ginger passed an agitated hand over his forehead.

"It's like this. . ."

"I hate to keep criticizing your appearance," said Sally, "and personally I like it; but, when you clutched your brow just then, you put about a pound of dust on it. Your hands are probably grubby."

Ginger inspected them.

"They are!"

"Why not make a really good job of it and have a wash?"

"Do you mind?"

"I'd prefer it."

"Thanks awfully. I mean to say it's your basin, you know, and all that. What I mean is, seem to be making myself pretty well at home."

"Oh, no."

"Touching the matter of soap. . ."

"Use mine. We Americans are famous for our hospitality."

"Thanks awfully."

"The towel is on your right."

"Thanks awfully."

"And I've a clothes brush in my bag."

"Thanks awfully."

Splashing followed like a sea-lion taking a dip. "Now, then," said Sally, "why were you hiding from Mrs. Meecher?"

A careworn, almost hunted look came into Ginger's face. "I say, you know, that woman is rather by way of being one of the lads, what! Scares me! Word was brought that she was on the prowl, so it seemed to me a judicious move to take cover till she sort of blew over. If she'd found me, she'd have made me take that dog of hers for a walk."

"Toto?"

"Toto. You know," said Ginger, with a strong sense of injury, "no dog's got a right to be a dog like that. I don't suppose there's anyone keener on dogs than I am, but a thing like a woolly rat." He shuddered slightly. "Well, one hates to be seen about with it in the public streets."

"Why couldn't you have refused in a firm but gentlemanly manner to take Toto out?"

"Ah! There you rather touch the spot. You see, the fact of the matter is, I'm a bit behind with the rent, and that makes it rather hard to take what you might call a firm stand."

"But how can you be behind with the rent? I only left here the Saturday before last and you weren't in the place then. You can't have been here more than a week."

"I've been here just a week. That's the week I'm behind with."

"But why? You were a millionaire when I left you at Roville."

"Well, the fact of the matter is, I went back to the tables that night and lost a goodish bit of what I'd won. And, somehow or another, when I got to America, the stuff seemed to slip away."

"What made you come to America at all?" said Sally, asking the question which, she felt, any sensible person would have asked at the opening of the conversation.

One of his familiar blushes raced over Ginger's face. "Oh, I thought I would. Land of opportunity, you know."

"Have you managed to find any of the opportunities yet?"

"Well, I have got a job of sorts, I'm a waiter at a rummy little place on Second Avenue. The salary isn't big, but I'd have wangled enough out of it to pay last week's rent, only they docked me a goodish bit for breaking plates and what not. The fact is, I'm making rather a hash of it."

"Oh, Ginger! You oughtn't to be a waiter!"

"That's what the boss seems to think."

"I mean, you ought to be doing something ever so much better."

P.G. WODEHOUSE

"But what? You've no notion how well all these blighters here seem to be able to get along without my help. I've tramped all over the place, offering my services, but they all say they'll try to carry on as they are."

Sally reflected.

"I know!"

"What?"

"I'll make Fillmore give you a job. I wonder I didn't think of it before."

"Fillmore?"

"My brother. Yes, he'll be able to use you."

"What as?"

Sally considered.

"As a—as a—oh, as his right-hand man."

"Does he want a right-hand man?"

"Sure to. He's a young fellow trying to get along. Sure to want a right-hand man."

"'M yes," said Ginger reflectively. "Of course, I've never been a right-hand man, you know."

"Oh, you'd pick it up. I'll take you round to him now. He's staying at the Astor."

"There's just one thing," said Ginger.

"What's that?"

"I might make a hash of it."

"Heavens, Ginger! There must be something in this world that you wouldn't make a hash of. Don't stand arguing any longer. Are you dry? and clean? Very well, then. Let's be off."

"Right ho."

Ginger took a step towards the door, then paused, rigid, with one leg in the air, as though some spell had been cast upon him. From the passage outside there had sounded a shrill yapping. Ginger looked at Sally. Then he looked—longingly—at the bed.

"Don't be such a coward," said Sally, severely.

"Yes, but. . ."

"How much do you owe Mrs. Meecher?"

"Round about twelve dollars, I think it is."

"I'll pay her."

Ginger flushed awkwardly.

"No, I'm hanged if you will! I mean," he stammered, "it's frightfully good of you and all that, and I can't tell you how grateful I am, but honestly, I couldn't. . ."

Sally did not press the point. She liked him the better for a rugged independence, which in the days of his impecuniousness her brother Fillmore had never dreamed of exhibiting.

"Very well," she said. "Have it your own way. Proud. That's me all over, Mabel. Ginger!" She broke off sharply. "Pull yourself together. Where is your manly spirit? I'd be ashamed to be such a coward."

"Awfully sorry, but, honestly, that woolly dog. . ."

"Never mind the dog. I'll see you through."

They came out into the passage almost on top of Toto, who was stalking phantom rats. Mrs. Meecher was manoeuvring in the background. Her face lit up grimly at the sight of Ginger.

"Mister Kemp! I been looking for you."

Sally intervened brightly.

"Oh, Mrs. Meecher," she said, shepherding her young charge through the danger zone, "I was so surprised to meet Mr. Kemp here. He is a great friend of mine. We met in France. We're going off now to have a long talk about old times, and then I'm taking him to see my brother. . ."

"Toto. . ."

"Dear little thing! You ought to take him for a walk," said Sally. "It's a lovely day. Mr. Kemp was saying just now that he would have liked to take him, but we're rather in a hurry and shall probably have to get into a taxi. You've no idea how busy my brother is just now. If we're late, he'll never forgive us."

She passed on down the stairs, leaving Mrs. Meecher dissatisfied but irresolute. There was something about Sally which even in her pre-wealthy days had always baffled Mrs. Meecher and cramped her style, and now that she was rich and independent she inspired in the chatelaine of the boarding-house an emotion which was almost awe. The front door had closed before Mrs. Meecher had collected her faculties; and Ginger, pausing on the sidewalk, drew a long breath.

"You know, you're wonderful!" he said, regarding Sally with unconcealed admiration.

She accepted the compliment composedly.

"Now we'll go and hunt up Fillmore," she said. "But there's no need to hurry, of course, really. We'll go for a walk first, and then call at the Astor and make him give us lunch. I want to hear all about you. I've heard something already. I met your cousin, Mr. Carmyle. He was on the train coming from Detroit. Did you know that he was in America?"

"No, I've—er—rather lost touch with the Family."

"So I gathered from Mr. Carmyle. And I feel hideously responsible. It was all through me that all this happened."

"Oh, no."

"Of course it was. I made you what you are to-day—I hope I'm satisfied—I dragged and dragged you down until the soul within you died, so to speak. I know perfectly well that you wouldn't have dreamed of savaging the Family as you seem to have done if it hadn't been for what I said to you at Roville. Ginger, tell me, what did happen? I'm dying to know. Mr. Carmyle said you insulted your uncle!"

"Donald. Yes, we did have a bit of a scrap, as a matter of fact. He made me go out to dinner with him and we—er—sort of disagreed. To start with, he wanted me to apologize to old Scrymgeour, and I rather gave it a miss."

"Noble fellow!"

"Scrymgeour?"

"No, silly! You."

"Oh, ah!" Ginger blushed. "And then there was all that about the soup, you know."

"How do you mean, 'all that about the soup'? What about the soup? What soup?"

"Well, things sort of hotted up a bit when the soup arrived."

"I don't understand."

"I mean, the trouble seemed to start, as it were, when the waiter had finished ladling out the mulligatawny. Thick soup, you know."

"I know mulligatawny is a thick soup. Yes?"

"Well, my old uncle—I'm not blaming him, don't you know—more his misfortune than his fault—I can see that now—but he's got a heavy moustache. Like a walrus, rather, and he's a bit apt to inhale the stuff through it. And I—well, I asked him not to. It was just a suggestion, you know. He cut up fairly rough, and by the time the fish came round we were more or less down on the mat chewing holes in one another. My fault, probably. I wasn't feeling particularly well-disposed towards the Family that night. I'd just had a talk with Bruce—my cousin, you know—in Piccadilly, and that had rather got the wind up me. Bruce always seems to get on my nerves a bit somehow and—Uncle Donald asking me to dinner and all that. By the way, did you get the books?"

"What books?"

"Bruce said he wanted to send you some books. That was why I gave him your address." Sally stared.

"He never sent me any books."

"Well, he said he was going to, and I had to tell him where to send them."

Sally walked on, a little thoughtfully. She was not a vain girl, but it was impossible not to perceive in the light of this fresh evidence that Mr. Carmyle had made a journey of three thousand miles with the sole object of renewing his acquaintance with her. It did not matter, of course, but it was vaguely disturbing. No girl cares to be dogged by a man she rather dislikes.

"Go on telling me about your uncle," she said.

"Well, there's not much more to tell. I'd happened to get that wireless of yours just before I started out to dinner with him, and I was more or less feeling that I wasn't going to stand any rot from the Family. I'd got to the fish course, hadn't I? Well, we managed to get through that somehow, but we didn't survive the fillet steak. One thing seemed to lead to another, and the show sort of bust up. He called me a good many things, and I got a bit fed-up, and finally I told him I hadn't any more use for the Family and was going to start out on my own. And— well, I did, don't you know. And here I am."

Sally listened to this saga breathlessly. More than ever did she feel responsible for her young protégé, and any faint qualms which she had entertained as to the wisdom of transferring practically the whole of her patrimony to the care of so erratic a financier as her brother vanished. It was her plain duty to see that Ginger was started well in the race of life, and Fillmore was going to come in uncommonly handy.

"We'll go to the Astor now," she said, "and I'll introduce you to Fillmore. He's a theatrical manager and he's sure to have something for you."

"It's awfully good of you to bother about me."

"Ginger," said Sally, "I regard you as a grandson. Hail that cab, will you?"

X

SALLY IN THE SHADOWS

1

IT SEEMED TO SALLY IN the weeks that followed her reunion with Ginger Kemp that a sort of golden age had set in. On all the frontiers of her little kingdom there was peace and prosperity, and she woke each morning in a world so neatly smoothed and ironed out that the most captious pessimist could hardly have found anything in it to criticize.

True, Gerald was still a thousand miles away. Going to Chicago to superintend the opening of "The Primrose Way"; for Fillmore had acceded to his friend Ike's suggestion in the matter of producing it first in Chicago, and he had been called in by a distracted manager to revise the work of a brother dramatist, whose comedy was in difficulties at one of the theatres in that city; and this meant he would have to remain on the spot for some time to come. It was disappointing, for Sally had been looking forward to having him back in New York in a few days; but she refused to allow herself to be depressed. Life as a whole was much too satisfactory for that. Life indeed, in every other respect, seemed perfect. Fillmore was going strong; Ginger was off her conscience; she had found an apartment; her new hat suited her; and "The Primrose Way" was a tremendous success. Chicago, it appeared from Fillmore's account, was paying little attention to anything except "The Primrose Way." National problems had ceased to interest the citizens. Local problems left them cold. Their minds were riveted to the exclusion of all else on the problem of how to secure seats. The production of the piece, according to Fillmore, had been the most terrific experience that had come to stir Chicago since the great fire.

Of all these satisfactory happenings, the most satisfactory, to Sally's thinking, was the fact that the problem of Ginger's future had been solved. Ginger had entered the service of the Fillmore Nicholas Theatrical Enterprises Ltd. (Managing Director, Fillmore Nicholas)— Fillmore would have made the title longer, only that was all that would go on the brass plate—and was to be found daily in the outer office, his duties consisting mainly, it seemed, in reading the evening papers.

What exactly he was, even Ginger hardly knew. Sometimes he felt like the man at the wheel, sometimes like a glorified office boy, and not so very glorified at that. For the most part he had to prevent the mob rushing and getting at Fillmore, who sat in semi-regal state in the inner office pondering great schemes.

But, though there might be an occasional passing uncertainty in Ginger's mind as to just what he was supposed to be doing in exchange for the fifty dollars he drew every Friday, there was nothing uncertain about his gratitude to Sally for having pulled the strings and enabled him to do it. He tried to thank her every time they met, and nowadays they were meeting frequently; for Ginger was helping her to furnish her new apartment. In this task, he spared no efforts. He said that it kept him in condition.

"And what I mean to say is," said Ginger, pausing in the act of carrying a massive easy chair to the third spot which Sally had selected in the last ten minutes, "if I didn't sweat about a bit and help you after the way you got me that job. . ."

"Ginger, desist," said Sally.

"Yes, but honestly. . ."

"If you don't stop it, I'll make you move that chair into the next room."

"Shall I?" Ginger rubbed his blistered hands and took a new grip. "Anything you say."

"Silly! Of course not. The only other rooms are my bedroom, the bathroom and the kitchen. What on earth would I want a great lumbering chair in them for? All the same, I believe the first we chose was the best."

"Back she goes, then, what?"

Sally reflected frowningly. This business of setting up house was causing her much thought.

"No," she decided. "By the window is better." She looked at him remorsefully. "I'm giving you a lot of trouble."

"Trouble!" Ginger, accompanied by a chair, staggered across the room. "The way I look at it is this." He wiped a bead of perspiration from his freckled forehead. "You got me that job, and. . ."

"Stop!"

"Right ho. . . Still, you did, you know."

Sally sat down in the armchair and stretched herself. Watching Ginger work had given her a vicarious fatigue. She surveyed the room proudly. It was certainly beginning to look cosy. The pictures were up, the carpet down, the furniture very neatly in order. For almost the first time in her life she had the restful sensation of being at home. She had always longed, during the past three years of boarding-house existence, for a settled abode, a place where she could lock the door on herself and be alone. The apartment was small, but it was undeniably a haven. She looked about her and could see no flaw in it. . . except. . . She had a sudden sense of something missing.

"Hullo!" she said. "Where's that photograph of me? I'm sure I put it on the mantelpiece yesterday."

His exertions seemed to have brought the blood to Ginger's face. He was a rich red. He inspected the mantelpiece narrowly.

"No. No photograph here."

"I know there isn't. But it was there yesterday. Or was it? I know I meant to put it there. Perhaps I forgot. It's the most beautiful thing you ever saw. Not a bit like me; but what of that? They touch 'em up in the dark-room, you know. I value it because it looks the way I should like to look if I could."

"I've never had a beautiful photograph taken of myself," said Ginger, solemnly, with gentle regret.

"Cheer up!"

"Oh, I don't mind. I only mentioned. . ."

"Ginger," said Sally, "pardon my interrupting your remarks, which I know are valuable, but this chair is—not—right! It ought to be where it was at the beginning. Could you give your imitation of a pack-mule just once more? And after that I'll make you some tea. If there's any tea—or milk—or cups."

"There are cups all right. I know, because I smashed two the day before yesterday. I'll nip round the corner for some milk, shall I?"

"Yes, please nip. All this hard work has taken it out of me terribly."

Over the tea-table Sally became inquisitive.

"What I can't understand about this job of yours. Ginger—which as you are just about to observe, I was noble enough to secure for you—is the amount of leisure that seems to go with it. How is it that you are able to spend your valuable time—Fillmore's valuable time, rather—juggling with my furniture every day?"

"Oh, I can usually get off."

"But oughtn't you to be at your post doing—whatever it is you do? What do you do?"

Ginger stirred his tea thoughtfully and gave his mind to the question.

"Well, I sort of mess about, you know." He pondered. "I interview divers blighters and tell 'em your brother is out and take their names and addresses and. . . oh, all that sort of thing."

"Does Fillmore consult you much?"

"He lets me read some of the plays that are sent in. Awful tosh most of them. Sometimes he sends me off to a vaudeville house of an evening."

"As a treat?"

"To see some special act, you know. To report on it. In case he might want to use it for this revue of his."

"Which revue?"

"Didn't you know he was going to put on a revue? Oh, rather. A whacking big affair. Going to cut out the Follies and all that sort of thing."

"But—my goodness!" Sally was alarmed. It was just like Fillmore, she felt, to go branching out into these expensive schemes when he ought to be moving warily and trying to consolidate the small success he had had. All his life he had thought in millions where the prudent man would have been content with hundreds. An inexhaustible fount of optimism bubbled eternally within him. "That's rather ambitious," she said.

"Yes. Ambitious sort of cove, your brother. Quite the Napoleon."

"I shall have to talk to him," said Sally decidedly. She was annoyed with Fillmore. Everything had been going so beautifully, with everybody peaceful and happy and prosperous and no anxiety anywhere, till he had spoiled things. Now she would have to start worrying again.

"Of course," argued Ginger, "there's money in revues. Over in London fellows make pots out of them."

Sally shook her head.

"It won't do," she said. "And I'll tell you another thing that won't do. This armchair. Of course it ought to be over by the window. You can see that yourself, can't you."

"Absolutely!" said Ginger, patiently preparing for action once more.

2

Sally's anxiety with regard to her ebullient brother was not lessened by the receipt shortly afterwards of a telegram from Miss Winch in Chicago.

Have you been feeding Fillmore meat?

the telegram ran: and, while Sally could not have claimed that she completely understood it, there was a sinister suggestion about the message which decided her to wait no longer before making investigations. She tore herself away from the joys of furnishing and went round to the headquarters of the Fillmore Nicholas Theatrical Enterprises Ltd. (Managing Director, Fillmore Nicholas) without delay.

Ginger, she discovered on arrival, was absent from his customary post, his place in the outer office being taken by a lad of tender years and pimply exterior, who thawed and cast off a proud reserve on hearing Sally's name, and told her to walk right in. Sally walked right in, and found Fillmore with his feet on an untidy desk, studying what appeared to be costume-designs.

"Ah, Sally!" he said in the distrait, tired voice which speaks of vast preoccupations. Prosperity was still putting in its silent, deadly work on the Hope of the American Theatre. What, even at as late an epoch as the return from Detroit, had been merely a smooth fullness around the angle of the jaw was now frankly and without disguise a double chin. He was wearing a new waistcoat and it was unbuttoned. "I am rather busy," he went on. "Always glad to see you, but I am rather busy. I have a hundred things to attend to."

"Well, attend to me. That'll only make a hundred and one. Fill, what's all this I hear about a revue?"

Fillmore looked as like a small boy caught in the act of stealing jam as it is possible for a great theatrical manager to look. He had been wondering in his darker moments what Sally would say about that project when she heard of it, and he had hoped that she would not hear of it until all the preparations were so complete that interference would be impossible. He was extremely fond of Sally, but there was, he knew, a lamentable vein of caution in her make-up which might lead her to criticize. And how can your man of affairs carry on if women are buzzing round criticizing all the time? He picked up a pen and put it down; buttoned his waistcoat and unbuttoned it; and scratched his ear with one of the costume-designs.

"Oh yes, the revue!"

"It's no good saying 'Oh yes!' You know perfectly well it's a crazy idea."

"Really. . . these business matters. . . this interference. . ."

"I don't want to run your affairs for you, Fill, but that money of mine does make me a sort of partner, I suppose, and I think I have a right to raise a loud yell of agony when I see you risking it on a. . ."

"Pardon me," said Fillmore loftily, looking happier. "Let me explain. Women never understand business matters. Your money is tied up exclusively in 'The Primrose Way,' which, as you know, is a tremendous success. You have nothing whatever to worry about as regards any new production I may make."

"I'm not worrying about the money. I'm worrying about you."

A tolerant smile played about the lower slopes of Fillmore's face.

"Don't be alarmed about me. I'm all right."

"You aren't all right. You've no business, when you've only just got started as a manager, to be rushing into an enormous production like this. You can't afford it."

"My dear child, as I said before, women cannot understand these things. A man in my position can always command money for a new venture."

"Do you mean to say you have found somebody silly enough to put up money?"

"Certainly. I don't know that there is any secret about it. Your friend, Mr. Carmyle, has taken an interest in some of my forthcoming productions."

"What!" Sally had been disturbed before, but she was aghast now.

This was something she had never anticipated. Bruce Carmyle seemed to be creeping into her life like an advancing tide. There appeared to be no eluding him. Wherever she turned, there he was, and she could do nothing but rage impotently. The situation was becoming impossible.

Fillmore misinterpreted the note of dismay in her voice.

"It's quite all right," he assured her. "He's a very rich man. Large private means, besides his big income. Even if anything goes wrong. . ."

"It isn't that. It's. . ."

The hopelessness of explaining to Fillmore stopped Sally. And while she was chafing at this new complication which had come to upset the orderly routine of her life there was an outburst of voices in the other office. Ginger's understudy seemed to be endeavouring to convince somebody that the Big Chief was engaged and not to be intruded upon. In this he was unsuccessful, for the door opened tempestuously and Miss Winch sailed in.

"Fillmore, you poor nut," said Miss Winch, for though she might wrap up her meaning somewhat obscurely in her telegraphic communications, when it came to the spoken word she was directness itself, "stop picking straws in your hair and listen to me. You're dippy!"

P.G. WODEHOUSE

The last time Sally had seen Fillmore's fiancée, she had been impressed by her imperturbable calm. Miss Winch, in Detroit, had seemed a girl whom nothing could ruffle. That she had lapsed now from this serene placidity, struck Sally as ominous. Slightly though she knew her, she felt that it could be no ordinary happening that had so animated her sister-in-law-to-be.

"Ah! Here you are!" said Fillmore. He had started to his feet indignantly at the opening of the door, like a lion bearded in its den, but calm had returned when he saw who the intruder was.

"Yes, here I am!" Miss Winch dropped despairingly into a swivel-chair, and endeavoured to restore herself with a stick of chewing-gum. "Fillmore, darling, you're the sweetest thing on earth, and I love you, but on present form you could just walk straight into Bloomingdale and they'd give you the royal suite."

"My dear girl. . ."

"What do you think?" demanded Miss Winch, turning to Sally.

"I've just been telling him," said Sally, welcoming this ally, "I think it's absurd at this stage of things for him to put on an enormous revue. . ."

"Revue?" Miss Winch stopped in the act of gnawing her gum. "What revue?" She flung up her arms. "I shall have to swallow this gum," she said. "You can't chew with your head going round. Are you putting on a revue too?"

Fillmore was buttoning and unbuttoning his waistcoat. He had a hounded look.

"Certainly, certainly," he replied in a tone of some feverishness. "I wish you girls would leave me to manage. . ."

"Dippy!" said Miss Winch once more. "Telegraphic address: Tea-Pot, Matteawan." She swivelled round to Sally again. "Say, listen! This boy must be stopped. We must form a gang in his best interests and get him put away. What do you think he proposes doing? I'll give you three guesses. Oh, what's the use? You'd never hit it. This poor wandering lad has got it all fixed up to star me—me—in a new show!"

Fillmore removed a hand from his waistcoat buttons and waved it protestingly.

"I have used my own judgment. . ."

"Yes, sir!" proceeded Miss Winch, riding over the interruption. "That's what he's planning to spring on an unsuspicious public. I'm sitting peacefully in my room at the hotel in Chicago, pronging a few cents' worth of scrambled eggs and reading the morning paper, when the telephone rings. Gentleman below would like to see me. Oh, ask him to wait. Business of flinging on a few clothes. Down in elevator. Bright sunrise effects in lobby."

"What on earth do you mean?"

"The gentleman had a head of red hair which had to be seen to be believed," explained Miss Winch. "Lit up the lobby. Management had switched off all the electrics for sake of economy. An Englishman he was. Nice fellow. Named Kemp."

"Oh, is Ginger in Chicago?" said Sally. "I wondered why he wasn't on his little chair in the outer office.

"I sent Kemp to Chicago," said Fillmore, "to have a look at the show. It is my policy, if I am unable to pay periodical visits myself, to send a representative. . ."

"Save it up for the long winter evenings," advised Miss Winch, cutting in on this statement of managerial tactics. "Mr. Kemp may have been there to look at the show, but his chief reason for coming was to tell me to beat it back to New York to enter into my kingdom. Fillmore wanted me on the spot, he told me, so that I could sit around in this office here, interviewing my supporting company. Me! Can you or can you not," inquired Miss Winch frankly, "tie it?"

"Well. . ." Sally hesitated.

"Don't say it! I know it just as well as you do. It's too sad for words."

"You persist in underestimating your abilities, Gladys," said Fillmore reproachfully. "I have had a certain amount of experience in theatrical matters—I have seen a good deal of acting—and I assure you that as a character-actress you. . ."

Miss Winch rose swiftly from her seat, kissed Fillmore energetically, and sat down again. She produced another stick of chewing-gum, then shook her head and replaced it in her bag.

"You're a darling old thing to talk like that," she said, "and I hate to wake you out of your daydreams, but, honestly, Fillmore, dear, do just step out of the padded cell for one moment and listen to reason. I know exactly what has been passing in your poor disordered bean. You took Elsa Doland out of a minor part and made her a star overnight. She goes to Chicago, and the critics and everybody else rave about her. As a matter of fact," she said to Sally with enthusiasm, for hers was an honest and generous nature, "you can't realize, not having seen her play there, what an amazing hit she has made. She really is a sensation. Everybody says she's going to be the biggest thing on record. Very well, then, what

P.G. WODEHOUSE

does Fillmore do? The poor fish claps his hand to his forehead and cries 'Gadzooks! An idea! I've done it before, I'll do it again. I'm the fellow who can make a star out of anything.' And he picks on me!"

"My dear girl. . ."

"Now, the flaw in the scheme is this. Elsa is a genius, and if he hadn't made her a star somebody else would have done. But little Gladys? That's something else again." She turned to Sally. "You've seen me in action, and let me tell you you've seen me at my best. Give me a maid's part, with a tray to carry on in act one and a couple of 'Yes, madam's' in act two, and I'm there! Ellen Terry hasn't anything on me when it comes to saying 'Yes, madam,' and I'm willing to back myself for gold, notes, or lima beans against Sarah Bernhardt as a tray-carrier. But there I finish. That lets me out. And anybody who thinks otherwise is going to lose a lot of money. Between ourselves the only thing I can do really well is to cook. . ."

"My dear Gladys!" cried Fillmore revolted.

"I'm a heaven-born cook, and I don't mind notifying the world to that effect. I can cook a chicken casserole so that you would leave home and mother for it. Also my English pork-pies! One of these days I'll take an afternoon off and assemble one for you. You'd be surprised! But acting—no. I can't do it, and I don't want to do it. I only went on the stage for fun, and my idea of fun isn't to plough through a star part with all the critics waving their axes in the front row, and me knowing all the time that it's taking money out of Fillmore's bankroll that ought to be going towards buying the little home with stationary wash-tubs. . . Well, that's that, Fillmore, old darling. I thought I'd just mention it."

Sally could not help being sorry for Fillmore. He was sitting with his chin on his hands, staring moodily before him—Napoleon at Elba. It was plain that this project of taking Miss Winch by the scruff of the neck and hurling her to the heights had been very near his heart.

"If that's how you feel," he said in a stricken voice, "there is nothing more to say."

"Oh, yes there is. We will now talk about this revue of yours. It's off!"

Fillmore bounded to his feet; he thumped the desk with a well-nourished fist. A man can stand just so much.

"It is not off! Great heavens! It's too much! I will not put up with this interference with my business concerns. I will not be tied and hampered. Here am I, a man of broad vision and. . . and. . . broad vision. . . I form my plans. . . my plans. . . I form them. . . I shape my schemes. . . and what happens? A horde of girls flock into my private office while I am endeavouring to concentrate. . . and concentrate. . . I won't stand it. Advice, yes. Interference, no. I. . . I. . . I. . . and kindly remember that!"

The door closed with a bang. A fainter detonation announced the whirlwind passage through the outer office. Footsteps died away down the corridor.

Sally looked at Miss Winch, stunned. A roused and militant Fillmore was new to her.

Miss Winch took out the stick of chewing-gum again and unwrapped it.

"Isn't he cute!" she said. "I hope he doesn't get the soft kind," she murmured, chewing reflectively.

"The soft kind."

"He'll be back soon with a box of candy," explained Miss Winch, "and he will get that sloshy, creamy sort, though I keep telling him I like the other. Well, one thing's certain. Fillmore's got it up his nose. He's beginning to hop about and sing in the sunlight. It's going to be hard work to get that boy down to earth again." Miss Winch heaved a gentle sigh. "I should like him to have enough left in the old stocking to pay the first year's rent when the wedding bells ring out." She bit meditatively on her chewing-gum. "Not," she said, "that it matters. I'd be just as happy in two rooms and a kitchenette, so long as Fillmore was there. You've no notion how dippy I am about him." Her freckled face glowed. "He grows on me like a darned drug. And the funny thing is that I keep right on admiring him though I can see all the while that he's the most perfect chump. He is a chump, you know. That's what I love about him. That and the way his ears wiggle when he gets excited. Chumps always make the best husbands. When you marry, Sally, grab a chump. Tap his forehead first, and if it rings solid, don't hesitate. All the unhappy marriages come from the husband having brains. What good are brains to a man? They only unsettle him." She broke off and scrutinized Sally closely. "Say, what do you do with your skin?"

She spoke with solemn earnestness which made Sally laugh.

"What do I do with my skin? I just carry it around with me."

"Well," said Miss Winch enviously, "I wish I could train my darned fool of a complexion to get that way. Freckles are the devil. When I was eight I had the finest collection in the Middle West, and I've been adding to it right along. Some folks say lemon-juice'll cure 'em. Mine lap up all I give 'em and ask for more. There's only one way of getting rid of freckles, and that is to saw the head off at the neck."

"But why do you want to get rid of them?"

"Why? Because a sensitive girl, anxious to retain her future husband's love, doesn't enjoy going about looking like something out of a dime museum."

"How absurd! Fillmore worships freckles."

"Did he tell you so?" asked Miss Winch eagerly.

"Not in so many words, but you can see it in his eye."

"Well, he certainly asked me to marry him, knowing all about them, I will say that. And, what's more, I don't think feminine loveliness means much to Fillmore, or he'd never have picked on me. Still, it is calculated to give a girl a jar, you must admit, when she picks up a magazine and reads an advertisement of a face-cream beginning, 'Your husband is growing cold to you. Can you blame him? Have you really tried to cure those unsightly blemishes?'—meaning what I've got. Still, I haven't noticed Fillmore growing cold to me, so maybe it's all right."

It was a subdued Sally who received Ginger when he called at her apartment a few days later on his return from Chicago. It seemed to her, thinking over the recent scene, that matters were even worse than she had feared. This absurd revue, which she had looked on as a mere isolated outbreak of foolishness, was, it would appear, only a specimen of the sort of thing her misguided brother proposed to do, a sample selected at random from a wholesale lot of frantic schemes. Fillmore, there was no longer any room for doubt, was preparing to express his great soul on a vast scale. And she could not dissuade him. A humiliating thought. She had grown so accustomed through the years to being the dominating mind that this revolt from her authority made her feel helpless and inadequate. Her self-confidence was shaken.

And Bruce Carmyle was financing him. . . It was illogical, but Sally could not help feeling that when—she had not the optimism to say "if"—he lost his money, she would somehow be under an obligation to him, as if the disaster had been her fault. She disliked, with a whole-hearted intensity, the thought of being under an obligation to Mr. Carmyle.

Ginger said he had looked in to inspect the furniture on the chance that Sally might want it shifted again: but Sally had no criticisms to make on that subject. Weightier matters occupied her mind. She sat Ginger down in the armchair and started to pour out her troubles. It soothed her to talk to him. In a world which had somehow become chaotic again after an all too brief period of peace, he was solid and consoling.

"I shouldn't worry," observed Ginger with Winch-like calm, when she had finished drawing for him the picture of a Fillmore rampant against a background of expensive revues. Sally nearly shook him.

"It's all very well to tell me not to worry," she cried. "How can I help worrying? Fillmore's simply a baby, and he's just playing the fool. He has lost his head completely. And I can't stop him! That is the awful part of it. I used to be able to look him in the eye, and he would wag his tail and crawl back into his basket, but now I seem to have no influence at all over him. He just snorts and goes on running round in circles, breathing fire."

Ginger did not abandon his attempts to indicate the silver lining.

"I think you are making too much of all this, you know. I mean to say, it's quite likely he's found some mug. . . what I mean is, it's just possible that your brother isn't standing the entire racket himself. Perhaps some rich Johnnie has breezed along with a pot of money. It often happens like that, you know. You read in the paper that some manager or other is putting on some show or other, when really the chap who's actually supplying the pieces of eight is some anonymous lad in the background."

"That is just what has happened, and it makes it worse than ever. Fillmore tells me that your cousin, Mr. Carmyle, is providing the money."

This did interest Ginger. He sat up with a jerk.

"Oh, I say!" he exclaimed.

"Yes," said Sally, still agitated but pleased that she had at last shaken him out of his trying attitude of detachment.

Ginger was scowling.

"That's a bit off," he observed.

"I think so, too."

"I don't like that."

"Nor do I."

"Do you know what I think?" said Ginger, ever a man of plain speech and a reckless plunger into delicate subjects. "The blighter's in love with you."

Sally flushed. After examining the evidence before her, she had reached the same conclusion in the privacy of her thoughts, but it embarrassed her to hear the thing put into bald words.

"I know Bruce," continued Ginger, "and, believe me, he isn't the sort of cove to take any kind of flutter without a jolly good motive. Of course, he's got tons of money. His old guvnor was the Carmyle of Carmyle, Brent & Co.—coal mines up in Wales, and all that sort of thing—and I suppose he must have left Bruce something like half a million. No need for the fellow to have worked at all, if he hadn't wanted to. As far as having the stuff goes, he's in a position to back all the shows he wants to. But the point is, it's right out of his line. He doesn't do that sort of thing. Not a drop of sporting blood in the chap. Why I've known him stick the whole family on to me just because it got noised about that I'd dropped a couple of quid on the Grand National. If he's really brought himself to the point of shelling out on a risky proposition like a show, it means something, take my word for it. And I don't see what else it can mean except. . . well, I mean to say, is it likely that he's doing it simply to make your brother look on him as a good egg and a pal, and all that sort of thing?"

"No, it's not," agreed Sally. "But don't let's talk about it any more. Tell me all about your trip to Chicago."

"All right. But, returning to this binge for a moment, I don't see how it matters to you one way or the other. You're engaged to another fellow, and when Bruce rolls up and says: 'What about it?' you've simply to tell him that the shot isn't on the board and will he kindly melt away. Then you hand him his hat and out he goes."

Sally gave a troubled laugh.

"You think that's simple, do you? I suppose you imagine that a girl enjoys that sort of thing? Oh, what's the use of talking about it? It's horrible, and no amount of arguing will make it anything else. Do let's change the subject. How did you like Chicago?"

"Oh, all right. Rather a grubby sort of place."

"So I've always heard. But you ought not to mind that, being a Londoner."

"Oh, I didn't mind it. As a matter of fact, I had rather a good time. Saw one or two shows, you know. Got in on my face as your brother's representative, which was all to the good. By the way, it's rummy how you run into people when you move about, isn't it?"

"You talk as if you had been dashing about the streets with your eyes shut. Did you meet somebody you knew?"

"Chap I hadn't seen for years. Was at school with him, as a matter of fact. Fellow named Foster. But I expect you know him, too, don't you? By name, at any rate. He wrote your brother's show."

Sally's heart jumped.

"Oh! Did you meet Gerald—Foster?"

"Ran into him one night at the theatre."

"And you were really at school with him?"

"Yes. He was in the footer team with me my last year."

"Was he a scrum-half, too?" asked Sally, dimpling.

Ginger looked shocked.

"You don't have two scrum-halves in a team," he said, pained at this ignorance on a vital matter. "The scrum-half is the half who works the scrum and. . ."

"Yes, you told me that at Roville. What was Gerald—Mr. Foster then? A six and seven-eighths, or something?"

"He was a wing-three," said Ginger with a gravity befitting his theme. "Rather fast, with a fairly decent swerve. But he would not learn to give the reverse pass inside to the centre."

"Ghastly!" said Sally.

"If," said Ginger earnestly, "a wing's bottled up by his wing and the back, the only thing he can do, if he doesn't want to be bundled into touch, is to give the reverse pass."

"I know," said Sally. "If I've thought that once, I've thought it a hundred times. How nice it must have been for you meeting again. I suppose you had all sorts of things to talk about?"

Ginger shook his head.

"Not such a frightful lot. We were never very thick. You see, this chap Foster was by way of being a bit of a worm."

"What!"

"A tick," explained Ginger. "A rotter. He was pretty generally barred at school. Personally, I never had any use for him at all."

Sally stiffened. She had liked Ginger up to that moment, and later on, no doubt, she would resume her liking for him: but in the immediate moment which followed these words she found herself regarding him with stormy hostility. How dare he sit there saying things like that about Gerald?

Ginger, who was lighting a cigarette without a care in the world, proceeded to develop his theme.

"It's a rummy thing about school. Generally, if a fellow's good at games—in the cricket team or the footer team and so forth—he can hardly help being fairly popular. But this blighter Foster somehow— nobody seemed very keen on him. Of course, he had a few of his own pals, but most of the chaps rather gave him a miss. It may have been because he was a bit sidey. . . had rather an edge on him, you know. . . Personally, the reason I barred him was because he wasn't straight. You didn't notice it if you weren't thrown a goodish bit with him, of course, but he and I were in the same house, and. . ."

Sally managed to control her voice, though it shook a little.

"I ought to tell you," she said, and her tone would have warned him had he been less occupied, "that Mr. Foster is a great friend of mine."

But Ginger was intent on the lighting of his cigarette, a delicate operation with the breeze blowing in through the open window. His head was bent, and he had formed his hands into a protective framework which half hid his face.

"If you take my tip," he mumbled, "you'll drop him. He's a wrong 'un."

He spoke with the absent-minded drawl of preoccupation, and Sally could keep the conflagration under no longer. She was aflame from head to foot.

"It may interest you to know," she said, shooting the words out like bullets from between clenched teeth, "that Gerald Foster is the man I am engaged to marry."

Ginger's head came slowly up from his cupped hands. Amazement was in his eyes, and a sort of horror. The cigarette hung limply from his mouth. He did not speak, but sat looking at her, dazed. Then the match burnt his fingers, and he dropped it with a start. The sharp sting of it seemed to wake him. He blinked.

"You're joking," he said, feebly. There was a note of wistfulness in his voice. "It isn't true?"

Sally kicked the leg of her chair irritably. She read insolent disapproval into the words. He was daring to criticize. . .

"Of course it's true. . ."

"But. . ." A look of hopeless misery came into Ginger's pleasant face. He hesitated. Then, with the air of a man bracing himself to a dreadful, but unavoidable, ordeal, he went on. He spoke gruffly, and his eyes, which had been fixed on Sally's, wandered down to the match on the carpet. It was still glowing, and mechanically he put a foot on it.

"Foster's married," he said shortly. "He was married the day before I left Chicago."

3

IT SEEMED TO GINGER THAT in the silence which followed, brooding over the room like a living presence, even the noises in the street had ceased, as though what he had said had been a spell cutting

Sally and himself off from the outer world. Only the little clock on the mantelpiece ticked—ticked—ticked, like a heart beating fast.

He stared straight before him, conscious of a strange rigidity. He felt incapable of movement, as he had sometimes felt in nightmares; and not for all the wealth of America could he have raised his eyes just then to Sally's face. He could see her hands. They had tightened on the arm of the chair. The knuckles were white.

He was blaming himself bitterly now for his oafish clumsiness in blurting out the news so abruptly. And yet, curiously, in his remorse there was something of elation. Never before had he felt so near to her. It was as though a barrier that had been between them had fallen.

Something moved. . . It was Sally's hand, slowly relaxing. The fingers loosened their grip, tightened again, then, as if reluctantly relaxed once more. The blood flowed back.

"Your cigarette's out."

Ginger started violently. Her voice, coming suddenly out of the silence, had struck him like a blow.

"Oh, thanks!"

He forced himself to light another match. It sputtered noisily in the stillness. He blew it out, and the uncanny quiet fell again.

Ginger drew at his cigarette mechanically. For an instant he had seen Sally's face, white-cheeked and bright-eyed, the chin tilted like a flag flying over a stricken field. His mood changed. All his emotions had crystallized into a dull, futile rage, a helpless fury directed at a man a thousand miles away.

Sally spoke again. Her voice sounded small and far off, an odd flatness in it.

"Married?"

Ginger threw his cigarette out of the window. He was shocked to find he was smoking. Nothing could have been farther from his intention than to smoke. He nodded.

"Whom has he married?"

Ginger coughed. Something was sticking in his throat, and speech was difficult.

"A girl called Doland."

"Oh, Elsa Doland?"

"Yes."

"Elsa Doland." Sally drummed with her fingers on the arm of the chair. "Oh, Elsa Doland?"

There was silence again. The little clock ticked fussily on the mantelpiece. Out in the street automobile horns were blowing. From somewhere in the distance came faintly the rumble of an elevated train. Familiar sounds, but they came to Sally now with a curious, unreal sense of novelty. She felt as though she had been projected into another world where everything was new and strange and horrible—everything except Ginger. About him, in the mere sight of him, there was something known and heartening.

Suddenly, she became aware that she was feeling that Ginger was behaving extremely well. She seemed to have been taken out of herself and to be regarding the scene from outside, regarding it coolly and critically; and it was plain to her that Ginger, in this upheaval of all things, was bearing himself perfectly. He had attempted no banal words of sympathy. He had said nothing and he was not looking at her. And Sally felt that sympathy just now would be torture, and that she could not have borne to be looked at.

Ginger was wonderful. In that curious, detached spirit that had come upon her, she examined him impartially, and gratitude welled up from the very depths of her. There he sat, saying nothing and doing nothing, as if he knew that all she needed, the only thing that could keep her sane in this world of nightmare, was the sight of that dear, flaming head of his that made her feel that the world had not slipped away from her altogether.

Ginger did not move. The room had grown almost dark now. A spear of light from a street lamp shone in through the window.

Sally got up abruptly. Slowly, gradually, inch by inch, the great suffocating cloud which had been crushing her had lifted. She felt alive again. Her black hour had gone, and she was back in the world of living things once more. She was afire with a fierce, tearing pain that tormented her almost beyond endurance, but dimly she sensed the fact that she had passed through something that was worse than pain, and, with Ginger's stolid presence to aid her, had passed triumphantly.

"Go and have dinner, Ginger," she said. "You must be starving."

Ginger came to life like a courtier in the palace of the Sleeping Beauty. He shook himself, and rose stiffly from his chair.

"Oh, no," he said. "Not a bit, really."

Sally switched on the light and set him blinking. She could bear to be looked at now.

"Go and dine," she said. "Dine lavishly and luxuriously. You've certainly earned. . ." Her voice faltered for a moment. She held out her hand. "Ginger," she said shakily, "I. . . Ginger, you're a pal."

When he had gone. Sally sat down and began to cry. Then she dried her eyes in a business-like manner.

"There, Miss Nicholas!" she said. "You couldn't have done that an hour ago. . . We will now boil you an egg for your dinner and see how that suits you!"

XI

Sally Runs Away

If Ginger Kemp had been asked to enumerate his good qualities, it is not probable that he would have drawn up a very lengthy list. He might have started by claiming for himself the virtue of meaning well, but after that he would have had to chew the pencil in prolonged meditation. And, even if he could eventually have added one or two further items to the catalogue, tact and delicacy of feeling would not have been among them.

Yet, by staying away from Sally during the next few days he showed considerable delicacy. It was not easy to stay away from her, but he forced himself to do so. He argued from his own tastes, and was strongly of opinion that in times of travail, solitude was what the sufferer most desired. In his time he, too, had had what he would have described as nasty jars, and on these occasions all he had asked was to be allowed to sit and think things over and fight his battle out by himself.

By Saturday, however, he had come to the conclusion that some form of action might now be taken. Saturday was rather a good day for picking up the threads again. He had not to go to the office, and, what was still more to the point, he had just drawn his week's salary. Mrs. Meecher had deftly taken a certain amount of this off him, but enough remained to enable him to attempt consolation on a fairly princely scale. There presented itself to him as a judicious move the idea of hiring a car and taking Sally out to dinner at one of the road-houses he had heard about up the Boston Post Road. He examined the scheme. The more he looked at it, the better it seemed.

He was helped to this decision by the extraordinary perfection of the weather. The weather of late had been a revelation to Ginger. It was his first experience of America's Indian Summer, and it had quite overcome him. As he stood on the roof of Mrs. Meecher's establishment on the Saturday morning, thrilled by the velvet wonder of the sunshine, it seemed to him that the only possible way of passing such a day was to take Sally for a ride in an open car.

The Maison Meecher was a lofty building on one of the side-streets at the lower end of the avenue. From its roof, after you had worked your way through the groves of washing which hung limply from the clothes-line, you could see many things of interest. To the left lay Washington Square, full of somnolent Italians and roller-skating children; to the right was a spectacle which never failed to intrigue Ginger, the high smoke-stacks of a Cunard liner moving slowly down the river, sticking up over the house-tops as if the boat was travelling down Ninth Avenue.

To-day there were four of these funnels, causing Ginger to deduce the Mauritania. As the boat on which he had come over from England, the Mauritania had a sentimental interest for him. He stood watching her stately progress till the higher buildings farther down the town shut her from his sight; then picked his way through the washing and went down to his room to get his hat. A quarter of an hour later he was in the hall-way of Sally's apartment house, gazing with ill-concealed disgust at the serge-clad back of his cousin Mr. Carmyle, who was engaged in conversation with a gentleman in overalls.

No care-free prospector, singing his way through the Mojave Desert and suddenly finding himself confronted by a rattlesnake, could have experienced so abrupt a change of mood as did Ginger at this revolting spectacle. Even in their native Piccadilly it had been unpleasant to run into Mr. Carmyle. To find him here now was nothing short of nauseating. Only one thing could have brought him to this place. Obviously, he must have come to see Sally; and with a sudden sinking of the heart Ginger remembered the shiny, expensive automobile which he had seen waiting at the door. He, it was clear, was not the only person to whom the idea had occurred of taking Sally for a drive on this golden day.

He was still standing there when Mr. Carmyle swung round with a frown on his dark face which seemed to say that he had not found the janitor's conversation entertaining. The sight of Ginger plainly did nothing to lighten his gloom.

"Hullo!" he said.

"Hullo!" said Ginger.

Uncomfortable silence followed these civilities.

"Have you come to see Miss Nicholas?"

"Why, yes."

"She isn't here," said Mr. Carmyle, and the fact that he had found someone to share the bad news, seemed to cheer him a little.

"Not here?"

"No. Apparently. . ." Bruce Carmyle's scowl betrayed that resentment which a well-balanced man cannot but feel at the unreasonableness of others. ". . . Apparently, for some extraordinary reason, she has taken it into her head to dash over to England."

Ginger tottered. The unexpectedness of the blow was crushing. He followed his cousin out into the sunshine in a sort of dream. Bruce Carmyle was addressing the driver of the expensive automobile.

"I find I shall not want the car. You can take it back to the garage."

The chauffeur, a moody man, opened one half-closed eye and spat cautiously. It was the way Rockefeller would have spat when approaching the crisis of some delicate financial negotiation.

"You'll have to pay just the same," he observed, opening his other eye to lend emphasis to the words.

"Of course I shall pay," snapped Mr. Carmyle, irritably. "How much is it?"

Money passed. The car rolled off.

"Gone to England?" said Ginger, dizzily.

"Yes, gone to England."

"But why?"

"How the devil do I know why?" Bruce Carmyle would have found his best friend trying at this moment. Gaping Ginger gave him almost a physical pain. "All I know is what the janitor told me, that she sailed on the Mauretania this morning."

The tragic irony of this overcame Ginger. That he should have stood on the roof, calmly watching the boat down the river. . .

He nodded absently to Mr. Carmyle and walked off. He had no further remarks to make. The warmth had gone out of the sunshine and all interest had departed from his life. He felt dull, listless, at a loose end. Not even the thought that his cousin, a careful man with his money, had had to pay a day's hire for a car which he could not use brought him any balm. He loafed aimlessly about the streets. He wandered in the Park and out again. The Park bored him. The streets bored him. The whole city bored him. A city without Sally in it was a drab, futile city, and nothing that the sun could do to brighten it could make it otherwise.

Night came at last, and with it a letter. It was the first even passably pleasant thing that had happened to Ginger in the whole of this dreary and unprofitable day: for the envelope bore the crest of the good ship Mauretania. He snatched it covetously from the letter-rack, and carried it upstairs to his room.

Very few of the rooms at Mrs. Meecher's boarding-house struck any note of luxury. Mrs. Meecher was not one of your fashionable interior decorators. She considered that when she had added a Morris chair to the essentials which make up a bedroom, she had gone as far in the direction of pomp as any guest at seven-and-a-half per could expect her to go. As a rule, the severity of his surroundings afflicted Ginger with a touch of gloom when he went to bed; but to-night—such is the magic of a letter from the right person—he was uplifted and almost gay. There are moments when even illuminated texts over the wash-stand cannot wholly quell us.

There was nothing of haste and much of ceremony in Ginger's method of approaching the perusal of his correspondence. He bore himself after the manner of a small boy in the presence of unexpected ice-cream, gloating for awhile before embarking on the treat, anxious to make it last out. His first move was to feel in the breast-pocket of his coat and produce the photograph of Sally which he had feloniously removed from her apartment. At this he looked long and earnestly before propping it up within easy reach against his basin, to be handy, if required, for purposes of reference. He then took off his coat, collar, and shoes, filled and lit a pipe, placed pouch and matches on the arm of the Morris chair, and drew that chair up so that he could sit with his feet on the bed. Having manoeuvred himself into a position of ease, he lit his pipe again and took up the letter. He looked at the crest, the handwriting of the address, and the postmark. He weighed it in his hand. It was a bulky letter.

He took Sally's photograph from the wash-stand and scrutinized it once more. Then he lit his pipe again, and, finally, wriggling himself into the depths of the chair, opened the envelope.

"Ginger, dear."

Having read so far, Ginger found it necessary to take up the photograph and study it with an even greater intentness than before. He gazed at it for many minutes, then laid it down and lit his pipe again. Then he went on with the letter.

"Ginger, dear—I'm afraid this address is going to give you rather a shock, and I'm feeling very guilty. I'm running away, and I haven't even stopped to say good-bye. I can't help it. I know it's weak and cowardly, but I simply can't help it. I stood it for a day or two, and then I saw that it was no good. (Thank you for leaving me alone and not coming round to see me. Nobody else but you would have done that. But then, nobody ever has been or ever could be so understanding as you.)"

Ginger found himself compelled at this point to look at the photograph again.

"There was too much in New York to remind me. That's the worst of being happy in a place. When things go wrong you find there are too many ghosts about. I just couldn't stand it. I tried, but I couldn't. I'm going away to get cured—if I can. Mr. Faucitt is over in England, and when I went down to Mrs. Meecher for my letters, I found one from him. His brother is dead, you know, and he has inherited, of all things, a fashionable dress-making place in Regent Street. His brother was Laurette et Cie. I suppose he will sell the business later on, but, just at present, the poor old dear is apparently quite bewildered and that doesn't seem to have occurred to him. He kept saying in his letter how much he wished I was with him, to help him, and I was tempted and ran. Anything to get away from the ghosts and have something to do. I don't suppose I shall feel much better in England, but, at least, every street corner won't have associations. Don't ever be happy anywhere, Ginger. It's too big a risk, much too big a risk.

"There was a letter from Elsa Doland, too. Bubbling over with affection. We had always been tremendous friends. Of course, she never knew anything about my being engaged to Gerald. I lent Fillmore the money to buy that piece, which gave Elsa her first big chance, and so she's very grateful. She says, if ever she gets the opportunity of doing me a good turn. . . Aren't things muddled?

"And there was a letter from Gerald. I was expecting one, of course, but. . . what would you have done, Ginger? Would you have read it? I sat with it in front of me for an hour, I should think, just looking at the envelope, and then. . . You see, what was the use? I could guess exactly the sort of thing that would be in it, and reading it would only have hurt a lot more. The thing was done, so why bother about explanations? What good are explanations, anyway? They don't help. They don't do anything. . . I burned it, Ginger. The last letter I shall ever get from him. I made a bonfire on the bathroom floor, and it smouldered and went brown, and then flared a little, and every now and then I lit another match and kept it burning, and at last it was just black ashes and a stain on the tiles. Just a mess!

"Ginger, burn this letter, too. I'm pouring out all the poison to you, hoping it will make me feel better. You don't mind, do you? But I know you don't. If ever anybody had a real pal. . .

"It's a dreadful thing, fascination, Ginger. It grips you and you are helpless. One can be so sensible and reasonable about other people's love affairs. When I was working at the dance place I told you about there was a girl who fell in love with the most awful little beast. He had a mean mouth and shiny black hair brushed straight back, and anybody would have seen what he was. But this girl wouldn't listen to a word. I talked to her by the hour. It makes me smile now when I think how sensible and level-headed I was. But she wouldn't listen. In some mysterious way this was the man she wanted, and, of course, everything happened that one knew would happen.

"If one could manage one's own life as well as one can manage other people's! If all this wretched thing of mine had happened to some other girl, how beautifully I could have proved that it was the best thing that could have happened, and that a man who could behave as Gerald has done wasn't worth worrying about. I can just hear myself. But, you see, whatever he has done, Gerald is still Gerald and Sally is still Sally and, however much I argue, I can't get away from that. All I can do is to come howling to my redheaded pal, when I know just as well as he does that a girl of any spirit would be dignified and keep her troubles to herself and be much too proud to let anyone know that she was hurt.

"Proud! That's the real trouble, Ginger. My pride has been battered and chopped up and broken into as many pieces as you broke Mr. Scrymgeour's stick! What pitiful creatures we are. Girls, I mean. At least, I suppose a good many girls are like me. If Gerald had died and I had lost him that way, I know quite well I shouldn't be feeling as I do now. I should have been broken-hearted, but it wouldn't have been the same. It's my pride that is hurt. I have always been a bossy, cocksure little creature, swaggering about the world like an English sparrow; and now I'm paying for it! Oh, Ginger, I'm paying for it! I wonder if running away is going to do me any good at all. Perhaps, if Mr. Faucitt has some real hard work for me to do. . .

"Of course, I know exactly how all this has come about. Elsa's pretty and attractive. But the point is that she is a success, and as a success she appeals to Gerald's weakest side. He worships success. She is going to have a marvellous career, and she can help Gerald on in his. He can write plays for her to star in. What have I to offer against that? Yes, I know it's grovelling and contemptible of me to say that, Ginger. I ought to be above it, oughtn't I—talking as if I were competing for some prize. . . But I haven't any pride left. Oh, well!

"There! I've poured it all out and I really do feel a little better just for the moment. It won't last, of course, but even a minute is something. Ginger, dear, I shan't see you for ever so long, even if we ever do meet again, but you'll try to remember that I'm thinking of you a whole lot, won't you? I feel responsible for you. You're my baby. You've got started now and you've only to stick to it. Please, please, please don't 'make a hash of it'! Good-bye. I never did find that photograph of me that we were looking for that afternoon in the apartment, or I would send it to you. Then you could have kept it on your mantelpiece, and whenever you felt inclined to make a hash of anything I would have caught your eye sternly and you would have pulled up.

"Good-bye, Ginger. I shall have to stop now. The mail is just closing.

"Always your pal, wherever I am.—SALLY."

Ginger laid the letter down, and a little sound escaped him that was half a sigh, half an oath. He was wondering whether even now some desirable end might not be achieved by going to Chicago and breaking Gerald Foster's neck. Abandoning this scheme as impracticable, and not being able to think of anything else to do he re-lit his pipe and started to read the letter again.

XII

SOME LETTERS FOR GINGER

Laurette et Cie,
Regent Street,
London, W.,
England.
January 21st

Dear Ginger,

I'm feeling better. As it's three months since I last wrote to you, no doubt you will say to yourself that I would be a poor, weak-minded creature if I wasn't. I suppose one ought to be able to get over anything in three months. Unfortunately, I'm afraid I haven't quite succeeded in doing that, but at least I have managed to get my troubles stowed away in the cellar, and I'm not dragging them out and looking at them all the time. That's something, isn't it?

I ought to give you all my impressions of London, I suppose; but I've grown so used to the place that I don't think I have any now. I seem to have been here years and years.

You will see by the address that Mr. Faucitt has not yet sold his inheritance. He expects to do so very soon, he tells me—there is a rich-looking man with whiskers and a keen eye whom he is always lunching with, and I think big deals are in progress. Poor dear! he is crazy to get away into the country and settle down and grow ducks and things. London has disappointed him. It is not the place it used to be. Until quite lately, when he grew resigned, he used to wander about in a disconsolate sort of way, trying to locate the landmarks of his youth. (He has not been in England for nearly thirty years!) The trouble is, it seems, that about once in every thirty years a sort of craze for change comes over London, and they paint a shop-front red instead of blue, and that upsets the returned exile dreadfully. Mr. Faucitt feels like Rip Van Winkle. His first shock was when he found that the Empire was a theatre now instead of a music-hall. Then he was told that another music-hall, the Tivoli, had been pulled down altogether. And when on top of that he went to look at the baker's shop in Rupert Street, over which he had lodgings in the eighties, and discovered that it had been turned into a dressmaker's, he grew very melancholy, and only cheered up a little when a lovely magenta fog came on and showed him that some things were still going along as in the good old days.

I am kept quite busy at Laurette et Cie., thank goodness. (Not being a French scholar like you—do you remember Jules?—I thought at first that Cie was the name of the junior partner, and looked forward to meeting him. "Miss Nicholas, shake hands with Mr. Cie, one of your greatest admirers.") I hold down the female equivalent of your job at the Fillmore Nicholas Theatrical Enterprises Ltd.—that is to say, I'm a sort of right-hand woman. I hang around and sidle up to the customers when they come in, and say, "Chawming weather, moddom!" (which is usually a black lie) and pass them on to the staff, who do the actual work. I shouldn't mind going on like this for the next few years, but Mr. Faucitt is determined to sell. I don't know if you are like that, but every other Englishman I've ever met seems to have an ambition to own a house and lot in Loamshire or Hants or Salop or somewhere. Their one object in life is to make some money and "buy back the old place"—which was sold, of course, at the end of act one to pay the heir's gambling debts.

Mr. Faucitt, when he was a small boy, used to live in a little village in Gloucestershire, near a place called Cirencester—at least, it isn't: it's called Cissister, which I bet you didn't know—and after forgetting about it for fifty years, he has suddenly been bitten by the desire to end his days there, surrounded by pigs and chickens. He took me down to see the place the other day. Oh, Ginger, this English country! Why any of you ever live in towns I can't think. Old, old grey stone houses with yellow haystacks and lovely squelchy muddy lanes and great fat trees and blue hills in the distance. The peace of it! If ever I sell my soul, I shall insist on the devil giving me at least forty years in some English country place in exchange.

Perhaps you will think from all this that I am too much occupied to remember your existence. Just to show how interested I am in you, let me tell you that, when I was reading the paper a week ago, I happened to see the headline, "International Match." It didn't seem to mean anything at first, and then I suddenly recollected. This was the thing you had once been a snip for! So I went down to a place called Twickenham, where this football game was to be, to see the sort of thing you used to do before I took charge of you and made you a respectable right-hand man. There was an enormous crowd there, and I was nearly squeezed to death, but I bore it for your sake. I found out that the English team were the ones wearing white shirts, and that the ones in red were the Welsh. I said to the man next to me, after he had finished yelling himself black in the face, "Could you kindly inform me which is the English scrum-half?" And just at that moment the players came quite near where I was, and about a dozen assassins in red hurled themselves violently on top of a meek-looking little fellow who had just fallen on the ball. Ginger, you are well out of it! That was the scrum-half, and I gathered that that sort of thing was a mere commonplace in his existence. Stopping a rush, it is called, and he is expected to do it all the time. The idea of you ever going in for such brutal sports! You thank your stars that you are safe on your little stool in Fillmore's outer office, and that, if anybody jumps on top of you now, you can call a cop. Do you mean to say you really used to do these daredevil feats? You must have hidden depths in you which I have never suspected.

As I was taking a ride down Piccadilly the other day on top of a bus, I saw somebody walking along who seemed familiar. It was Mr. Carmyle. So he's back in England again. He didn't see me, thank goodness. I don't want to meet anybody just at present who reminds me of New York.

Thanks for telling me all the news, but please don't do it again. It makes me remember, and I don't want to. It's this way, Ginger. Let me write to you, because it really does relieve me, but don't answer my letters. Do you mind? I'm sure you'll understand.

So Fillmore and Gladys Winch are married! From what I have seen of her, it's the best thing that has ever happened to Brother F. She is a splendid girl. I must write to him. . .

Laurette et Cie.
London
March 12th

Dear Ginger,

I saw in a Sunday paper last week that "The Primrose Way" had been produced in New York, and was a great success. Well, I'm very glad. But I don't think the papers ought to print things like that. It's unsettling.

Next day, I did one of those funny things you do when you're feeling blue and lonely and a long way away from everybody. I called at your club and asked for you! Such a nice old man in uniform at the desk said in a fatherly way that you hadn't been in lately, and he rather fancied you were out of town, but would I take a seat while he inquired. He then summoned a tiny boy, also in uniform, and the child skipped off chanting, "Mister Kemp! Mister Kemp!" in a shrill treble. It gave me such an odd feeling to hear your name echoing in the distance. I felt so ashamed for giving them all that trouble; and when the boy came back I slipped twopence into his palm, which I suppose was against all the rules, though he seemed to like it.

Mr. Faucitt has sold the business and retired to the country, and I am rather at a loose end. . .

Monk's Crofton,
(whatever that means)
Much Middleford,
Salop,
(slang for Shropshire)
England

April 18th

Dear Ginger,

What's the use? What is the use? I do all I can to get right away from New York, and New York comes after me and tracks me down in my hiding-place. A week or so ago, as I was walking down the Strand in an aimless sort of way, out there came right on top of me—who do you think? Fillmore, arm in arm with Mr. Carmyle! I couldn't dodge. In the first place, Mr. Carmyle had seen me; in the second place, it is a day's journey to dodge poor dear Fillmore now. I blushed for him. Ginger! Right there in the Strand I blushed for him. In my worst dreams I had never pictured him so enormous. Upon what meat doth this our Fillmore feed that he is grown so great? Poor Gladys! When she looks at him she must feel like a bigamist.

Apparently Fillmore is still full of big schemes, for he talked airily about buying all sorts of English plays. He has come over, as I suppose you know, to arrange about putting on "The Primrose Way" over here. He is staying at the Savoy, and they took me off there to lunch, whooping joyfully as over a strayed lamb. It was the worst thing that could possibly have happened to me. Fillmore talked Broadway without a pause, till by the time he had worked his way past the French pastry and was lolling back, breathing a little stertorously, waiting for the coffee and liqueurs, he had got me so homesick that, if it hadn't been that I didn't want to make a public exhibition of myself, I should have broken down and howled. It was crazy of me ever to go near the Savoy. Of course, it's simply an annex to Broadway. There were Americans at every table as far as the eye could reach. I might just as well have been at the Astor.

Well, if Fate insists in bringing New York to England for my special discomfiture, I suppose I have got to put up with it. I just let events take their course, and I have been drifting ever since. Two days ago I drifted here. Mr. Carmyle invited Fillmore—he seems to love Fillmore—and me to Monk's Crofton, and I hadn't even the shadow of an excuse for refusing. So I came, and I am now sitting writing to you in an enormous bedroom with an open fire and armchairs and every other sort of luxury. Fillmore is out golfing. He sails for New York on Saturday on the Mauretania. I am horrified to hear from him that, in addition to all his other big schemes, he is now promoting a fight for the light-weight championship in Jersey City, and guaranteeing enormous sums to both boxers. It's no good arguing with him. If you do, he simply quotes figures to show the fortunes other people have made out of these things. Besides, it's too late now, anyway. As far as I can make out, the fight is going to take place in another week or two. All the same, it makes my flesh creep.

Well, it's no use worrying, I suppose. Let's change the subject. Do you know Monk's Crofton? Probably you don't, as I seem to remember hearing something said about it being a recent purchase. Mr. Carmyle bought it from some lord or other who had been losing money on the Stock Exchange. I hope you haven't seen it, anyway, because I want to describe it at great length. I want to pour out my soul about it. Ginger, what has England ever done to deserve such paradises? I thought, in my ignorance, that Mr. Faucitt's Cissister place was pretty good, but it doesn't even begin. It can't compete. Of course, his is just an ordinary country house, and this is a Seat. Monk's Crofton is the sort of place they used to write about in the English novels. You know. "The sunset was falling on the walls of G—— Castle, in B——shire, hard by the picturesque village of H——, and not a stone's throw from the hamlet of J——." I can imagine Tennyson's Maud living here. It is one of the stately homes of England; how beautiful they stand, and I'm crazy about it.

You motor up from the station, and after you have gone about three miles, you turn in at a big iron gate with stone posts on each side with stone beasts on them. Close by the gate is the cutest little house with an old man inside it who pops out and touches his hat. This is only the lodge, really, but you think you have arrived; so you get all ready to jump out, and then the car goes rolling on for another fifty miles or so through beech woods full of rabbits and open meadows with deer in them. Finally, just as you think you are going on for ever, you whizz round a corner, and there's the house. You don't get a glimpse of it till then, because the trees are too thick.

It's very large, and sort of low and square, with a kind of tower at one side and the most fascinating upper porch sort of thing with battlements. I suppose in the old days you used to stand on this and drop molten lead on visitors' heads. Wonderful lawns all round, and shrubberies and a lake that you can just see where the ground dips beyond the fields. Of course it's too early yet for them to be out, but to the left of the house there's a place where there will be about a million roses when June comes round, and all along the side of the rose-garden is a high wall of old red brick which shuts off the kitchen garden. I went exploring there this morning. It's an enormous place, with hothouses and things, and there's the cunningest farm at one end with a stable yard full of puppies that just tear the heart out of you, they're so sweet. And a big, sleepy cat, which sits and blinks in the sun and lets the puppies run all over her. And there's a lovely stillness, and you can hear everything growing. And thrushes and blackbirds. . . Oh, Ginger, it's heavenly!

But there's a catch. It's a case of "Where every prospect pleases and only man is vile." At least, not exactly vile, I suppose, but terribly stodgy. I can see now why you couldn't hit it off with the Family. Because I've seen 'em all! They're here! Yes, Uncle Donald and all of them. Is it a habit of your family to collect in gangs, or have I just happened to stumble into an accidental Old Home Week? When I came down to dinner the first evening, the drawing-room was full to bursting point— not simply because Fillmore was there, but because there were uncles and aunts all over the place. I felt like a small lion in a den of Daniels. I know exactly now what you mean about the Family. They look at you! Of course, it's all right for me, because I am snowy white clear through, but I can just imagine what it must have been like for you with your permanently guilty conscience. You must have had an awful time.

By the way, it's going to be a delicate business getting this letter through to you—rather like carrying the despatches through the enemy's lines in a Civil War play. You're supposed to leave letters on the table in the hall, and someone collects them in the afternoon and takes them down to the village on a bicycle. But, if I do that some aunt or uncle is bound to see it, and I shall be an object of loathing, for it is no light matter, my lad, to be caught having correspondence with a human Jimpson weed like you. It would blast me socially. At least, so I gather from the way they behaved when your name came up at dinner last night. Somebody mentioned you, and the most awful roasting party broke loose. Uncle Donald acting as cheer-leader. I said feebly that I had met you and had found you part human, and there was an awful silence till they all started at the same time to show me where I was wrong, and how cruelly my girlish inexperience had deceived me. A young and innocent half-portion like me, it appears, is absolutely incapable of suspecting the true infamy of the dregs of society. You aren't fit to speak to the likes of me, being at the kindest estimate little more than a blot on the human race. I tell you this in case you may imagine you're popular with the Family. You're not.

So I shall have to exercise a good deal of snaky craft in smuggling this letter through. I'll take it down to the village myself if I can sneak away. But it's going to be pretty difficult, because for some reason I seem to be a centre of attraction. Except when I take refuge in my room, hardly a moment passes without an aunt or an uncle popping out and having a cosy talk with me. It sometimes seems as though they were weighing me in the balance. Well, let 'em weigh!

Time to dress for dinner now. Good-bye.

Yours in the balance,
Sally

P.S.—You were perfectly right about your Uncle Donald's moustache, but I don't agree with you that it is more his misfortune than his fault. I think he does it on purpose.

(Just for the moment)
Monk's Crofton,
Much Middleford,
Salop,
England

April 20th

Dear Ginger,

Leaving here to-day. In disgrace. Hard, cold looks from the family. Strained silences. Uncle Donald far from chummy. You can guess what has happened. I might have seen it coming. I can see now that it was in the air all along.

Fillmore knows nothing about it. He left just before it happened. I shall see him very soon, for I have decided to come back and stop running away from things any longer. It's cowardly to skulk about over here. Besides, I'm feeling so much better that I believe I can face the ghosts. Anyway, I'm going to try. See you almost as soon as you get this.

I shall mail this in London, and I suppose it will come over by the same boat as me. It's hardly worth writing, really, of course, but I have sneaked up to my room to wait till the motor arrives to take me to the station, and it's something to do. I can hear muffled voices. The Family talking me over, probably. Saying they never really liked me all along. Oh, well!

Yours moving in an orderly manner to the exit,
Sally

XIII

STRANGE BEHAVIOUR OF A SPARRING-PARTNER

1

SALLY'S EMOTIONS, AS SHE SAT in her apartment on the morning of her return to New York, resembled somewhat those of a swimmer who, after wavering on a raw morning at the brink of a chill pool, nerves himself to the plunge. She was aching, but she knew that she had done well. If she wanted happiness, she must fight for it, and for all these months she had been shirking the fight. She had done with wavering on the brink, and here she was, in mid-stream, ready for whatever might befall. It hurt, this coming to grips. She had expected it to hurt. But it was a pain that stimulated, not a dull melancholy that smothered. She felt alive and defiant.

She had finished unpacking and tidying up. The next move was certainly to go and see Ginger. She had suddenly become aware that she wanted very badly to see Ginger. His stolid friendliness would be a support and a prop. She wished now that she had sent him a cable, so that he could have met her at the dock. It had been rather terrible at the dock. The echoing customs sheds had sapped her valour and she felt alone and forlorn.

She looked at her watch, and was surprised to find how early it was. She could catch him at the office and make him take her out to lunch. She put on her hat and went out.

The restless hand of change, always active in New York, had not spared the outer office of the Fillmore Nicholas Theatrical Enterprises Ltd. in the months of her absence. She was greeted on her arrival by an entirely new and original stripling in the place of the one with whom at her last visit she had established such cordial relations. Like his predecessor he was generously pimpled, but there the resemblance stopped. He was a grim boy, and his manner was stern and suspicious. He peered narrowly at Sally for a moment as if he had caught her in the act of purloining the office blotting-paper, then, with no little acerbity, desired her to state her business.

"I want Mr. Kemp," said Sally.

The office-boy scratched his cheek dourly with a ruler. No one would have guessed, so austere was his aspect, that a moment before her entrance he had been trying to balance it on his chin, juggling the while with a pair of paper-weights. For, impervious as he seemed to human weaknesses, it was this lad's ambition one day to go into vaudeville.

"What name?" he said, coldly.

"Nicholas," said Sally. "I am Mr. Nicholas' sister."

On a previous occasion when she had made this announcement, disastrous results had ensued; but to-day it went well. It seemed to hit the office-boy like a bullet. He started convulsively, opened his mouth, and dropped the ruler. In the interval of stooping and recovering it he was able to pull himself together. He had not been curious about Sally's name. What he had wished was to have the name of the person for whom she was asking repeated. He now perceived that he had had a bit of luck. A wearying period of disappointment in the matter of keeping the paper-weights circulating while balancing the ruler, had left him peevish, and it had been his intention to work off his ill-humour on the young visitor. The discovery that it was the boss's sister who was taking up his time, suggested the advisability of a radical change of tactics. He had stooped with a frown: he returned to the perpendicular with a smile that was positively winning. It was like the sun suddenly bursting through a London fog.

"Will you take a seat, lady?" he said, with polished courtesy even unbending so far as to reach out and dust one with the sleeve of his coat. He added that the morning was a fine one.

"Thank you," said Sally. "Will you tell him I'm here."

"Mr. Nicholas is out, miss," said the office-boy, with gentlemanly regret. "He's back in New York, but he's gone out."

"I don't want Mr. Nicholas. I want Mr. Kemp."

"Mr. Kemp?"

"Yes, Mr. Kemp."

Sorrow at his inability to oblige shone from every hill-top on the boy's face.

"Don't know of anyone of that name around here," he said, apologetically.

"But surely. . ." Sally broke off suddenly. A grim foreboding had come to her. "How long have you been here?" she asked.

"All day, ma'am," said the office-boy, with the manner of a Casablanca.

"I mean, how long have you been employed here?"

"Just over a month, miss."

"Hasn't Mr. Kemp been in the office all that time?"

"Name's new to me, lady. Does he look like anything? I meanter say, what's he look like?"

"He has very red hair."

"Never seen him in here," said the office-boy. The truth shone coldly on Sally. She blamed herself for ever having gone away, and told herself that she might have known what would happen. Left to his own resources, the unhappy Ginger had once more made a hash of it. And this hash must have been a more notable and outstanding hash than any of his previous efforts, for, surely, Fillmore would not lightly have dismissed one who had come to him under her special protection.

"Where is Mr. Nicholas?" she asked. It seemed to her that Fillmore was the only possible source of information. "Did you say he was out?"

"Really out, miss," said the office-boy, with engaging candour. "He went off to White Plains in his automobile half-an-hour ago."

"White Plains? What for?"

The pimpled stripling had now given himself up wholeheartedly to social chit-chat. Usually he liked his time to himself and resented the intrusion of the outer world, for he who had chosen jugglery for his walk in life must neglect no opportunity of practising: but so favourable was the impression which Sally had made on his plastic mind that he was delighted to converse with her as long as she wished.

"I guess what's happened is, he's gone up to take a look at Bugs Butler," he said.

"Whose butler?" said Sally mystified.

The office-boy smiled a tolerant smile. Though an admirer of the sex, he was aware that women were seldom hep to the really important things in life. He did not blame them. That was the way they were constructed, and one simply had to accept it.

"Bugs Butler is training up at White Plains, miss."

"Who is Bugs Butler?"

Something of his former bleakness of aspect returned to the office-boy. Sally's question had opened up a subject on which he felt deeply.

"Ah!" he replied, losing his air of respectful deference as he approached the topic. "Who is he! That's what they're all saying, all the wise guys. Who has Bugs Butler ever licked?"

"I don't know," said Sally, for he had fixed her with a penetrating gaze and seemed to be pausing for a reply.

"Nor nobody else," said the stripling vehemently. "A lot of stiffs out on the coast, that's all. Ginks nobody has ever heard of, except Cyclone Mullins, and it took that false alarm fifteen rounds to get a referee's decision over him. The boss would go and give him a chance against the champ, but I could have told him that the legitimate contender was K-leg Binns. K-leg put Cyclone Mullins out in the fifth. Well," said the office-boy in the overwrought tone of one chafing at human folly, "if anybody thinks Bugs Butler can last six rounds with Lew Lucas, I've two bucks right here in my vest pocket that says it ain't so."

Sally began to see daylight.

"Oh, Bugs—Mr. Butler is one of the boxers in this fight that my brother is interested in?"

"That's right. He's going up against the lightweight champ. Lew Lucas is the lightweight champ. He's a bird!"

"Yes?" said Sally. This youth had a way of looking at her with his head cocked on one side as though he expected her to say something.

"Yes, sir!" said the stripling with emphasis. "Lew Lucas is a hot sketch. He used to live on the next street to me," he added as clinching evidence of his hero's prowess. "I've seen his old mother as close as I am to you. Say, I seen her a hundred times. Is any stiff of a Bugs Butler going to lick a fellow like that?"

"It doesn't seem likely."

"You spoke it!" said the lad crisply, striking unsuccessfully at a fly which had settled on the blotting-paper.

There was a pause. Sally started to rise.

"And there's another thing," said the office-boy, loath to close the subject. "Can Bugs Butler make a hundred and thirty-five ringside without being weak?"

"It sounds awfully difficult."

"They say he's clever." The expert laughed satirically. "Well, what's that going to get him? The poor fish can't punch a hole in a nut-sundae."

"You don't seem to like Mr. Butler."

"Oh, I've nothing against him," said the office-boy magnanimously. "I'm only saying he's no licence to be mixing it with Lew Lucas."

Sally got up. Absorbing as this chat on current form was, more important matters claimed her attention.

"How shall I find my brother when I get to White Plains?" she asked.

"Oh, anybody'll show you the way to the training-camp. If you hurry, there's a train you can make now."

"Thank you very much."

"You're welcome."

He opened the door for her with an old-world politeness which disuse had rendered a little rusty: then, with an air of getting back to business after a pleasant but frivolous interlude, he took up the paper-weights once more and placed the ruler with nice care on his upturned chin.

2

FILLMORE HEAVED A SIGH OF relief and began to sidle from the room. It was a large room, half barn, half gymnasium. Athletic appliances of various kinds hung on the walls and in the middle there was a wide roped-off space, around which a small crowd had distributed itself with an air of expectancy. This is a commercial age, and the days when a prominent pugilist's training activities used to be hidden from the public gaze are over. To-day, if the public can lay its hands on fifty cents, it may come and gaze its fill. This afternoon, plutocrats to the number of about forty had assembled, though not all of these, to the regret of Mr. Lester Burrowes, the manager of the eminent Bugs Butler, had parted with solid coin. Many of those present were newspaper representatives and on the free list—writers who would polish up Mr. Butler's somewhat crude prognostications as to what he proposed to do to Mr. Lew Lucas, and would report him as saying, "I am in really superb condition and feel little apprehension of the issue," and artists who would depict him in a state of semi-nudity with feet several sizes too large for any man.

The reason for Fillmore's relief was that Mr. Burrowes, who was a great talker and had buttonholed him a quarter of an hour ago, had at last had his attention distracted elsewhere, and had gone off to investigate some matter that called for his personal handling, leaving Fillmore free to slide away to the hotel and get a bite to eat, which he sorely needed. The zeal which had brought him to the training-camp to inspect the final day of Mr. Butler's preparation—for the fight was to take place on the morrow—had been so great that he had omitted to lunch before leaving New York.

So Fillmore made thankfully for the door. And it was at the door that he encountered Sally. He was looking over his shoulder at the moment, and was not aware of her presence till she spoke.

"Hallo, Fillmore!"

Sally had spoken softly, but a dynamite explosion could not have shattered her brother's composure with more completeness. In the leaping twist which brought him facing her, he rose a clear three inches from the floor. He had a confused sensation, as though his nervous system had been stirred up with a pole. He struggled for breath and moistened his lips with the tip of his tongue, staring at her continuously during the process.

Great men, in their moments of weakness, are to be pitied rather than scorned. If ever a man had an excuse for leaping like a young ram, Fillmore had it. He had left Sally not much than a week ago in England, in Shropshire, at Monk's Crofton. She had said nothing of any intention on her part of leaving the country, the county, or the house. Yet here she was, in Bugs Butler's training-camp at White Plains, in the State of New York, speaking softly in his ear without even going through the preliminary of tapping him on the shoulder to advertise her presence. No wonder that Fillmore was startled. And no wonder that, as he adjusted his faculties to the situation, there crept upon him a chill apprehension.

For Fillmore had not been blind to the significance of that invitation to Monk's Crofton. Nowadays your wooer does not formally approach a girl's nearest relative and ask permission to pay his addresses; but, when he invites her and that nearest relative to his country home and collects all the rest of the family to meet her, the thing may be said to have advanced beyond the realms of mere speculation. Shrewdly Fillmore had deduced that Bruce Carmyle was in love with Sally, and mentally he had joined their hands and given them a brother's blessing. And now it was only too plain that disaster must have occurred. If the invitation could mean only one thing, so also could Sally's presence at White Plains mean only one thing.

"Sally!" A croaking whisper was the best he could achieve. "What. . . what. . . ?"

"Did I startle you? I'm sorry."

"What are you doing here? Why aren't you at Monk's Crofton?"

Sally glanced past him at the ring and the crowd around it.

"I decided I wanted to get back to America. Circumstances arose which made it pleasanter to leave Monk's Crofton."

"Do you mean to say. . . ?"

"Yes. Don't let's talk about it."

"Do you mean to say," persisted Fillmore, "that Carmyle proposed to you and you turned him down?"

Sally flushed.

"I don't think it's particularly nice to talk about that sort of thing, but—yes."

A feeling of desolation overcame Fillmore. That conviction, which saddens us at all times, of the wilful bone-headedness of our fellows swept coldly upon him. Everything had been so perfect, the whole arrangement so ideal, that it had never occurred to him as a possibility that Sally might take it into her head to spoil it by declining to play the part allotted to her. The match was so obviously the best thing that could happen. It was not merely the suitor's impressive wealth that made him hold this opinion, though it would be idle to deny that the prospect of having a brother-in-lawful claim on the Carmyle bank-balance had cast a rosy glamour over the future as he had envisaged it. He honestly liked and respected the man. He appreciated his quiet and aristocratic reserve. A well-bred fellow, sensible withal, just the sort of husband a girl like Sally needed. And now she had ruined everything. With the capricious perversity which so characterizes her otherwise delightful sex, she had spilled the beans.

"But why?"

"Oh, Fill!" Sally had expected that realization of the facts would produce these symptoms in him, but now that they had presented themselves she was finding them rasping to the nerves. "I should have thought the reason was obvious."

"You mean you don't like him?"

"I don't know whether I do or not. I certainly don't like him enough to marry him."

"He's a darned good fellow."

"Is he? You say so. I don't know."

The imperious desire for bodily sustenance began to compete successfully for Fillmore's notice with his spiritual anguish.

"Let's go to the hotel and talk it over. We'll go to the hotel and I'll give you something to eat."

"I don't want anything to eat, thanks."

"You don't want anything to eat?" said Fillmore incredulously. He supposed in a vague sort of way that there were eccentric people of this sort, but it was hard to realize that he had met one of them. "I'm starving."

"Well, run along then."

"Yes, but I want to talk. . ."

He was not the only person who wanted to talk. At the moment a small man of sporting exterior hurried up. He wore what his tailor's advertisements would have called a "nobbly" suit of checked tweed and—in defiance of popular prejudice—a brown bowler hat. Mr. Lester Burrowes, having dealt with the business which had interrupted their conversation a few minutes before, was anxious to resume his remarks on the subject of the supreme excellence in every respect of his young charge.

"Say, Mr. Nicholas, you ain't going'? Bugs is just getting ready to spar."

He glanced inquiringly at Sally.

"My sister—Mr. Burrowes," said Fillmore faintly. "Mr. Burrowes is Bugs Butler's manager."

"How do you do?" said Sally.

"Pleased to meecher," said Mr. Burrowes. "Say. . ."

"I was just going to the hotel to get something to eat," said Fillmore.

Mr. Burrowes clutched at his coat-button with a swoop, and held him with a glittering eye.

"Yes, but, say, before-you-go-lemme-tell-ya-somef'n. You've never seen this boy of mine, not when he was feeling right. Believe me, he's there! He's a wizard. He's a Hindoo! Say, he's been practising up a left shift that. . ."

Fillmore's eye met Sally's wanly, and she pitied him. Presently she would require him to explain to her how he had dared to dismiss Ginger from his employment—and make that explanation a good one: but in the meantime she remembered that he was her brother and was suffering.

"He's the cleverest lightweight," proceeded Mr. Burrowes fervently, "since Joe Gans. I'm telling you and I know! He. . ."

"Can he make a hundred and thirty-five ringside without being weak?" asked Sally.

The effect of this simple question on Mr. Burrowes was stupendous. He dropped away from Fillmore's coat-button like an exhausted bivalve, and his small mouth opened feebly. It was as if a child had suddenly propounded to an eminent mathematician some abstruse problem in the higher algebra. Females who took an interest in boxing had come into Mr. Burrowes' life before-—in his younger days, when he was a famous featherweight, the first of his three wives had been accustomed to sit at the ringside during his contests and urge him in language of the severest technicality to knock opponents' blocks off—but somehow he had not supposed from her appearance and manner that Sally was one of the elect. He gaped at her, and the relieved Fillmore sidled off like a bird hopping from the compelling gaze of a snake. He was not quite sure that he was acting correctly in allowing his sister to roam at large among the somewhat Bohemian surroundings of a training-camp, but the instinct of self-preservation turned the scale. He had breakfasted early, and if he did not eat right speedily it seemed to him that dissolution would set in.

"Whazzat?" said Mr. Burrowes feebly.

"It took him fifteen rounds to get a referee's decision over Cyclone Mullins," said Sally severely, "and K-leg Binns. . ."

Mr. Burrowes rallies.

"You ain't got it right" he protested. "Say, you mustn't believe what you see in the papers. The referee was dead against us, and Cyclone was down once for all of half a minute and they wouldn't count him out. Gee! You got to kill a guy in some towns before they'll give you a decision. At that, they couldn't do nothing so raw as make it anything but a win for my boy, after him leading by a mile all the way. Have you ever seen Bugs, ma'am?"

Sally had to admit that she had not had that privilege. Mr. Burrowes with growing excitement felt in his breast-pocket and produced a picture-postcard, which he thrust into her hand.

"That's Bugs," he said. "Take a slant at that and then tell me if he don't look the goods."

The photograph represented a young man in the irreducible minimum of clothing who crouched painfully, as though stricken with one of the acuter forms of gastritis.

"I'll call him over and have him sign it for you," said Mr. Burrowes, before Sally had had time to grasp the fact that this work of art was a gift and no mere loan. "Here, Bugs—wantcher."

A youth enveloped in a bath-robe, who had been talking to a group of admirers near the ring, turned, started languidly towards them, then, seeing Sally, quickened his pace. He was an admirer of the sex.

Mr. Burrowes did the honours.

"Bugs, this is Miss Nicholas, come to see you work out. I have been telling her she's going to have a treat." And to Sally. "Shake hands with Bugs Butler, ma'am, the coming lightweight champion of the world."

Mr. Butler's photograph, Sally considered, had flattered him. He was, in the flesh, a singularly repellent young man. There was a mean and cruel curve to his lips and a cold arrogance in his eye; a something dangerous and sinister in the atmosphere he radiated. Moreover, she did not like the way he smirked at her.

However, she exerted herself to be amiable.

"I hope you are going to win, Mr. Butler," she said.

The smile which she forced as she spoke the words removed the coming champion's doubts, though they had never been serious. He was convinced now that he had made a hit. He always did, he reflected, with the girls. It was something about him. His chest swelled complacently beneath the bath-robe.

"You betcher," he asserted briefly.

Mr. Burrows looked at his watch.

"Time you were starting, Bugs."

The coming champion removed his gaze from Sally's face, into which he had been peering in a conquering manner, and cast a disparaging glance at the audience. It was far from being as large as he could have wished, and at least a third of it was composed of non-payers from the newspapers.

"All right," he said, bored.

His languor left him, as his gaze fell on Sally again, and his spirits revived somewhat. After all, small though the numbers of spectators might be, bright eyes would watch and admire him.

"I'll go a couple of rounds with Reddy for a starter," he said. "Seen him anywheres? He's never around when he's wanted."

"I'll fetch him," said Mr. Burrowes. "He's back there somewheres."

"I'm going to show that guy up this afternoon," said Mr. Butler coldly. "He's been getting too fresh."

The manager bustled off, and Bugs Butler, with a final smirk, left Sally and dived under the ropes. There was a stir of interest in the audience, though the newspaper men, blasé through familiarity, exhibited no emotion. Presently Mr. Burrowes reappeared, shepherding a young man whose face was hidden by the sweater which he was pulling over his head. He was a sturdily built young man. The sweater, moving from his body, revealed a good pair of shoulders.

A last tug, and the sweater was off. Red hair flashed into view, tousled and disordered: and, as she saw it, Sally uttered an involuntary gasp of astonishment which caused many eyes to turn towards her. And the red-headed young man, who had been stooping to pick up his gloves, straightened himself with a jerk and stood staring at her blankly and incredulously, his face slowly crimsoning.

It was the energetic Mr. Burrowes who broke the spell.

"Come on, come on," he said impatiently. "Li'l speed there, Reddy."

Ginger Kemp started like a sleep-walker awakened; then recovering himself, slowly began to pull on the gloves. Embarrassment was stamped on his agreeable features. His face matched his hair.

Sally plucked at the little manager's elbow. He turned irritably, but beamed in a distrait sort of manner when he perceived the source of the interruption.

"Who—him?" he said in answer to Sally's whispered question. "He's just one of Bugs' sparring-partners."

"But. . ."

Mr. Burrowes, fussy now that the time had come for action, interrupted her.

"You'll excuse me, miss, but I have to hold the watch. We mustn't waste any time."

Sally drew back. She felt like an infidel who intrudes upon the celebration of strange rites. This was Man's hour, and women must keep in the background. She had the sensation of being very small and yet very much in the way, like a puppy who has wandered into a church. The novelty and solemnity of the scene awed her.

She looked at Ginger, who with averted gaze was fiddling with his clothes in the opposite corner of the ring. He was as removed from communication as if he had been in another world. She continued to stare, wide-eyed, and Ginger, shuffling his feet self-consciously, plucked at his gloves.

Mr. Butler, meanwhile, having doffed his bath-robe, stretched himself, and with leisurely nonchalance put on a second pair of gloves, was filling in the time with a little shadow boxing. He moved rhythmically to and fro, now ducking his head, now striking out with his muffled hands, and a sickening realization of the man's animal power swept over Sally and turned her cold. Swathed in his bath-robe, Bugs Butler had conveyed an atmosphere of dangerousness: in the boxing-tights which showed up every rippling muscle, he was horrible and sinister, a machine built for destruction, a human panther.

So he appeared to Sally, but a stout and bulbous eyed man standing at her side was not equally impressed. Obviously one of the Wise Guys of whom her friend the sporting office-boy had spoken, he was frankly dissatisfied with the exhibition.

"Shadow-boxing," he observed in a cavilling spirit to his companion. "Yes, he can do that all right, just like I can fox-trot if I ain't got a partner to get in the way. But one good wallop, and then watch him."

His friend, also plainly a guy of established wisdom, assented with a curt nod.

"Ah!" he agreed.

"Lew Lucas," said the first wise guy, "is just as shifty, and he can punch."

"Ah!" said the second wise guy.

"Just because he beats up a few poor mutts of sparring-partners," said the first wise guy disparagingly, "he thinks he's someone."

"Ah!" said the second wise guy.

As far as Sally could interpret these remarks, the full meaning of which was shrouded from her, they seemed to be reassuring. For a comforting moment she ceased to regard Ginger as a martyr waiting to be devoured by a lion. Mr. Butler, she gathered, was not so formidable as he appeared. But her relief was not to be long-lived.

"Of course he'll eat this red-headed gink," went on the first wise guy. "That's the thing he does best, killing his sparring-partners. But Lew Lucas. . ."

Sally was not interested in Lew Lucas. That numbing fear had come back to her. Even these cognoscenti, little as they esteemed Mr. Butler, had plainly no doubts as what he would do to Ginger. She tried to tear herself away, but something stronger than her own will kept her there standing where she was, holding on to the rope and staring forlornly into the ring.

"Ready, Bugs?" asked Mr. Burrowes.

The coming champion nodded carelessly.

"Go to it," said Mr. Burrowes.

Ginger ceased to pluck at his gloves and advanced into the ring.

4

OF ALL THE LEARNED PROFESSIONS, pugilism is the one in which the trained expert is most sharply divided from the mere dabbler. In other fields the amateur may occasionally hope to compete successfully with the man who has made a business of what is to him but a sport, but at boxing never: and the whole demeanour of Bugs Butler showed that he had laid this truth to heart. It would be too little to say that his bearing was confident: he comported himself with the care-free jauntiness of an infant about to demolish a Noah's Ark with a tack-hammer. Cyclone Mullinses might withstand him for fifteen rounds where they yielded to a K-leg Binns in the fifth, but, when it came to beating up a sparring-partner and an amateur at that, Bugs Butler knew his potentialities. He was there forty ways and he did not attempt to conceal it. Crouching as was his wont, he uncoiled himself like a striking rattlesnake and flicked Ginger lightly over his guard. Then he returned to his crouch and circled sinuously about the ring with the amiable intention of showing the crowd, payers and deadheads alike, what real footwork was. If there was one thing on which Bugs Butler prided himself, it was footwork.

The adverb "lightly" is a relative term, and the blow which had just planted a dull patch on Ginger's cheekbone affected those present in different degrees. Ginger himself appeared stolidly callous. Sally shuddered to the core of her being and had to hold more tightly to the rope to support herself. The two wise guys mocked openly. To the wise guys, expert connoisseurs of swat, the thing had appeared richly farcical. They seemed to consider the blow, administered to a third party and not to themselves, hardly worth calling a blow at all. Two more, landing as quickly and neatly as the first, left them equally cold.

"Call that punching?" said the first wise guy.

"Ah!" said the second wise guy.

But Mr. Butler, if he heard this criticism—and it is probable that he did—for the wise ones had been restrained by no delicacy of feeling from raising their voices, was in no way discommoded by it. Bugs Butler knew what he was about. Bright eyes were watching him, and he meant to give them a treat. The girls like smooth work. Any roughneck could sail into a guy and knock the daylights out of him, but how few could be clever and flashy and scientific? Few, few, indeed, thought Mr. Butler as he slid in and led once more.

Something solid smote Mr. Butler's nose, rocking him on to his heels and inducing an unpleasant smarting sensation about his eyes. He backed away and regarded Ginger with astonishment, almost with pain. Until this moment he had scarcely considered him as an active participant in the scene at all, and he felt strongly that this sort of thing was bad form. It was not being done by sparring-partners.

P.G. WODEHOUSE

A juster man might have reflected that he himself was to blame. He had undeniably been careless. In the very act of leading he had allowed his eyes to flicker sideways to see how Sally was taking this exhibition of science, and he had paid the penalty. Nevertheless, he was piqued. He shimmered about the ring, thinking it over. And the more he thought it over, the less did he approve of his young assistant's conduct. Hard thoughts towards Ginger began to float in his mind.

Ginger, too, was thinking hard thoughts. He had not had an easy time since he had come to the training camp, but never till to-day had he experienced any resentment towards his employer. Until this afternoon Bugs Butler had pounded him honestly and without malice, and he had gone through it, as the other sparring-partners did, phlegmatically, taking it as part of the day's work. But this afternoon there had been a difference. Those careless flicks had been an insult, a deliberate offence. The man was trying to make a fool of him, playing to the gallery: and the thought of who was in that gallery inflamed Ginger past thought of consequences. No one, not even Mr. Butler, was more keenly alive than he to the fact that in a serious conflict with a man who to-morrow night might be light-weight champion of the world he stood no chance whatever: but he did not intend to be made an exhibition of in front of Sally without doing something to hold his end up. He proposed to go down with his flag flying, and in pursuance of this object he dug Mr. Butler heavily in the lower ribs with his right, causing that expert to clinch and the two wise guys to utter sharp barking sounds expressive of derision.

"Say, what the hell d'ya think you're getting at?" demanded the aggrieved pugilist in a heated whisper in Ginger's ear as they fell into the embrace. "What's the idea, you jelly bean?"

Ginger maintained a pink silence. His jaw was set, and the temper which Nature had bestowed upon him to go with his hair had reached white heat. He dodged a vicious right which whizzed up at his chin out of the breaking clinch, and rushed. A left hook shook him, but was too high to do more. There was rough work in the far corner, and suddenly with startling abruptness Bugs Butler, bothered by the ropes at his back and trying to side-step, ran into a swing and fell.

"Time!" shouted the scandalized Mr. Burrowes, utterly aghast at this frightful misadventure. In the whole course of his professional experience he could recall no such devastating occurrence.

The audience was no less startled. There was audible gasping. The newspaper men looked at each other with a wild surmise and conjured up pleasant pictures of their sporting editors receiving this sensational item of news later on over the telephone. The two wise guys, continuing to pursue Mr. Butler with their dislike, emitted loud and raucous laughs, and one of them, forming his hands into a megaphone, urged the fallen warrior to go away and get a rep. As for Sally, she was conscious of a sudden, fierce, cave-womanly rush of happiness which swept away completely the sickening qualms of the last few minutes. Her teeth were clenched and her eyes blazed with joyous excitement. She looked at Ginger yearningly, longing to forget a gentle upbringing and shout congratulation to him. She was proud of him. And mingled with the pride was a curious feeling that was almost fear. This was not the mild and amiable young man whom she was wont to mother through the difficulties of a world in which he was unfitted to struggle for himself. This was a new Ginger, a stranger to her.

On the rare occasions on which he had been knocked down in the past, it had been Bugs Butler's canny practice to pause for a while and rest before rising and continuing the argument, but now he was up almost before he had touched the boards, and the satire of the second wise guy, who had begun to saw the air with his hand and count loudly, lost its point. It was only too plain that Mr. Butler's motto was that a man may be down, but he is never out. And, indeed, the knock-down had been largely a stumble. Bugs Butler's educated feet, which had carried him unscathed through so many contests, had for this single occasion managed to get themselves crossed just as Ginger's blow landed, and it was to his lack of balance rather than the force of the swing that his downfall had been due.

"Time!" he snarled, casting a malevolent side-glance at his manager. "Like hell it's time!"

And in a whirlwind of flying gloves he flung himself upon Ginger, driving him across the ring, while Mr. Burrowes, watch in hand, stared with dropping jaw. If Ginger had seemed a new Ginger to Sally, still more did this seem a new Bugs Butler to Mr. Burrowes, and the manager groaned in spirit. Coolness, skill and science—these had been the qualities in his protégé which had always so endeared him to Mr. Lester Burrowes and had so enriched their respective bank accounts: and now, on the eve of the most important fight in his life, before an audience of newspaper men, he had thrown them all aside and was making an exhibition of himself with a common sparring-partner.

That was the bitter blow to Mr. Burrowes. Had this lapse into the unscientific primitive happened in a regular fight, he might have mourned and poured reproof into Bug's ear when he got him back in his corner at the end of the round; but he would not have experienced this feeling of helpless horror—the sort of horror an elder of the church might feel if he saw his favourite bishop yielding in public to the fascination of jazz. It was the fact that Bugs Butler was lowering himself to extend his powers against a sparring-partner that shocked Mr. Burrowes. There is an etiquette in these things. A champion may batter his sparring-partners into insensibility if he pleases, but he must do it with nonchalance. He must not appear to be really trying.

And nothing could be more manifest than that Bugs Butler was trying. His whole fighting soul was in his efforts to corner Ginger and destroy him. The battle was raging across the ring and down the ring, and up the ring and back again; yet always Ginger, like a storm-driven ship, contrived somehow to weather the tempest. Out of the flurry of swinging arms he emerged time after time bruised, bleeding, but fighting hard.

For Bugs Butler's fury was defeating its object. Had he remained his cool and scientific self, he could have demolished Ginger and cut through his defence in a matter of seconds. But he had lapsed back into the methods of his unskilled novitiate. He swung and missed, swung and missed again, struck but found no vital spot. And now there was blood on his face, too. In some wild mêlée the sacred fount had been tapped, and his teeth gleamed through a crimson mist.

The Wise Guys were beyond speech. They were leaning against one another, punching each other feebly in the back. One was crying.

And then suddenly the end came, as swiftly and unexpectedly as the thing had begun. His wild swings had tired Bugs Butler, and with fatigue prudence returned to him. His feet began once more their subtle weaving in and out. Twice his left hand flickered home. A quick feint, a short, jolting stab, and Ginger's guard was down and he was swaying in the middle of the ring, his hands hanging and his knees a-quiver.

Bugs Butler measured his distance, and Sally shut her eyes.

XIV

MR. ABRAHAMS RE-ENGAGES AN OLD EMPLOYEE

1

THE ONLY REAL HAPPINESS, WE are told, is to be obtained by bringing happiness to others. Bugs Butler's mood, accordingly, when some thirty hours after the painful episode recorded in the last chapter he awoke from a state of coma in the ring at Jersey City to discover that Mr. Lew Lucas had knocked him out in the middle of the third round, should have been one of quiet contentment. His inability to block a short left-hook followed by a right to the point of the jaw had ameliorated quite a number of existences.

Mr. Lew Lucas, for one, was noticeably pleased. So were Mr. Lucas's seconds, one of whom went so far as to kiss him. And most of the crowd, who had betted heavily on the champion, were delighted. Yet Bugs Butler did not rejoice. It is not too much to say that his peevish bearing struck a jarring note in the general gaiety. A heavy frown disfigured his face as he slouched from the ring.

But the happiness which he had spread went on spreading. The two Wise Guys, who had been unable to attend the fight in person, received the result on the ticker and exuberantly proclaimed themselves the richer by five hundred dollars. The pimpled office-boy at the Fillmore Nicholas Theatrical Enterprises Ltd. caused remark in the Subway by whooping gleefully when he read the news in his morning paper, for he, too, had been rendered wealthier by the brittleness of Mr. Butler's chin. And it was with fierce satisfaction that Sally, breakfasting in her little apartment, informed herself through the sporting page of the details of the contender's downfall. She was not a girl who disliked many people, but she had acquired a lively distaste for Bugs Butler.

Lew Lucas seemed a man after her own heart. If he had been a personal friend of Ginger's he could not, considering the brief time at his disposal, have avenged him with more thoroughness. In round one he had done all sorts of diverting things to Mr. Butler's left eye: in round two he had continued the good work on that gentleman's body;

and in round three he had knocked him out. Could anyone have done more? Sally thought not, and she drank Lew Lucas's health in a cup of coffee and hoped his old mother was proud of him.

The telephone bell rang at her elbow. She unhooked the receiver.

"Hullo?"

"Oh, hullo," said a voice.

"Ginger!" cried Sally delightedly.

"I say, I'm awfully glad you're back. I only got your letter this morning. Found it at the boarding-house. I happened to look in there and. . ."

"Ginger," interrupted Sally, "your voice is music, but I want to see you. Where are you?"

"I'm at a chemist's shop across the street. I was wondering if. . ."

"Come here at once!"

"I say, may I? I was just going to ask."

"You miserable creature, why haven't you been round to see me before?"

"Well, as a matter of fact, I haven't been going about much for the last day. You see. . ."

"I know. Of course." Quick sympathy came into Sally's voice. She gave a sidelong glance of approval and gratitude at the large picture of Lew Lucas which beamed up at her from the morning paper. "You poor thing! How are you?"

"Oh, all right, thanks."

"Well, hurry."

There was a slight pause at the other end of the wire.

"I say."

"Well?"

"I'm not much to look at, you know."

"You never were. Stop talking and hurry over."

"I mean to say. . ."

Sally hung up the receiver firmly. She waited eagerly for some minutes, and then footsteps came along the passage. They stopped at her door and the bell rang. Sally ran to the door, flung it open, and recoiled in consternation.

"Oh, Ginger!"

He had stated the facts accurately when he had said that he was not much to look at. He gazed at her devotedly out of an unblemished right eye, but the other was hidden altogether by a puffy swelling of dull purple. A great bruise marred his left cheek-bone, and he spoke with some difficulty through swollen lips.

"It's all right, you know," he assured her.

"It isn't. It's awful! Oh, you poor darling!" She clenched her teeth viciously. "I wish he had killed him!"

"Eh?"

"I wish Lew Lucas or whatever his name is had murdered him. Brute!"

"Oh, I don't know, you know." Ginger's sense of fairness compelled him to defend his late employer against these harsh sentiments. "He isn't a bad sort of chap, really. Bugs Butler, I mean."

"Do you seriously mean to stand there and tell me you don't loathe the creature?"

"Oh, he's all right. See his point of view and all that. Can't blame him, if you come to think of it, for getting the wind up a bit in the circs. Bit thick, I mean to say, a sparring-partner going at him like that. Naturally he didn't think it much of a wheeze. It was my fault right along. Oughtn't to have done it, of course, but somehow, when he started making an ass of me and I knew you were looking on. . . well, it seemed a good idea to have a dash at doing something on my own. No right to, of course. A sparring-partner isn't supposed. . ."

"Sit down," said Sally.

Ginger sat down.

"Ginger," said Sally, "you're too good to live."

"Oh, I say!"

"I believe if someone sandbagged you and stole your watch and chain you'd say there were faults on both sides or something. I'm just a cat, and I say I wish your beast of a Bugs Butler had perished miserably. I'd have gone and danced on his grave. . . But whatever made you go in for that sort of thing?"

"Well, it seemed the only job that was going at the moment. I've always done a goodish bit of boxing and I was very fit and so on, and it looked to me rather an opening. Gave me something to get along with. You get paid quite fairly decently, you know, and it's rather a jolly life. . ."

"Jolly? Being hammered about like that?"

"Oh, you don't notice it much. I've always enjoyed scrapping rather. And, you see, when your brother gave me the push. . ."

Sally uttered an exclamation.

"What an extraordinary thing it is—I went all the way out to White Plains that afternoon to find Fillmore and tackle him about that and I didn't say a word about it. And I haven't seen or been able to get hold of him since."

"No? Busy sort of cove, your brother."

"Why did Fillmore let you go?"

"Let me go? Oh, you mean. . . well, there was a sort of mix-up. A kind of misunderstanding."

"What happened?"

"Oh, it was nothing. Just a. . ."

"What happened?"

Ginger's disfigured countenance betrayed embarrassment. He looked awkwardly about the room.

"It's not worth talking about."

"It is worth talking about. I've a right to know. It was I who sent you to Fillmore. . ."

"Now that," said Ginger, "was jolly decent of you."

"Don't interrupt! I sent you to Fillmore, and he had no business to let you go without saying a word to me. What happened?"

Ginger twiddled his fingers unhappily.

"Well, it was rather unfortunate. You see, his wife—I don't know if you know her? . . ."

"Of course I know her."

"Why, yes, you would, wouldn't you? Your brother's wife, I mean," said Ginger acutely. "Though, as a matter of fact, you often find sisters-in-law who won't have anything to do with one another. I know a fellow. . ."

"Ginger," said Sally, "it's no good your thinking you can get out of telling me by rambling off on other subjects. I'm grim and resolute and relentless, and I mean to get this story out of you if I have to use a corkscrew. Fillmore's wife, you were saying. . ."

Ginger came back reluctantly to the main theme.

"Well, she came into the office one morning, and we started fooling about. . ."

"Fooling about?"

"Well, kind of chivvying each other."

"Chivvying?"

"At least I was."

"You were what?"

"Sort of chasing her a bit, you know."

Sally regarded this apostle of frivolity with amazement.

"What do you mean?"

Ginger's embarrassment increased.

"The thing was, you see, she happened to trickle in rather quietly when I happened to be looking at something, and I didn't know she was there till she suddenly grabbed it. . ."

"Grabbed what?"

"The thing. The thing I happened to be looking at. She bagged it. . . collared it. . . took it away from me, you know, and wouldn't give it back and generally started to rot about a bit, so I rather began to chivvy her to some extent, and I'd just caught her when your brother happened to roll in. I suppose," said Ginger, putting two and two together, "he had really come with her to the office and had happened to hang back for a minute or two, to talk to somebody or something. . . well, of course, he was considerably fed to see me apparently doing jiu-jitsu with his wife. Enough to rattle any man, if you come to think of it," said Ginger, ever fair-minded. "Well, he didn't say anything at the time, but a bit later in the day he called me in and administered the push."

Sally shook her head.

"It sounds the craziest story to me. What was it that Mrs. Fillmore took from you?"

"Oh, just something."

Sally rapped the table imperiously.

"Ginger!"

"Well, as a matter of fact," said her goaded visitor, "It was a photograph."

"Who of? Or, if you're particular, of whom?"

"Well. . . you, to be absolutely accurate."

"Me?" Sally stared. "But I've never given you a photograph of myself."

Ginger's face was a study in scarlet and purple.

"You didn't exactly give it to me," he mumbled. "When I say give, I mean. . ."

"Good gracious!" Sudden enlightenment came upon Sally. "That photograph we were hunting for when I first came here! Had you stolen it all the time?"

"Why, yes, I did sort of pinch it. . ."

"You fraud! You humbug! And you pretended to help me look for it." She gazed at him almost with respect. "I never knew you were so deep and snaky. I'm discovering all sorts of new things about you."

There was a brief silence. Ginger, confession over, seemed a trifle happier.

"I hope you're not frightfully sick about it?" he said at length. "It was lying about, you know, and I rather felt I must have it. Hadn't the cheek to ask you for it, so. . ."

"Don't apologize," said Sally cordially. "Great compliment. So I have caused your downfall again, have I? I'm certainly your evil genius, Ginger. I'm beginning to feel like a regular rag and a bone and a hank of hair. First I egged you on to insult your family—oh, by the way, I want to thank you about that. Now that I've met your Uncle Donald I can see how public-spirited you were. I ruined your prospects there, and now my fatal beauty—cabinet size—has led to your destruction once more. It's certainly up to me to find you another job, I can see that."

"No, really, I say, you mustn't bother. I shall be all right."

"It's my duty. Now what is there that you really can do? Burglary, of course, but it's not respectable. You've tried being a waiter and a prize-fighter and a right-hand man, and none of those seems to be just right. Can't you suggest anything?"

Ginger shook his head.

"I shall wangle something, I expect.'"

"Yes, but what? It must be something good this time. I don't want to be walking along Broadway and come on you suddenly as a street-cleaner. I don't want to send for an express-man and find you popping up. My idea would be to go to my bank to arrange an overdraft and be told the president could give me two minutes and crawl in humbly and find you prezzing away to beat the band in a big chair. Isn't there anything in the world that you can do that's solid and substantial and will keep you out of the poor-house in your old age? Think!"

"Of course, if I had a bit of capital. . ."

"Ah! The business man! And what," inquired Sally, "would you do, Mr. Morgan, if you had a bit of capital?"

"Run a dog-thingummy," said Ginger promptly.

"What's a dog-thingummy?"

"Why, a thingamajig. For dogs, you know."

Sally nodded.

"Oh, a thingamajig for dogs? Now I understand. You will put things so obscurely at first. Ginger, you poor fish, what are you raving about? What on earth is a thingamajig for dogs?"

"I mean a sort of place like fellows have. Breeding dogs, you know, and selling them and winning prizes and all that. There are lots of them about."

"Oh, a kennels?"

"Yes, a kennels."

"What a weird mind you have, Ginger. You couldn't say kennels at first, could you? That wouldn't have made it difficult enough. I suppose, if anyone asked you where you had your lunch, you would say, 'Oh, at a thingamajig for mutton chops' . . . Ginger, my lad, there is something in this. I believe for the first time in our acquaintance you have spoken something very nearly resembling a mouthful. You're wonderful with dogs, aren't you?"

"I'm dashed keen on them, and I've studied them a bit. As a matter of fact, though it seems rather like swanking, there isn't much about dogs that I don't know."

"Of course. I believe you're a sort of honorary dog yourself. I could tell it by the way you stopped that fight at Roville. You plunged into a howling mass of about a million hounds of all species and just whispered in their ears and they stopped at once. Why, the more one examines this, the better it looks. I do believe it's the one thing you couldn't help making a success of. It's very paying, isn't it?"

"Works out at about a hundred per cent on the original outlay, I've been told."

"A hundred per cent? That sounds too much like something of Fillmore's for comfort. Let's say ninety-nine and be conservative. Ginger, you have hit it. Say no more. You shall be the Dog King, the biggest thingamajigger for dogs in the country. But how do you start?"

"Well, as a matter of fact, while I was up at White Plains, I ran into a cove who had a place of the sort and wanted to sell out. That was what made me think of it."

"You must start to-day. Or early to-morrow."

"Yes," said Ginger doubtfully. "Of course, there's the catch, you know."

"What catch?"

"The capital. You've got to have that. This fellow wouldn't sell out under five thousand dollars."

"I'll lend you five thousand dollars."

"No!" said Ginger.

Sally looked at him with exasperation. "Ginger, I'd like to slap you," she said. It was maddening, this intrusion of sentiment into business affairs. Why, simply because he was a man and she was a woman, should she be restrained from investing money in a sound commercial undertaking? If Columbus had taken up this bone-headed stand towards Queen Isabella, America would never have been discovered.

"I can't take five thousand dollars off you," said Ginger firmly.

"Who's talking of taking it off me, as you call it?" stormed Sally. "Can't you forget your burglarious career for a second? This isn't the same thing as going about stealing defenceless girls' photographs. This is business. I think you would make an enormous success of a dog-place, and you admit you're good, so why make frivolous objections? Why shouldn't I put money into a good thing? Don't you want me to get rich, or what is it?"

Ginger was becoming confused. Argument had never been his strong point.

"But it's such a lot of money."

"To you, perhaps. Not to me. I'm a plutocrat. Five thousand dollars! What's five thousand dollars? I feed it to the birds."

Ginger pondered woodenly for a while. His was a literal mind, and he knew nothing of Sally's finances beyond the fact that when he had first met her she had come into a legacy of some kind. Moreover, he had been hugely impressed by Fillmore's magnificence. It seemed plain enough that the Nicholases were a wealthy family.

"I don't like it, you know," he said.

"You don't have to like it," said Sally. "You just do it."

A consoling thought flashed upon Ginger.

"You'd have to let me pay you interest."

"Let you? My lad, you'll have to pay me interest. What do you think this is—a round game? It's a cold business deal."

"Topping!" said Ginger relieved. "How about twenty-five per cent."

"Don't be silly," said Sally quickly. "I want three."

"No, that's all rot," protested Ginger. "I mean to say—three. I don't," he went on, making a concession, "mind saying twenty."

"If you insist, I'll make it five. Not more."

"Well, ten, then?"

"Five!"

"Suppose," said Ginger insinuatingly, "I said seven?"

"I never saw anyone like you for haggling," said Sally with disapproval. "Listen! Six. And that's my last word."

"Six?"

"Six."

Ginger did sums in his head.

"But that would only work out at three hundred dollars a year. It isn't enough."

"What do you know about it? As if I hadn't been handling this sort of deal in my life. Six! Do you agree?"

"I suppose so."

"Then that's settled. Is this man you talk about in New York?"

"No, he's down on Long Island at a place on the south shore."

"I mean, can you get him on the 'phone and clinch the thing?"

"Oh, yes. I know his address, and I suppose his number's in the book."

"Then go off at once and settle with him before somebody else snaps him up. Don't waste a minute."

Ginger paused at the door.

"I say, you're absolutely sure about this?"

"Of course."

"I mean to say. . ."

"Get on," said Sally.

2

THE WINDOW OF SALLY'S SITTING-ROOM looked out on to a street which, while not one of the city's important arteries, was capable, nevertheless, of affording a certain amount of entertainment to the observer: and after Ginger had left, she carried the morning paper to the window-sill and proceeded to divide her attention between a third reading of the fight-report and a lazy survey of the outer world. It was a beautiful day, and the outer world was looking its best.

She had not been at her post for many minutes when a taxi-cab stopped at the apartment-house, and she was surprised and interested to see her brother Fillmore heave himself out of the interior. He paid the driver, and the cab moved off, leaving him on the sidewalk casting a large shadow in the sunshine. Sally was on the point of calling to him, when his behaviour became so odd that astonishment checked her.

From where she sat Fillmore had all the appearance of a man practising the steps of a new dance, and sheer curiosity as to what he would do next kept Sally watching in silence. First, he moved in a resolute sort of way towards the front door; then, suddenly stopping, scuttled back. This movement he repeated twice, after which he stood in deep thought before making another dash for the door, which, like the others, came to an abrupt end as though he had run into some invisible obstacle. And, finally, wheeling sharply, he bustled off down the street and was lost to view.

Sally could make nothing of it. If Fillmore had taken the trouble to come in a taxi-cab, obviously to call upon her, why had he abandoned the idea at her very threshold? She was still speculating on this mystery when the telephone-bell rang, and her brother's voice spoke huskily in her ear.

"Sally?"

"Hullo, Fill. What are you going to call it?"

"What am I. . . Call what?"

"The dance you were doing outside here just now. It's your own invention, isn't it?"

"Did you see me?" said Fillmore, upset.

"Of course I saw you. I was fascinated."

"I—er—I was coming to have a talk with you. Sally. . ."

Fillmore's voice trailed off.

"Well, why didn't you?"

There was a pause—on Fillmore's part, if the timbre of at his voice correctly indicated his feelings, a pause of discomfort. Something was plainly vexing Fillmore's great mind.

"Sally," he said at last, and coughed hollowly into the receiver.

"Yes."

"I—that is to say, I have asked Gladys. . . Gladys will be coming to see you very shortly. Will you be in?"

"I'll stay in. How is Gladys? I'm longing to see her again."

"She is very well. A trifle—a little upset."

"Upset? What about?"

"She will tell you when she arrives. I have just been 'phoning to her. She is coming at once." There was another pause. "I'm afraid she has bad news."

"What news?"

There was silence at the other end of the wire.

"What news?" repeated Sally, a little sharply. She hated mysteries.

But Fillmore had rung off. Sally hung up the receiver thoughtfully. She was puzzled and anxious. However, there being nothing to be gained by worrying, she carried the breakfast things into the kitchen and tried to divert herself by washing up. Presently a ring at the door-bell brought her out, to find her sister-in-law.

Marriage, even though it had brought with it the lofty position of partnership with the Hope of the American Stage, had effected no noticeable alteration in the former Miss Winch. As Mrs. Fillmore she was the same square, friendly creature. She hugged Sally in a muscular manner and went on in the sitting-room.

"Well, it's great seeing you again," she said. "I began to think you were never coming back. What was the big idea, springing over to England like that?"

Sally had been expecting the question, and answered it with composure.

"I wanted to help Mr. Faucitt."

"Who's Mr. Faucitt?"

"Hasn't Fillmore ever mentioned him? He was a dear old man at the boarding-house, and his brother died and left him a dressmaking establishment in London. He screamed to me to come and tell him what to do about it. He has sold it now and is quite happy in the country."

"Well, the trip's done you good," said Mrs. Fillmore. "You're prettier than ever."

There was a pause. Already, in these trivial opening exchanges, Sally had sensed a suggestion of unwonted gravity in her companion. She missed that careless whimsicality which had been the chief characteristic of Miss Gladys Winch and seemed to have been cast off by Mrs. Fillmore Nicholas. At their meeting, before she had spoken, Sally had not noticed this, but now it was apparent that something was weighing on her companion. Mrs. Fillmore's honest eyes were troubled.

"What's the bad news?" asked Sally abruptly. She wanted to end the suspense. "Fillmore was telling me over the 'phone that you had some bad news for me."

Mrs. Fillmore scratched at the carpet for a moment with the end of her parasol without replying. When she spoke it was not in answer to the question.

"Sally, who's this man Carmyle over in England?"

"Oh, did Fillmore tell you about him?"

"He told me there was a rich fellow over in England who was crazy about you and had asked you to marry him, and that you had turned him down."

Sally's momentary annoyance faded. She could hardly, she felt, have expected Fillmore to refrain from mentioning the matter to his wife.

"Yes," she said. "That's true."

"You couldn't write and say you've changed your mind?"

Sally's annoyance returned. All her life she had been intensely independent, resentful of interference with her private concerns.

"I suppose I could if I had—but I haven't. Did Fillmore tell you to try to talk me round?"

"Oh, I'm not trying to talk you round," said Mrs. Fillmore quickly. "Goodness knows, I'm the last person to try and jolly anyone into marrying anybody if they didn't feel like it. I've seen too many marriages go wrong to do that. Look at Elsa Doland."

Sally's heart jumped as if an exposed nerve had been touched.

"Elsa?" she stammered, and hated herself because her voice shook. "Has—has her marriage gone wrong?"

"Gone all to bits," said Mrs. Fillmore shortly. "You remember she married Gerald Foster, the man who wrote 'The Primrose Way'?"

Sally with an effort repressed an hysterical laugh.

"Yes, I remember," she said.

"Well, it's all gone bloo-ey. I'll tell you about that in a minute. Coming back to this man in England, if you're in any doubt about it. . . I mean, you can't always tell right away whether you're fond of a man or not. . . When first I met Fillmore, I couldn't see him with a spy-glass, and now he's just the whole shooting-match. . . But that's not what I wanted to talk about. I was saying one doesn't always know one's own mind at first, and if this fellow really is a good fellow. . . and Fillmore tells me he's got all the money in the world. . ."

Sally stopped her.

"No, it's no good. I don't want to marry Mr. Carmyle."

"That's that, then," said Mrs. Fillmore. "It's a pity, though."

"Why are you taking it so much to heart?" said Sally with a nervous laugh.

"Well. . ." Mrs. Fillmore paused. Sally's anxiety was growing. It must, she realized, be something very serious indeed that had happened if it had the power to make her forthright sister-in-law disjointed in her talk. "You see. . ." went on Mrs. Fillmore, and stopped again. "Gee! I'm hating this!" she murmured.

"What is it? I don't understand."

"You'll find it's all too darned clear by the time I'm through," said Mrs. Fillmore mournfully. "If I'm going to explain this thing, I guess I'd best start at the beginning. You remember that revue of Fillmore's—the one we both begged him not to put on. It flopped!"

"Oh!"

"Yes. It flopped on the road and died there. Never got to New York at all. Ike Schumann wouldn't let Fillmore have a theatre. The book wanted fixing and the numbers wanted fixing and the scenery wasn't right: and while they were tinkering with all that there was trouble about the cast and the Actors Equity closed the show. Best thing that could have happened, really, and I was glad at the time, because going on with it would only have meant wasting more money, and it had cost a fortune already. After that Fillmore put on a play of Gerald Foster's and that was a frost, too. It ran a week at the Booth. I hear the new piece he's got in rehearsal now is no good either. It's called 'The Wild Rose,' or something. But Fillmore's got nothing to do with that."

"But. . ." Sally tried to speak, but Mrs. Fillmore went on.

"Don't talk just yet, or I shall never get this thing straight. Well, you know Fillmore, poor darling. Anyone else would have pulled in his horns and gone slow for a spell, but he's one of those fellows whose horse is always going to win the next race. The big killing is always just round the corner with him. Funny how you can see what a chump a man is and yet love him to death. . . I remember saying something like that to you before. . . He thought he could get it all back by staging this fight of his that came off in Jersey City last night. And if everything had gone right he might have got afloat again. But it seems as if he can't touch anything without it turning to mud. On the very day before the fight was to come off, the poor mutt who was going against the champion goes and lets a sparring-partner of his own knock him down and fool around with him. With all the newspaper men there too! You probably saw about it in the papers. It made a great story for them. Well, that killed the whole thing. The public had never been any too sure that this fellow Bugs Butler had a chance of putting up a scrap with the champion that would be worth paying to see; and, when they read that he couldn't even stop his sparring-partners slamming him all around the place they simply decided to stay away. Poor old Fill! It was a finisher for him. The house wasn't a quarter full, and after he'd paid these two pluguglies their guarantees, which they insisted on having before they'd so much as go into the ring, he was just about cleaned out. So there you are!"

Sally had listened with dismay to this catalogue of misfortunes.

"Oh, poor Fill!" she cried. "How dreadful!"

"Pretty tough."

"But 'The Primrose Way' is a big success, isn't it?" said Sally, anxious to discover something of brightness in the situation.

"It was." Mrs. Fillmore flushed again. "This is the part I hate having to tell you."

"It was? Do you mean it isn't still? I thought Elsa had made such a tremendous hit. I read about it when I was over in London. It was even in one of the English papers."

"Yes, she made a hit all right," said Mrs. Fillmore drily. "She made such a hit that all the other managements in New York were after her right away, and Fillmore had hardly sailed when she handed in her notice and signed up with Goble and Cohn for a new piece they are starring her in."

"Ah, she couldn't!" cried Sally.

"My dear, she did! She's out on the road with it now. I had to break the news to poor old Fillmore at the dock when he landed. It was rather a blow. I must say it wasn't what I would call playing the game. I know there isn't supposed to be any sentiment in business, but after all we had given Elsa her big chance. But Fillmore wouldn't put her name up over the theatre in electrics, and Goble and Cohn made it a clause in her contract that they would, so nothing else mattered. People are like that."

"But Elsa. . . She used not to be like that."

"They all get that way. They must grab success if it's to be grabbed. I suppose you can't blame them. You might just as well expect a cat to keep off catnip. Still, she might have waited to the end of the New York run." Mrs. Fillmore put out her hand and touched Sally's. "Well, I've got it out now," she said, "and, believe me, it was one rotten job. You don't know how sorry I am. Sally. I wouldn't have had it happen for a million dollars. Nor would Fillmore. I'm not sure that I blame him for getting cold feet and backing out of telling you himself. He just hadn't the nerve to come and confess that he had fooled away your money. He was hoping all along that this fight would pan out big and that he'd be able to pay you back what you had loaned him, but things didn't happen right."

Sally was silent. She was thinking how strange it was that this room in which she had hoped to be so happy had been from the first moment of her occupancy a storm centre of bad news and miserable disillusionment. In this first shock of the tidings, it was the disillusionment that hurt most. She had always been so fond of Elsa, and Elsa had always seemed so fond of her. She remembered that letter of Elsa's with all its protestations of gratitude. . . It wasn't straight. It was horrible. Callous, selfish, altogether horrible. . .

"It's. . ." She choked, as a rush of indignation brought the tears to her eyes. "It's. . . beastly! I'm. . . I'm not thinking about my money. That's just bad luck. But Elsa. . ."

Mrs. Fillmore shrugged her square shoulders.

"Well, it's happening all the time in the show business," she said. "And in every other business, too, I guess, if one only knew enough about them to be able to say. Of course, it hits you hard because Elsa was a pal of yours, and you're thinking she might have considered you after all you've done for her. I can't say I'm much surprised myself." Mrs. Fillmore was talking rapidly, and dimly Sally understood that she was talking so that talk would carry her over this bad moment. Silence now would have been unendurable. "I was in the company with her, and it sometimes seems to me as if you can't get to know a person right through till you've been in the same company with them. Elsa's all right, but she's two people really, like these dual identity cases you read about. She's awfully fond of you. I know she is. She was always saying so, and it was quite genuine. If it didn't interfere with business there's nothing she wouldn't do for you. But when it's a case of her career you don't count. Nobody counts. Not even her husband. Now that's funny. If you think that sort of thing funny. Personally, it gives me the willies."

"What's funny?" asked Sally, dully.

"Well, you weren't there, so you didn't see it, but I was on the spot all the time, and I know as well as I know anything that he simply married her because he thought she could get him on in the game. He hardly paid any attention to her at all till she was such a riot in Chicago, and then he was all over her. And now he's got stung. She throws down his show and goes off to another fellow's. It's like marrying for money and finding the girl hasn't any. And she's got stung, too, in a way, because I'm pretty sure she married him mostly because she thought he was going to be the next big man in the play-writing business and could boost her up the ladder. And now it doesn't look as though he had another success in him. The result is they're at outs. I hear he's drinking. Somebody who'd seen him told me he had gone all to pieces. You haven't seen him, I suppose?"

"No."

"I thought maybe you might have run into him. He lives right opposite."

Sally clutched at the arm of her chair.

"Lives right opposite? Gerald Foster? What do you mean?"

"Across the passage there," said Mrs. Fillmore, jerking her thumb at the door. "Didn't you know? That's right, I suppose you didn't. They moved in after you had beaten it for England. Elsa wanted to be near you, and she was tickled to death when she found there was an apartment to be had right across from you. Now, that just proves what I was saying a while ago about Elsa. If she wasn't fond of you, would she go out of her way to camp next door? And yet, though she's so fond of you, she doesn't hesitate about wrecking your property by quitting the show when she sees a chance of doing herself a bit of good. It's funny, isn't it?"

The telephone-bell, tinkling sharply, rescued Sally from the necessity of a reply. She forced herself across the room to answer it.

"Hullo?"

Ginger's voice spoke jubilantly.

"Hullo. Are you there? I say, it's all right, about that binge, you know."

"Oh, yes?"

"That dog fellow, you know," said Ginger, with a slight diminution of exuberance. His sensitive ear had seemed to detect a lack of animation in her voice. "I've just been talking to him over the 'phone, and it's all settled. If," he added, with a touch of doubt, "you still feel like going into it, I mean."

There was an instant in which Sally hesitated, but it was only an instant.

"Why, of course," she said, steadily. "Why should you think I had changed my mind?"

"Well, I thought. . . that is to say, you seemed. . . oh, I don't know."

"You imagine things. I was a little worried about something when you called me up, and my mind wasn't working properly. Of course, go ahead with it. Ginger. I'm delighted."

"I say, I'm awfully sorry you're worried."

"Oh. it's all right."

"Something bad?"

"Nothing that'll kill me. I'm young and strong."

Ginger was silent for a moment.

"I say, I don't want to butt in, but can I do anything?"

"No, really, Ginger, I know you would do anything you could, but this is just something I must worry through by myself. When do you go down to this place?"

"I was thinking of popping down this afternoon, just to take a look round."

"Let me know what train you're making and I'll come and see you off."

"That's ripping of you. Right ho. Well, so long."

"So long," said Sally.

Mrs. Fillmore, who had been sitting in that state of suspended animation which comes upon people who are present at a telephone conversation which has nothing to do with themselves, came to life as Sally replaced the receiver.

"Sally," she said, "I think we ought to have a talk now about what you're going to do."

Sally was not feeling equal to any discussion of the future. All she asked of the world at the moment was to be left alone.

"Oh, that's all right. I shall manage. You ought to be worrying about Fillmore."

"Fillmore's got me to look after him," said Gladys, with quiet determination. "You're the one that's on my mind. I lay awake all last night thinking about you. As far as I can make out from Fillmore, you've still a few thousand dollars left. Well, as it happens, I can put you on to a really good thing. I know a girl. . ."

"I'm afraid," interrupted Sally, "all the rest of my money, what there is of it, is tied up."

"You can't get hold of it?"

"No."

"But listen," said Mrs. Fillmore, urgently. "This is a really good thing. This girl I know started an interior decorating business some time ago and is pulling in the money in handfuls. But she wants more capital, and she's willing to let go of a third of the business to anyone who'll put in a few thousand. She won't have any difficulty getting it, but I 'phoned her this morning to hold off till I'd heard from you. Honestly, Sally, it's the chance of a lifetime. It would put you right on easy street. Isn't there really any way you could get your money out of this other thing and take on this deal?"

"There really isn't. I'm awfully obliged to you, Gladys dear, but it's impossible."

"Well," said Mrs. Fillmore, prodding the carpet energetically with her parasol, "I don't know what you've gone into, but, unless they've given you a share in the Mint or something, you'll be losing by not making the switch. You're sure you can't do it?"

"I really can't."

Mrs. Fillmore rose, plainly disappointed.

"Well, you know best, of course. Gosh! What a muddle everything is. Sally," she said, suddenly stopping at the door, "you're not going to hate poor old Fillmore over this, are you?"

"Why, of course not. The whole thing was just bad luck."

"He's worried stiff about it."

"Well, give him my love, and tell him not to be so silly."

Mrs. Fillmore crossed the room and kissed Sally impulsively.

"You're an angel," she said. "I wish there were more like you. But I guess they've lost the pattern. Well, I'll go back and tell Fillmore that. It'll relieve him."

The door closed, and Sally sat down with her chin in her hands to think.

3

MR. ISADORE ABRAHAMS, THE FOUNDER AND proprietor of that deservedly popular dancing resort poetically named "The Flower Garden," leaned back in his chair with a contented sigh and laid down the knife and fork with which he had been assailing a plateful of succulent goulash. He was dining, as was his admirable custom, in the bosom of his family at his residence at Far Rockaway. Across the table, his wife, Rebecca, beamed at him over her comfortable plinth of chins, and round the table his children, David, Jacob, Morris and Saide, would have beamed at him if they had not been too busy at the moment ingurgitating goulash. A genial, honest, domestic man was Mr. Abrahams, a credit to the community.

"Mother," he said.

"Pa?" said Mrs. Abrahams.

"Knew there was something I'd meant to tell you," said Mr. Abrahams, absently chasing a piece of bread round his plate with a stout finger. "You remember that girl I told you about some time back—girl working at the Garden—girl called Nicholas, who came into a bit of money and threw up her job. . ."

"I remember. You liked her. Jakie, dear, don't gobble."

"Ain't gobbling," said Master Abrahams.

"Everybody liked her," said Mr. Abrahams. "The nicest girl I ever hired, and I don't hire none but nice girls, because the Garden's a nice place, and I like to run it nice. I wouldn't give you a nickel for any of your tough joints where you get nothing but low-lifes and scare away all the real folks. Everybody liked Sally Nicholas. Always pleasant and always smiling, and never anything but the lady. It was a treat to have her around. Well, what do you think?"

"Dead?" inquired Mrs. Abrahams, apprehensively. The story had sounded to her as though it were heading that way. "Wipe your mouth, Jakie dear."

"No, not dead," said Mr. Abrahams, conscious for the first time that the remainder of his narrative might be considered by a critic something of an anti-climax and lacking in drama. "But she was in to see me this afternoon and wants her job back."

"Ah!" said Mrs. Abrahams, rather tonelessly. An ardent supporter of the local motion-picture palace, she had hoped for a slightly more gingery denouement, something with a bit more punch.

"Yes, but don't it show you?" continued Mr. Abrahams, gallantly trying to work up the interest. "There's this girl, goes out of my place not more'n a year ago, with a good bank-roll in her pocket, and here she is, back again, all of it spent. Don't it show you what a tragedy life is, if you see what I mean, and how careful one ought to be about money? It's what I call a human document. Goodness knows how she's been and gone and spent it all. I'd never have thought she was the sort of girl to go gadding around. Always seemed to me to be kind of sensible."

"What's gadding, Pop?" asked Master Jakie, the goulash having ceased to chain his interest.

"Well, she wanted her job back and I gave it to her, and glad to get her back again. There's class to that girl. She's the sort of girl I want in the place. Don't seem quite to have so much get-up in her as she used to. . . seems kind of quieted down. . . but she's got class, and I'm glad she's back. I hope she'll stay. But don't it show you?"

"Ah!" said Mrs. Abrahams, with more enthusiasm than before. It had not worked out such a bad story after all. In its essentials it was not unlike the film she had seen the previous evening—Gloria Gooch in "A Girl against the World."

"Pop!" said Master Abrahams.

"Yes, Jakie?"

"When I'm grown up, I won't never lose no money. I'll put it in the bank and save it."

The slight depression caused by the contemplation of Sally's troubles left Mr. Abrahams as mist melts beneath a sunbeam.

"That's a good boy, Jakie," he said.

He felt in his waistcoat pocket, found a dime, put it back again, and bent forward and patted Master Abrahams on the head.

P.G. WODEHOUSE

XV

UNCLE DONALD SPEAKS HIS MIND

There is in certain men—and Bruce Carmyle was one of them—a quality of resilience, a sturdy refusal to acknowledge defeat, which aids them as effectively in affairs of the heart as in encounters of a sterner and more practical kind. As a wooer, Bruce Carmyle resembled that durable type of pugilist who can only give of his best after he has received at least one substantial wallop on some tender spot. Although Sally had refused his offer of marriage quite definitely at Monk's Crofton, it had never occurred to him to consider the episode closed. All his life he had been accustomed to getting what he wanted, and he meant to get it now.

He was quite sure that he wanted Sally. There had been moments when he had been conscious of certain doubts, but in the smart of temporary defeat these had vanished. That streak of Bohemianism in her which from time to time since their first meeting had jarred upon his orderly mind was forgotten; and all that Mr. Carmyle could remember was the brightness of her eyes, the jaunty lift of her chin, and the gallant trimness of her. Her gay prettiness seemed to flick at him like a whip in the darkness of wakeful nights, lashing him to pursuit. And quietly and methodically, like a respectable wolf settling on the trail of a Red Riding Hood, he prepared to pursue. Delicacy and imagination might have kept him back, but in these qualities he had never been strong. One cannot have everything.

His preparations for departure, though he did his best to make them swiftly and secretly, did not escape the notice of the Family. In many English families there seems to exist a system of inter-communication and news-distribution like that of those savage tribes in Africa who pass the latest item of news and interest from point to point over miles of intervening jungle by some telepathic method never properly explained. On his last night in London, there entered to Bruce Carmyle at his apartment in South Audley Street, the Family's chosen representative, the man to whom the Family pointed with pride—Uncle Donald, in the flesh.

There were two hundred and forty pounds of the flesh Uncle Donald was in, and the chair in which he deposited it creaked beneath its burden.

Once, at Monk's Crofton, Sally had spoiled a whole morning for her brother Fillmore, by indicating Uncle Donald as the exact image of what he would be when he grew up. A superstition, cherished from early schooldays, that he had a weak heart had caused the Family's managing director to abstain from every form of exercise for nearly fifty years; and, as he combined with a distaste for exercise one of the three heartiest appetites in the south-western postal division of London, Uncle Donald, at sixty-two, was not a man one would willingly have lounging in one's armchairs. Bruce Carmyle's customary respectfulness was tinged with something approaching dislike as he looked at him.

Uncle Donald's walrus moustache heaved gently upon his laboured breath, like seaweed on a ground-swell. There had been stairs to climb.

"What's this? What's this?" he contrived to exclaim at last. "You packing?"

"Yes," said Mr. Carmyle, shortly. For the first time in his life he was conscious of that sensation of furtive guilt which was habitual with his cousin Ginger when in the presence of this large, mackerel-eyed man.

"You going away?"

"Yes."

"Where you going?"

"America."

"When you going?"

"To-morrow morning."

"Why you going?"

This dialogue has been set down as though it had been as brisk and snappy as any cross-talk between vaudeville comedians, but in reality Uncle Donald's peculiar methods of conversation had stretched it over a period of nearly three minutes: for after each reply and before each question he had puffed and sighed and inhaled his moustache with such painful deliberation that his companion's nerves were finding it difficult to bear up under the strain.

"You're going after that girl," said Uncle Donald, accusingly.

Bruce Carmyle flushed darkly. And it is interesting to record that at this moment there flitted through his mind the thought that Ginger's behaviour at Bleke's Coffee House, on a certain notable occasion, had not been so utterly inexcusable as he had supposed. There was no doubt that the Family's Chosen One could be trying.

"Will you have a whisky and soda, Uncle Donald?" he said, by way of changing the conversation.

"Yes," said his relative, in pursuance of a vow he had made in the early eighties never to refuse an offer of this kind. "Gimme!"

You would have thought that that would have put matters on a pleasanter footing. But no. Having lapped up the restorative, Uncle Donald returned to the attack quite un-softened.

"Never thought you were a fool before," he said severely.

Bruce Carmyle's proud spirit chafed. This sort of interview, which had become a commonplace with his cousin Ginger, was new to him. Hitherto, his actions had received neither criticism nor been subjected to it.

"I'm not a fool."

"You are a fool. A damn fool," continued Uncle Donald, specifying more exactly. "Don't like the girl. Never did. Not a nice girl. Didn't like her. Right from the first."

"Need we discuss this?" said Bruce Carmyle, dropping, as he was apt to do, into the grand manner.

The Head of the Family drank in a layer of moustache and blew it out again.

"Need we discuss it?" he said with asperity. "We're going to discuss it! Whatch think I climbed all these blasted stairs for with my weak heart? Gimme another!"

Mr. Carmyle gave him another.

"'S a bad business," moaned Uncle Donald, having gone through the movements once more. "Shocking bad business. If your poor father were alive, whatch think he'd say to your tearing across the world after this girl? I'll tell you what he'd say. He'd say. . . What kind of whisky's this?"

"O'Rafferty Special."

"New to me. Not bad. Quite good. Sound. Mellow. Wherej get it?"

"Bilby's in Oxford Street."

"Must order some. Mellow. He'd say. . . well, God knows what he'd say. Whatch doing it for? Whatch doing it for? That's what I can't see. None of us can see. Puzzles your uncle George. Baffles your aunt Geraldine. Nobody can understand it. Girl's simply after your money. Anyone can see that."

"Pardon me, Uncle Donald," said Mr. Carmyle, stiffly, "but that is surely rather absurd. If that were the case, why should she have refused me at Monk's Crofton?"

"Drawing you on," said Uncle Donald, promptly. "Luring you on. Well-known trick. Girl in 1881, when I was at Oxford, tried to lure me on. If

I hadn't had some sense and a weak heart. . . Whatch know of this girl? Whatch know of her? That's the point. Who is she? Wherej meet her?"

"I met her at Roville, in France."

"Travelling with her family?"

"Travelling alone," said Bruce Carmyle, reluctantly.

"Not even with that brother of hers? Bad!" said Uncle Donald. "Bad, bad!"

"American girls are accustomed to more independence than English girls."

"That young man," said Uncle Donald, pursuing a train of thought, "is going to be fat one of these days, if he doesn't look out. Travelling alone, was she? What did you do? Catch her eye on the pier?"

"Really, Uncle Donald!"

"Well, must have got to know her somehow."

"I was introduced to her by Lancelot. She was a friend of his."

"Lancelot!" exploded Uncle Donald, quivering all over like a smitten jelly at the loathed name. "Well, that shows you what sort of a girl she is. Any girl that would be a friend of. . . Unpack!"

"I beg your pardon?"

"Unpack! Mustn't go on with this foolery. Out of the question. Find some girl make you a good wife. Your aunt Mary's been meeting some people name of Bassington-Bassington, related Kent Bassington-Bassingtons. . . eldest daughter charming girl, just do for you."

Outside the pages of the more old-fashioned type of fiction nobody ever really ground his teeth, but Bruce Carmyle came nearer to it at that moment than anyone had ever come before. He scowled blackly, and the last trace of suavity left him.

"I shall do nothing of the kind," he said briefly. "I sail to-morrow."

Uncle Donald had had a previous experience of being defied by a nephew, but it had not accustomed him to the sensation. He was aware of an unpleasant feeling of impotence. Nothing is harder than to know what to do next when defied.

"Eh?" he said.

Mr. Carmyle having started to defy, evidently decided to make a good job of it.

"I am over twenty-one," said he. "I am financially independent. I shall do as I please."

"But, consider!" pleaded Uncle Donald, painfully conscious of the weakness of his words. "Reflect!"

"I have reflected."

"Your position in the county. . ."

"I've thought of that."

"You could marry anyone you pleased."

"I'm going to."

"You are determined to go running off to God-knows-where after this Miss I-can't-even-remember-her-dam-name?"

"Yes."

"Have you considered," said Uncle Donald, portentously, "that you owe a duty to the Family."

Bruce Carmyle's patience snapped and he sank like a stone to absolutely Gingerian depths of plain-spokenness.

"Oh, damn the Family!" he cried.

There was a painful silence, broken only by the relieved sigh of the armchair as Uncle Donald heaved himself out of it.

"After that," said Uncle Donald, "I have nothing more to say."

"Good!" said Mr. Carmyle rudely, lost to all shame.

"'Cept this. If you come back married to that girl, I'll cut you in Piccadilly. By George, I will!"

He moved to the door. Bruce Carmyle looked down his nose without speaking. A tense moment.

"What," asked Uncle Donald, his fingers on the handle, "did you say it was called?"

"What was what called?"

"That whisky."

"O'Rafferty Special."

"And wherj get it?"

"Bilby's, in Oxford Street."

"I'll make a note of it," said Uncle Donald.

XVI

At the Flower Garden

1

"And after all I've done for her," said Mr. Reginald Cracknell, his voice tremulous with self-pity and his eyes moist with the combined effects of anguish and over-indulgence in his celebrated private stock, "after all I've done for her she throws me down."

Sally did not reply. The orchestra of the Flower Garden was of a calibre that discouraged vocal competition; and she was having, moreover, too much difficulty in adjusting her feet to Mr. Cracknell's erratic dance-steps to employ her attention elsewhere. They manoeuvred jerkily past the table where Miss Mabel Hobson, the Flower Garden's newest "hostess," sat watching the revels with a distant hauteur. Miss Hobson was looking her most regal in old gold and black, and a sorrowful gulp escaped the stricken Mr. Cracknell as he shambled beneath her eye.

"If I told you," he moaned in Sally's ear, "what. . . was that your ankle? Sorry! Don't know what I'm doing to-night. . . If I told you what I had spent on that woman, you wouldn't believe it. And then she throws me down. And all because I said I didn't like her in that hat. She hasn't spoken to me for a week, and won't answer when I call up on the 'phone. And I was right, too. It was a rotten hat. Didn't suit her a bit. But that," said Mr. Cracknell, morosely, "is a woman all over!"

Sally uttered a stifled exclamation as his wandering foot descended on hers before she could get it out of the way. Mr. Cracknell interpreted the exclamation as a protest against the sweeping harshness of his last remark, and gallantly tried to make amends.

"I don't mean you're like that," he said. "You're different. I could see that directly I saw you. You have a sympathetic nature. That's why I'm telling you all this. You're a sensible and broad-minded girl and can understand. I've done everything for that woman. I got her this job as hostess here—you wouldn't believe what they pay her. I starred her in a show once. Did you see those pearls she was wearing? I gave her those. And she won't speak to me. Just because I didn't like her hat. I wish you could have seen that hat. You would agree with me, I know, because you're a sensible, broad-minded girl and understand hats. I don't know what to do. I come here every night." Sally was aware of this. She had seen him often, but this was the first time that Lee Schoenstein, the gentlemanly master of ceremonies, had inflicted him on her. "I come here every night and dance past her table, but she won't look at me. What," asked Mr. Cracknell, tears welling in his pale eyes, "would you do about it?"

"I don't know," said Sally, frankly.

"Nor do I. I thought you wouldn't, because you're a sensible, broad-minded. . . I mean, nor do I. I'm having one last try to-night, if you can keep a secret. You won't tell anyone, will you?" pleaded Mr. Cracknell, urgently. "But I know you won't because you're a sensible. . . I'm giving her a little present. Having it brought here to-night. Little present. That ought to soften her, don't you think?"

"A big one would do it better."

Mr. Cracknell kicked her on the shin in a dismayed sort of way.

"I never thought of that. Perhaps you're right. But it's too late now. Still, it might. Or wouldn't it? Which do you think?"

"Yes," said Sally.

"I thought as much," said Mr. Cracknell.

The orchestra stopped with a thump and a bang, leaving Mr. Cracknell clapping feebly in the middle of the floor. Sally slipped back to her table. Her late partner, after an uncertain glance about him, as if he had mislaid something but could not remember what, zigzagged off in search of his own seat. The noise of many conversations, drowned by the music, broke out with renewed vigour. The hot, close air was full of voices; and Sally, pressing her hands on her closed eyes, was reminded once more that she had a headache.

Nearly a month had passed since her return to Mr. Abrahams' employment. It had been a dull, leaden month, a monotonous succession of lifeless days during which life had become a bad dream. In some strange nightmare fashion, she seemed nowadays to be cut off from her kind. It was weeks since she had seen a familiar face. None of the companions of her old boarding-house days had crossed her path. Fillmore, no doubt from uneasiness of conscience, had not sought her out, and Ginger was working out his destiny on the south shore of Long Island.

She lowered her hands and opened her eyes and looked at the room. It was crowded, as always. The Flower Garden was one of the many establishments of the same kind which had swum to popularity on the rising flood of New York's dancing craze; and doubtless because, as its proprietor had claimed, it was a nice place and run nice, it had continued, unlike many of its rivals, to enjoy unvarying prosperity. In its advertisement, it described itself as "a supper-club for after-theatre dining and dancing," adding that "large and spacious, and sumptuously appointed," it was "one of the town's wonder-places, with its incomparable dance-floor, enchanting music, cuisine, and service de luxe." From which it may be gathered, even without his personal statements to that effect, that Isadore Abrahams thought well of the place.

There had been a time when Sally had liked it, too. In her first period of employment there she had found it diverting, stimulating and full of entertainment. But in those days she had never had headaches or, what was worse, this dreadful listless depression which weighed her down and made her nightly work a burden.

"Miss Nicholas."

The orchestra, never silent for long at the Flower Garden, had started again, and Lee Schoenstein, the master of ceremonies, was presenting a new partner. She got up mechanically.

"This is the first time I have been in this place," said the man, as they bumped over the crowded floor. He was big and clumsy, of course. To-night it seemed to Sally that the whole world was big and clumsy. "It's a swell place. I come from up-state myself. We got nothing like this where I come from." He cleared a space before him, using Sally as a battering-ram, and Sally, though she had not enjoyed her recent excursion with Mr. Cracknell, now began to look back to it almost with wistfulness. This man was undoubtedly the worst dancer in America.

"Give me li'l old New York," said the man from up-state, unpatriotically. "It's good enough for me. I been to some swell shows since I got to town. You seen this year's 'Follies'?"

"No."

"You go," said the man earnestly. "You go! Take it from me, it's a swell show. You seen 'Myrtle takes a Turkish Bath'?"

"I don't go to many theatres."

"You go! It's a scream. I been to a show every night since I got here. Every night regular. Swell shows all of 'em, except this last one. I cert'nly picked a lemon to-night all right. I was taking a chance, y'see, because it was an opening. Thought it would be something to say, when I got home, that I'd been to a New York opening. Set me back two-seventy-five, including tax, and I wish I'd got it in my kick right now. 'The Wild Rose,' they called it," he said satirically, as if exposing a low subterfuge

P.G. WODEHOUSE

on the part of the management. "'The Wild Rose!' It sure made me wild all right. Two dollars seventy-five tossed away, just like that."

Something stirred in Sally's memory. Why did that title seem so familiar? Then, with a shock, she remembered. It was Gerald's new play. For some time after her return to New York, she had been haunted by the fear lest, coming out of her apartment, she might meet him coming out of his; and then she had seen a paragraph in her morning paper which had relieved her of this apprehension. Gerald was out on the road with a new play, and "The Wild Rose," she was almost sure, was the name of it.

"Is that Gerald Foster's play?" she asked quickly.

"I don't know who wrote it," said her partner, "but let me tell you he's one lucky guy to get away alive. There's fellows breaking stones on the Ossining Road that's done a lot less to deserve a sentence. Wild Rose! I'll tell the world it made me go good and wild," said the man from up-state, an economical soul who disliked waste and was accustomed to spread out his humorous efforts so as to give them every chance. "Why, before the second act was over, the people were beating it for the exits, and if it hadn't been for someone shouting 'Women and children first' there'd have been a panic."

Sally found herself back at her table without knowing clearly how she had got there.

"Miss Nicholas."

She started to rise, and was aware suddenly that this was not the voice of duty calling her once more through the gold teeth of Mr. Schoenstein. The man who had spoken her name had seated himself beside her, and was talking in precise, clipped accents, oddly familiar. The mist cleared from her eyes and she recognized Bruce Carmyle.

2

"I CALLED AT YOUR PLACE," Mr. Carmyle was saying, "and the hall porter told me that you were here, so I ventured to follow you. I hope you do not mind? May I smoke?"

He lit a cigarette with something of an air. His fingers trembled as he raised the match, but he flattered himself that there was nothing else in his demeanour to indicate that he was violently excited. Bruce Carmyle's ideal was the strong man who can rise superior to his emotions. He was alive to the fact that this was an embarrassing moment, but he was determined not to show that he appreciated it. He cast a sideways glance at Sally, and thought that never, not even in the garden at Monk's Crofton on a certain momentous occasion, had he seen her looking prettier. Her face was flushed and her eyes aflame. The stout wraith of Uncle Donald, which had accompanied Mr. Carmyle on this expedition of his, faded into nothingness as he gazed.

There was a pause. Mr. Carmyle, having lighted his cigarette, puffed vigorously.

"When did you land?" asked Sally, feeling the need of saying something. Her mind was confused. She could not have said whether she was glad or sorry that he was there. Glad, she thought, on the whole. There was something in his dark, cool, stiff English aspect that gave her a curious feeling of relief. He was so unlike Mr. Cracknell and the man from up-state and so calmly remote from the feverish atmosphere in which she lived her nights that it was restful to look at him.

"I landed to-night," said Bruce Carmyle, turning and faced her squarely.

"To-night!"

"We docked at ten."

He turned away again. He had made his effect, and was content to leave her to think it over.

Sally was silent. The significance of his words had not escaped her. She realized that his presence there was a challenge which she must answer. And yet it hardly stirred her. She had been fighting so long, and she felt utterly inert. She was like a swimmer who can battle no longer and prepares to yield to the numbness of exhaustion. The heat of the room pressed down on her like a smothering blanket. Her tired nerves cried out under the blare of music and the clatter of voices.

"Shall we dance this?" he asked.

The orchestra had started to play again, a sensuous, creamy melody which was making the most of its brief reign as Broadway's leading song-hit, overfamiliar to her from a hundred repetitions.

"If you like."

Efficiency was Bruce Carmyle's gospel. He was one of these men who do not attempt anything which they cannot accomplish to perfection. Dancing, he had decided early in his life, was a part of a gentleman's education, and he had seen to it that he was educated thoroughly. Sally, who, as they swept out on to the floor, had braced herself automatically for a repetition of the usual bumping struggle which dancing at the

P.G. WODEHOUSE

Flower Garden had come to mean for her, found herself in the arms of a masterful expert, a man who danced better than she did, and suddenly there came to her a feeling that was almost gratitude, a miraculous slackening of her taut nerves, a delicious peace. Soothed and contented, she yielded herself with eyes half closed to the rhythm of the melody, finding it now robbed in some mysterious manner of all its stale cheapness, and in that moment her whole attitude towards Bruce Carmyle underwent a complete change.

She had never troubled to examine with any minuteness her feelings towards him: but one thing she had known clearly since their first meeting—that he was physically distasteful to her. For all his good looks, and in his rather sinister way he was a handsome man, she had shrunk from him. Now, spirited away by the magic of the dance, that repugnance had left her. It was as if some barrier had been broken down between them.

"Sally!"

She felt his arm tighten about her, the muscles quivering. She caught sight of his face. His dark eyes suddenly blazed into hers and she stumbled with an odd feeling of helplessness; realizing with a shock that brought her with a jerk out of the half-dream into which she had been lulled that this dance had not postponed the moment of decision, as she had looked to it to do. In a hot whisper, the words swept away on the flood of the music which had suddenly become raucous and blaring once more, he was repeating what he had said under the trees at Monk's Crofton on that far-off morning in the English springtime. Dizzily she knew that she was resenting the unfairness of the attack at such a moment, but her mind seemed numbed.

The music stopped abruptly. Insistent clapping started it again, but Sally moved away to her table, and he followed her like a shadow. Neither spoke. Bruce Carmyle had said his say, and Sally was sitting staring before her, trying to think. She was tired, tired. Her eyes were burning. She tried to force herself to face the situation squarely. Was it worth struggling? Was anything in the world worth a struggle? She only knew that she was tired, desperately tired, tired to the very depths of her soul.

The music stopped. There was more clapping, but this time the orchestra did not respond. Gradually the floor emptied. The shuffling of feet ceased. The Flower Garden was as quiet as it was ever able to be. Even the voices of the babblers seemed strangely hushed. Sally closed her eyes, and as she did so from somewhere up near the roof there came the song of a bird.

Isadore Abrahams was a man of his word. He advertised a Flower Garden, and he had tried to give the public something as closely resembling a flower-garden as it was possible for an overcrowded, overheated, overnoisy Broadway dancing-resort to achieve. Paper roses festooned the walls; genuine tulips bloomed in tubs by every pillar; and from the roof hung cages with birds in them. One of these, stirred by the sudden cessation of the tumult below, had began to sing.

Sally had often pitied these birds, and more than once had pleaded in vain with Abrahams for a remission of their sentence, but somehow at this moment it did not occur to her that this one was merely praying in its own language, as she often had prayed in her thoughts, to be taken out of this place. To her, sitting there wrestling with Fate, the song seemed cheerful. It soothed her. It healed her to listen to it. And suddenly before her eyes there rose a vision of Monk's Crofton, cool, green, and peaceful under the mild English sun, luring her as an oasis seen in the distance lures the desert traveller. . .

She became aware that the master of Monk's Crofton had placed his hand on hers and was holding it in a tightening grip. She looked down and gave a little shiver. She had always disliked Bruce Carmyle's hands. They were strong and bony and black hair grew on the back of them. One of the earliest feelings regarding him had been that she would hate to have those hands touching her. But she did not move. Again that vision of the old garden had flickered across her mind. . . a haven where she could rest. . .

He was leaning towards her, whispering in her ear. The room was hotter than it had ever been, noisier than it had ever been, fuller than it had ever been. The bird on the roof was singing again and now she understood what it said. "Take me out of this!" Did anything matter except that? What did it matter how one was taken, or where, or by whom, so that one was taken.

Monk's Crofton was looking cool and green and peaceful. . .

"Very well," said Sally.

3

BRUCE CARMYLE, IN THE CAPACITY of accepted suitor, found himself at something of a loss. He had a dissatisfied feeling. It was not the manner of Sally's acceptance that caused this. It would, of course, have pleased him better if she had shown more warmth, but he was prepared to wait for warmth. What did trouble him was the fact that his correct mind perceived now for the first time that he had chosen an unsuitable moment and place for his outburst of emotion. He belonged to the orthodox school of thought which looks on moonlight and solitude as the proper setting for a proposal of marriage; and the surroundings of the Flower Garden, for all its nice-ness and the nice manner in which it was conducted, jarred upon him profoundly.

Music had begun again, but it was not the soft music such as a lover demands if he is to give of his best. It was a brassy, clashy rendering of a ribald one-step, enough to choke the eloquence of the most ardent. Couples were dipping and swaying and bumping into one another as far as the eye could reach; while just behind him two waiters had halted in order to thrash out one of those voluble arguments in which waiters love to indulge. To continue the scene at the proper emotional level was impossible, and Bruce Carmyle began his career as an engaged man by dropping into Smalltalk.

"Deuce of a lot of noise," he said querulously.

"Yes," agreed Sally.

"Is it always like this?"

"Oh, yes."

"Infernal racket!"

"Yes."

The romantic side of Mr. Carmyle's nature could have cried aloud at the hideous unworthiness of these banalities. In the visions which he had had of himself as a successful wooer, it had always been in the moments immediately succeeding the all-important question and its whispered reply that he had come out particularly strong. He had been accustomed to picture himself bending with a proud tenderness over his partner in the scene and murmuring some notably good things to her bowed head. How could any man murmur in a pandemonium like this. From tenderness Bruce Carmyle descended with a sharp swoop to irritability.

"Do you often come here?"

"Yes."

"What for?"

"To dance."

Mr. Carmyle chafed helplessly. The scene, which should be so romantic, had suddenly reminded him of the occasion when, at the age of twenty, he had attended his first ball and had sat in a corner behind a potted palm perspiring shyly and endeavouring to make conversation to a formidable nymph in pink. It was one of the few occasions in his life at which he had ever been at a complete disadvantage. He could still remember the clammy discomfort of his too high collar as it melted on him. Most certainly it was not a scene which he enjoyed recalling; and that he should be forced to recall it now, at what ought to have been the supreme moment of his life, annoyed him intensely. Almost angrily he endeavoured to jerk the conversation to a higher level.

"Darling," he murmured, for by moving his chair two feet to the right and bending sideways he found that he was in a position to murmur, "you have made me so. . ."

"Batti, batti! I presto ravioli hollandaise," cried one of the disputing waiters at his back—or to Bruce Carmyle's prejudiced hearing it sounded like that.

"La Donna e mobile spaghetti napoli Tettrazina," rejoined the second waiter with spirit.

". . . you have made me so. . ."

"Infanta Isabella lope de Vegas mulligatawny Toronto," said the first waiter, weak but coming back pluckily.

". . . so happy. . ."

"Funiculi funicula Vincente y Blasco Ibanez vermicelli sul campo della gloria risotto!" said the second waiter clinchingly, and scored a technical knockout.

Bruce Carmyle gave it up, and lit a moody cigarette. He was oppressed by that feeling which so many of us have felt in our time, that it was all wrong.

The music stopped. The two leading citizens of Little Italy vanished and went their way, probably to start a vendetta. There followed comparative calm. But Bruce Carmyle's emotions, like sweet bells jangled, were out of tune, and he could not recapture the first fine careless rapture. He found nothing within him but small-talk.

"What has become of your party?" he asked.

"My party?"

"The people you are with," said Mr. Carmyle. Even in the stress of his emotion this problem had been exercising him. In his correctly ordered world girls did not go to restaurants alone.

"I'm not with anybody."

"You came here by yourself?" exclaimed Bruce Carmyle, frankly aghast. And, as he spoke, the wraith of Uncle Donald, banished till

P.G. WODEHOUSE

now, returned as large as ever, puffing disapproval through a walrus moustache.

"I am employed here," said Sally.

Mr. Carmyle started violently.

"Employed here?"

"As a dancer, you know. I. . ."

Sally broke off, her attention abruptly diverted to something which had just caught her eye at a table on the other side of the room. That something was a red-headed young man of sturdy build who had just appeared beside the chair in which Mr. Reginald Cracknell was sitting in huddled gloom. In one hand he carried a basket, and from this basket, rising above the din of conversation, there came a sudden sharp yapping. Mr. Cracknell roused himself from his stupor, took the basket, raised the lid. The yapping increased in volume.

Mr. Cracknell rose, the basket in his arms. With uncertain steps and a look on his face like that of those who lead forlorn hopes he crossed the floor to where Miss Mabel Hobson sat, proud and aloof. The next moment that haughty lady, the centre of an admiring and curious crowd, was hugging to her bosom a protesting Pekingese puppy, and Mr. Cracknell, seizing his opportunity like a good general, had deposited himself in a chair at her side. The course of true love was running smooth again.

The red-headed young man was gazing fixedly at Sally.

"As a dancer!" exclaimed Mr. Carmyle. Of all those within sight of the moving drama which had just taken place, he alone had paid no attention to it. Replete as it was with human interest, sex-appeal, the punch, and all the other qualities which a drama should possess, it had failed to grip him. His thoughts had been elsewhere. The accusing figure of Uncle Donald refused to vanish from his mental eye. The stern voice of Uncle Donald seemed still to ring in his ear.

A dancer! A professional dancer at a Broadway restaurant! Hideous doubts began to creep like snakes into Bruce Carmyle's mind. What, he asked himself, did he really know of this girl on whom he had bestowed the priceless boon of his society for life? How did he know what she was—he could not find the exact adjective to express his meaning, but he knew what he meant. Was she worthy of the boon? That was what it amounted to. All his life he had had a prim shrinking from the section of the feminine world which is connected with the light-life of large cities. Club acquaintances of his in London had from time to time married into the Gaiety Chorus, and Mr. Carmyle, though he had no objection to the Gaiety Chorus in its proper place—on the other side of the footlights—had always looked on these young men after as social outcasts. The fine dashing frenzy which had brought him all the way from South Audley Street to win Sally was ebbing fast.

Sally, hearing him speak, had turned. And there was a candid honesty in her gaze which for a moment sent all those creeping doubts scuttling away into the darkness whence they had come. He had not made a fool of himself, he protested to the lowering phantom of Uncle Donald. Who, he demanded, could look at Sally and think for an instant that she was not all that was perfect and lovable? A warm revulsion of feeling swept over Bruce Carmyle like a returning tide.

"You see, I lost my money and had to do something," said Sally.

"I see, I see," murmured Mr. Carmyle; and if only Fate had left him alone who knows to what heights of tenderness he might not have soared? But at this moment Fate, being no respecter of persons, sent into his life the disturbing personality of George Washington Williams.

George Washington Williams was the talented coloured gentleman who had been extracted from small-time vaudeville by Mr. Abrahams to do a nightly speciality at the Flower Garden. He was, in fact, a trap-drummer: and it was his amiable practice, after he had done a few minutes trap-drumming, to rise from his seat and make a circular tour of the tables on the edge of the dancing-floor, whimsically pretending to clip the locks of the male patrons with a pair of drumsticks held scissor-wise. And so it came about that, just as Mr. Carmyle was bending towards Sally in an access of manly sentiment, and was on the very verge of pouring out his soul in a series of well-phrased remarks, he was surprised and annoyed to find an Ethiopian to whom he had never been introduced leaning over him and taking quite unpardonable liberties with his back hair.

One says that Mr. Carmyle was annoyed. The word is weak. The interruption coming at such a moment jarred every ganglion in his body. The clicking noise of the drumsticks maddened him. And the gleaming whiteness of Mr. Williams' friendly and benignant smile was the last straw. His dignity writhed beneath this abominable infliction. People at other tables were laughing. At him. A loathing for the Flower Garden flowed over Bruce Carmyle, and with it a feeling of suspicion and disapproval of everyone connected with the establishment. He sprang to his feet.

"I think I will be going," he said.

Sally did not reply. She was watching Ginger, who still stood beside the table recently vacated by Reginald Cracknell.

"Good night," said Mr. Carmyle between his teeth.

"Oh, are you going?" said Sally with a start. She felt embarrassed. Try as she would, she was unable to find words of any intimacy. She tried to realize that she had promised to marry this man, but never before had he seemed so much a stranger to her, so little a part of her life. It came to her with a sensation of the incredible that she had done this thing, taken this irrevocable step.

The sudden sight of Ginger had shaken her. It was as though in the last half-hour she had forgotten him and only now realized what marriage with Bruce Carmyle would mean to their comradeship. From now on he was dead to her. If anything in this world was certain that was. Sally Nicholas was Ginger's pal, but Mrs. Carmyle, she realized, would never be allowed to see him again. A devastating feeling of loss smote her like a blow.

"Yes, I've had enough of this place," Bruce Carmyle was saying.

"Good night," said Sally. She hesitated. "When shall I see you?" she asked awkwardly.

It occurred to Bruce Carmyle that he was not showing himself at his best. He had, he perceived, allowed his nerves to run away with him.

"You don't mind if I go?" he said more amiably. "The fact is, I can't stand this place any longer. I'll tell you one thing, I'm going to take you out of here quick."

"I'm afraid I can't leave at a moment's notice," said Sally, loyal to her obligations.

"We'll talk over that to-morrow. I'll call for you in the morning and take you for a drive somewhere in a car. You want some fresh air after this." Mr. Carmyle looked about him in stiff disgust, and expressed his unalterable sentiments concerning the Flower Garden, that apple of Isadore Abrahams' eye, in a snort of loathing. "My God! What a place!"

He walked quickly away and disappeared. And Ginger, beaming happily, swooped on Sally's table like a homing pigeon.

4

"Good Lord, I say, what ho!" cried Ginger. "Fancy meeting you here. What a bit of luck!" He glanced over his shoulder warily. "Has that blighter pipped?"

"Pipped?"

"Popped," explained Ginger. "I mean to say, he isn't coming back or any rot like that, is he?"

"Mr. Carmyle? No, he has gone."

"Sound egg!" said Ginger with satisfaction. "For a moment, when I saw you yarning away together, I thought he might be with your party. What on earth is he doing over here at all, confound him? He's got all Europe to play about in, why should he come infesting New York? I say, it really is ripping, seeing you again. It seems years. . . Of course, one get's a certain amount of satisfaction writing letters, but it's not the same. Besides, I write such rotten letters. I say, this really is rather priceless. Can't I get you something? A cup of coffee, I mean, or an egg or something? By jove! this really is top-hole."

His homely, honest face glowed with pleasure, and it seemed to Sally as though she had come out of a winter's night into a warm friendly room. Her mercurial spirits soared.

"Oh, Ginger! If you knew what it's like seeing you!"

"No, really? Do you mean, honestly, you're braced?"

"I should say I am braced."

"Well, isn't that fine! I was afraid you might have forgotten me."

"Forgotten you!"

With something of the effect of a revelation it suddenly struck Sally how far she had been from forgetting him, how large was the place he had occupied in her thoughts.

"I've missed you dreadfully," she said, and felt the words inadequate as she uttered them.

"What ho!" said Ginger, also internally condemning the poverty of speech as a vehicle for conveying thought.

There was a brief silence. The first exhilaration of the reunion over, Sally deep down in her heart was aware of a troubled feeling as though the world were out of joint. She forced herself to ignore it, but it would not be ignored. It grew. Dimly she was beginning to realize what Ginger meant to her, and she fought to keep herself from realizing it. Strange things were happening to her to-night, strange emotions stirring her. Ginger seemed somehow different, as if she were really seeing him for the first time.

"You're looking wonderfully well," she said trying to keep the conversation on a pedestrian level.

"I am well," said Ginger. "Never felt fitter in my life. Been out in the open all day long. . . simple life and all that. . . working like blazes. I say, business is booming. Did you see me just now, handing over Percy the Pup to what's-his-name? Five hundred dollars on that one deal. Got the cheque in my pocket. But what an extraordinarily rummy thing that I should have come to this place to deliver the goods just when you happened to be here. I couldn't believe my eyes at first. I say, I hope the people you're with won't think I'm butting in. You'll have to explain that we're old pals and that you started me in business and all that sort of thing. Look here," he said lowering his voice, "I know how you hate being thanked, but I simply must say how terrifically decent. . ."

"Miss Nicholas."

Lee Schoenstein was standing at the table, and by his side an expectant youth with a small moustache and pince-nez. Sally got up, and the next moment Ginger was alone, gaping perplexedly after her as she vanished and reappeared in the jogging throng on the dancing floor. It was the nearest thing Ginger had seen to a conjuring trick, and at that moment he was ill-attuned to conjuring tricks. He brooded, fuming, at what seemed to him the supremest exhibition of pure cheek, of monumental nerve, and of undiluted crust that had ever come within his notice. To come and charge into a private conversation like that and whisk her away without a word. . .

"Who was that blighter?" he demanded with heat, when the music ceased and Sally limped back.

"That was Mr. Schoenstein."

"And who was the other?"

"The one I danced with? I don't know."

"You don't know?"

Sally perceived that the conversation had arrived at an embarrassing point. There was nothing for it but candour.

"Ginger," she said, "you remember my telling you when we first met that I used to dance in a Broadway place? This is the place. I'm working again."

Complete unintelligence showed itself on Ginger's every feature.

"I don't understand," he said—unnecessarily, for his face revealed the fact.

"I've got my old job back."

"But why?"

"Well, I had to do something." She went on rapidly. Already a light dimly resembling the light of understanding was beginning to appear in Ginger's eyes. "Fillmore went smash, you know—it wasn't his fault, poor dear. He had the worst kind of luck—and most of my money was tied up in his business, so you see. . ."

She broke off confused by the look in his eyes, conscious of an absurd feeling of guilt. There was amazement in that look and a sort of incredulous horror.

"Do you mean to say. . ." Ginger gulped and started again. "Do you mean to tell me that you let me have. . . all that money. . . for the dog-business. . . when you were broke? Do you mean to say. . ."

Sally stole a glance at his crimson face and looked away again quickly. There was an electric silence.

"Look here," exploded Ginger with sudden violence, "you've got to marry me. You've jolly well got to marry me! I don't mean that," he added quickly. "I mean to say I know you're going to marry whoever you please. . . but won't you marry me? Sally, for God's sake have a dash at it! I've been keeping it in all this time because it seemed rather rotten to bother you about it, but now. . . Oh, dammit, I wish I could put it into words. I always was rotten at talking. But. . . well, look here, what I mean is, I know I'm not much of a chap, but it seems to me you must care for me a bit to do a thing like that for a fellow. . . and. . . I've loved you like the dickens ever since I met you. . . I do wish you'd have a stab at it, Sally. At least I could look after you, you know, and all that. . . I mean to say, work like the deuce and try to give you a good time. . . I'm not such an ass as to think a girl like you could ever really. . . er. . . love a blighter like me, but. . ."

Sally laid her hand on his.

"Ginger, dear," she said, "I do love you. I ought to have known it all along, but I seem to be understanding myself to-night for the first time." She got up and bent over him for a swift moment, whispering in his ear, "I shall never love anyone but you, Ginger. Will you try to remember that." She was moving away, but he caught at her arm and stopped her.

"Sally. . ."

She pulled her arm away, her face working as she fought against the tears that would not keep back.

"I've made a fool of myself," she said. "Ginger, your cousin. . . Mr. Carmyle. . . just now he asked me to marry him, and I said I would."

She was gone, flitting among the tables like some wild creature running to its home: and Ginger, motionless, watched her go.

5

THE TELEPHONE-BELL IN SALLY'S LITTLE sitting-room was ringing jerkily as she let herself in at the front door. She guessed who it was at the other end of the wire, and the noise of the bell sounded to her like the voice of a friend in distress crying for help. Without stopping to close the door, she ran to the table and unhooked the receiver. Muffled, plaintive sounds were coming over the wire.

"Hullo. . . Hullo. . . I say. . . Hullo. . ."

"Hullo, Ginger," said Sally quietly.

An exclamation that was half a shout and half gurgle answered her.

"Sally! Is that you?"

"Yes, here I am, Ginger."

"I've been trying to get you for ages."

"I've only just come in. I walked home."

There was a pause.

"Hullo."

"Yes?"

"Well, I mean. . ." Ginger seemed to be finding his usual difficulty in expressing himself. "About that, you know. What you said."

"Yes?" said Sally, trying to keep her voice from shaking.

"You said. . ." Again Ginger's vocabulary failed him. "You said you loved me."

"Yes," said Sally simply.

Another odd sound floated over the wire, and there was a moment of silence before Ginger found himself able to resume.

"I. . . I. . . Well, we can talk about that when we meet. I mean, it's no good trying to say what I think over the 'phone, I'm sort of knocked out. I never dreamed. . . But, I say, what did you mean about Bruce?"

"I told you, I told you." Sally's face was twisted and the receiver shook in her hand. "I've made a fool of myself. I never realized. . . And now it's too late."

"Good God!" Ginger's voice rose in a sharp wail. "You can't mean you really. . . You don't seriously intend to marry the man?"

"I must. I've promised."

"But, good heavens. . ."

"It's no good. I must."

"But the man's a blighter!"

"I can't break my word."

"I never heard such rot," said Ginger vehemently. "Of course you can. A girl isn't expected. . ."

"I can't, Ginger dear, I really can't."

"But look here. . ."

"It's really no good talking about it any more, really it isn't. . . Where are you staying to-night?"

"Staying? Me? At the Plaza. But look here. . ."

Sally found herself laughing weakly.

"At the Plaza! Oh, Ginger, you really do want somebody to look after you. Squandering your pennies like that. . . Well, don't talk any more now. It's so late and I'm so tired. I'll come and see you to-morrow. Good night."

She hung up the receiver quickly, to cut short a fresh outburst of protest. And as she turned away a voice spoke behind her.

"Sally!"

Gerald Foster was standing in the doorway.

XVII

SALLY LAYS A GHOST

1

THE BLOOD FLOWED SLOWLY BACK into Sally's face, and her heart, which had leaped madly for an instant at the sound of his voice, resumed its normal beat. The suddenness of the shock over, she was surprised to find herself perfectly calm. Always when she had imagined this meeting, knowing that it would have to take place sooner or later, she had felt something akin to panic: but now that it had actually occurred it hardly seemed to stir her. The events of the night had left her incapable of any violent emotion.

"Hullo, Sally!" said Gerald.

He spoke thickly, and there was a foolish smile on his face as he stood swaying with one hand on the door. He was in his shirt-sleeves, collarless: and it was plain that he had been drinking heavily. His face was white and puffy, and about him there hung like a nimbus a sodden disreputableness.

Sally did not speak. Weighed down before by a numbing exhaustion, she seemed now to have passed into that second phase in which over-tired nerves enter upon a sort of Indian summer of abnormal alertness. She looked at him quietly, coolly and altogether dispassionately, as if he had been a stranger.

"Hullo!" said Gerald again.

"What do you want?" said Sally.

"Heard your voice. Saw the door open. Thought I'd come in."

"What do you want?"

The weak smile which had seemed pinned on Gerald's face vanished. A tear rolled down his cheek. His intoxication had reached the maudlin stage.

"Sally. . . S-Sally. . . I'm very miserable." He slurred awkwardly over the difficult syllables. "Heard your voice. Saw the door open. Thought I'd come in."

Something flicked at the back of Sally's mind. She seemed to have been through all this before. Then she remembered. This was simply Mr. Reginald Cracknell over again.

"I think you had better go to bed, Gerald," she said steadily. Nothing about him seemed to touch her now, neither the sight of him nor his shameless misery.

"What's the use? Can't sleep. No good. Couldn't sleep. Sally, you don't know how worried I am. I see what a fool I've been."

Sally made a quick gesture, to check what she supposed was about to develop into a belated expression of regret for his treatment of herself. She did not want to stand there listening to Gerald apologizing with tears for having done his best to wreck her life. But it seemed that it was not this that was weighing upon his soul.

"I was a fool ever to try writing plays," he went on. "Got a winner first time, but can't repeat. It's no good. Ought to have stuck to newspaper work. I'm good at that. Shall have to go back to it. Had another frost to-night. No good trying any more. Shall have to go back to the old grind, damn it."

He wept softly, full of pity for his hard case.

"Very miserable," he murmured.

He came forward a step into the room, lurched, and retreated to the safe support of the door. For an instant Sally's artificial calm was shot through by a swift stab of contempt. It passed, and she was back again in her armour of indifference.

"Go to bed, Gerald," she said. "You'll feel better in the morning."

Perhaps some inkling of how he was going to feel in the morning worked through to Gerald's muddled intelligence, for he winced, and his manner took on a deeper melancholy.

"May not be alive in the morning," he said solemnly. "Good mind to end it all. End it all!" he repeated with the beginning of a sweeping gesture which was cut off abruptly as he clutched at the friendly door.

Sally was not in the mood for melodrama.

"Oh, go to bed," she said impatiently. The strange frozen indifference which had gripped her was beginning to pass, leaving in its place a growing feeling of resentment—resentment against Gerald for degrading himself like this, against herself for ever having found glamour in the man. It humiliated her to remember how utterly she had once allowed his personality to master hers. And under the sting of this humiliation she felt hard and pitiless. Dimly she was aware that a curious change had come over her to-night. Normally, the sight of any living thing in distress was enough to stir her quick sympathy: but Gerald mourning over the prospect of having to go back to regular work made no appeal to her—a fact which the sufferer noted and commented upon.

"You're very unsymp. . . unsympathetic," he complained.

"I'm sorry," said Sally. She walked briskly to the door and gave it a push. Gerald, still clinging to his chosen support, moved out into the passage, attached to the handle, with the air of a man the foundations of whose world have suddenly lost their stability. He released the handle and moved uncertainly across the passage. Finding his own door open before him, he staggered over the threshold; and Sally, having watched him safely to his journey's end, went into her bedroom with the intention of terminating this disturbing night by going to sleep.

Almost immediately she changed her mind. Sleep was out of the question. A fever of restlessness had come upon her. She put on a kimono, and went into the kitchen to ascertain whether her commissariat arrangements would permit of a glass of hot milk.

She had just remembered that she had that morning presented the last of the milk to a sandy cat with a purposeful eye which had dropped in through the window to take breakfast with her, when her regrets for this thriftless hospitality were interrupted by a muffled crash.

She listened intently. The sound had seemed to come from across the passage. She hurried to the door and opened it. As she did so, from behind the door of the apartment opposite there came a perfect fusillade of crashes, each seeming to her strained hearing louder and more appalling than the last.

There is something about sudden, loud noises in the stillness of the night which shatters the most rigid detachment. A short while before, Gerald, toying with the idea of ending his sorrows by violence, had left Sally unmoved: but now her mind leapt back to what he had said, and apprehension succeeded indifference. There was no disputing the fact that Gerald was in an irresponsible mood, under the influence of which he was capable of doing almost anything. Sally, listening in the doorway, felt a momentary panic.

A brief silence had succeeded the fusillade, but, as she stood there hesitating, the noise broke out again; and this time it was so loud and compelling that Sally hesitated no longer. She ran across the passage and beat on the door.

2

WHATEVER DEVASTATING HAPPENINGS HAD BEEN going on in his home, it was plain a moment later that Gerald had managed to survive them: for there came the sound of a dragging footstep, and the door opened. Gerald stood on the threshold, the weak smile back on his face.

"Hullo, Sally!"

At the sight of him, disreputable and obviously unscathed, Sally's brief alarm died away, leaving in its place the old feeling of impatient resentment. In addition to her other grievances against him, he had apparently frightened her unnecessarily.

"Whatever was all that noise?" she demanded.

"Noise?" said Gerald, considering the point open-mouthed.

"Yes, noise," snapped Sally.

"I've been cleaning house," said Gerald with the owl-like gravity of a man just conscious that he is not wholly himself.

Sally pushed her way past him. The apartment in which she found herself was almost an exact replica of her own, and it was evident that Elsa Doland had taken pains to make it pretty and comfortable in a niggly feminine way. Amateur interior decoration had always been a hobby of hers. Even in the unpromising surroundings of her bedroom at Mrs. Meecher's boarding-house she had contrived to create a certain daintiness which Sally, who had no ability in that direction herself, had always rather envied. As a decorator Elsa's mind ran in the direction of small, fragile ornaments, and she was not afraid of over-furnishing. Pictures jostled one another on the walls: china of all description stood about on little tables: there was a profusion of lamps with shades of parti-coloured glass: and plates were ranged along a series of shelves.

One says that the plates were ranged and the pictures jostled one another, but it would be more correct to put it they had jostled and had been ranged, for it was only by guess-work that Sally was able to reconstruct the scene as it must have appeared before Gerald had started, as he put it, to clean house. She had walked into the flat briskly enough, but she pulled up short as she crossed the threshold, appalled by the majestic ruin that met her gaze. A shell bursting in the little sitting-room could hardly have created more havoc.

The psychology of a man of weak character under the influence of alcohol and disappointed ambition is not easy to plumb, for his moods follow one another with a rapidity which baffles the observer. Ten minutes before, Gerald Foster had been in the grip of a clammy self-pity, and it seemed from his aspect at the present moment that this phase had returned. But in the interval there had manifestly occurred a brief but adequate spasm of what would appear to have been an almost

Berserk fury. What had caused it and why it should have expended itself so abruptly, Sally was not psychologist enough to explain; but that it had existed there was ocular evidence of the most convincing kind. A heavy niblick, flung petulantly—or remorsefully—into a corner, showed by what medium the destruction had been accomplished.

Bleak chaos appeared on every side. The floor was littered with every imaginable shape and size of broken glass and china. Fragments of pictures, looking as if they had been chewed by some prehistoric animal, lay amid heaps of shattered statuettes and vases. As Sally moved slowly into the room after her involuntary pause, china crackled beneath her feet. She surveyed the stripped walls with a wondering eye, and turned to Gerald for an explanation.

Gerald had subsided on to an occasional table, and was weeping softly again. It had come over him once more that he had been very, very badly treated.

"Well!" said Sally with a gasp. "You've certainly made a good job of it!"

There was a sharp crack as the occasional table, never designed by its maker to bear heavy weights, gave way in a splintering flurry of broken legs under the pressure of the master of the house: and Sally's mood underwent an abrupt change. There are few situations in life which do not hold equal potentialities for both tragedy and farce, and it was the ludicrous side of this drama that chanced to appeal to Sally at this moment. Her sense of humour was tickled. It was, if she could have analysed her feelings, at herself that she was mocking—at the feeble sentimental Sally who had once conceived the absurd idea of taking this preposterous man seriously. She felt light-hearted and light-headed, and she sank into a chair with a gurgling laugh.

The shock of his fall appeared to have had the desirable effect of restoring Gerald to something approaching intelligence. He picked himself up from the remains of a set of water-colours, gazing at Sally with growing disapproval.

"No sympathy," he said austerely.

"I can't help it," cried Sally. "It's too funny."

"Not funny," corrected Gerald, his brain beginning to cloud once more. "What did you do it for?"

Gerald returned for a moment to that mood of honest indignation, which had so strengthened his arm when wielding the niblick. He bethought him once again of his grievance.

"Wasn't going to stand for it any longer," he said heatedly. "A fellow's wife goes and lets him down. . . ruins his show by going off and playing in another show. . . why shouldn't I smash her things? Why should I stand for that sort of treatment? Why should I?"

"Well, you haven't," said Sally, "so there's no need to discuss it. You seem to have acted in a thoroughly manly and independent way."

"That's it. Manly independent." He waggled his finger impressively. "Don't care what she says," he continued. "Don't care if she never comes back. That woman. . ."

Sally was not prepared to embark with him upon a discussion of the absent Elsa. Already the amusing aspect of the affair had begun to fade, and her hilarity was giving way to a tired distaste for the sordidness of the whole business. She had become aware that she could not endure the society of Gerald Foster much longer. She got up and spoke decidedly.

"And now," she said, "I'm going to tidy up."

Gerald had other views.

"No," he said with sudden solemnity. "No! Nothing of the kind. Leave it for her to find. Leave it as it is."

"Don't be silly. All this has got to be cleaned up. I'll do it. You go and sit in my apartment. I'll come and tell you when you can come back."

"No!" said Gerald, wagging his head.

Sally stamped her foot among the crackling ruins. Quite suddenly the sight of him had become intolerable.

"Do as I tell you," she cried.

Gerald wavered for a moment, but his brief militant mood was ebbing fast. After a faint protest he shuffled off, and Sally heard him go into her room. She breathed a deep breath of relief and turned to her task.

A visit to the kitchen revealed a long-handled broom, and, armed with this, Sally was soon busy. She was an efficient little person, and presently out of chaos there began to emerge a certain order. Nothing short of complete re-decoration would ever make the place look habitable again, but at the end of half an hour she had cleared the floor, and the fragments of vases, plates, lamp-shades, pictures and glasses were stacked in tiny heaps against the walls. She returned the broom to the kitchen, and, going back into the sitting-room, flung open the window and stood looking out.

With a sense of unreality she perceived that the night had gone.

P.G. WODEHOUSE

Over the quiet street below there brooded that strange, metallic light which ushers in the dawn of a fine day. A cold breeze whispered to and fro. Above the house-tops the sky was a faint, level blue.

She left the window and started to cross the room. And suddenly there came over her a feeling of utter weakness. She stumbled to a chair, conscious only of being tired beyond the possibility of a further effort. Her eyes closed, and almost before her head had touched the cushions she was asleep.

3

SALLY WOKE. SUNSHINE WAS STREAMING through the open window, and with it the myriad noises of a city awake and about its business. Footsteps clattered on the sidewalk, automobile horns were sounding, and she could hear the clank of street cars as they passed over the points. She could only guess at the hour, but it was evident that the morning was well advanced. She got up stiffly. Her head was aching.

She went into the bathroom, bathed her face, and felt better. The dull oppression which comes of a bad night was leaving her. She leaned out of the window, revelling in the fresh air, then crossed the passage and entered her own apartment. Stertorous breathing greeted her, and she perceived that Gerald Foster had also passed the night in a chair. He was sprawling by the window with his legs stretched out and his head resting on one of the arms, an unlovely spectacle.

Sally stood regarding him for a moment with a return of the distaste which she had felt on the previous night. And yet, mingled with the distaste, there was a certain elation. A black chapter of her life was closed for ever. Whatever the years to come might bring to her, they would be free from any wistful yearnings for the man who had once been woven so inextricably into the fabric of her life. She had thought that his personality had gripped her too strongly ever to be dislodged, but now she could look at him calmly and feel only a faint half-pity, half-contempt. The glamour had departed.

She shook him gently, and he sat up with a start, blinking in the strong light. His mouth was still open. He stared at Sally foolishly, then scrambled awkwardly out of the chair.

"Oh, my God!" said Gerald, pressing both his hands to his forehead and sitting down again. He licked his lips with a dry tongue and moaned. "Oh, I've got a headache!"

Sally might have pointed out to him that he had certainly earned one, but she refrained.

"You'd better go and have a wash," she suggested.

"Yes," said Gerald, heaving himself up again.

"Would you like some breakfast?"

"Don't!" said Gerald faintly, and tottered off to the bathroom.

Sally sat down in the chair he had vacated. She had never felt quite like this before in her life. Everything seemed dreamlike. The splashing of water in the bathroom came faintly to her, and she realized that she had been on the point of falling asleep again. She got up and opened the window, and once more the air acted as a restorative. She watched the activities of the street with a distant interest. They, too, seemed dreamlike and unreal. People were hurrying up and down on mysterious errands. An inscrutable cat picked its way daintily across the road. At the door of the apartment house an open car purred sleepily.

She was roused by a ring at the bell. She went to the door and opened it, and found Bruce Carmyle standing on the threshold. He wore a light motor-coat, and he was plainly endeavouring to soften the severity of his saturnine face with a smile of beaming kindliness.

"Well, here I am!" said Bruce Carmyle cheerily. "Are you ready?"

With the coming of daylight a certain penitence had descended on Mr. Carmyle. Thinking things over while shaving and subsequently in his bath, he had come to the conclusion that his behaviour overnight had not been all that could have been desired. He had not actually been brutal, perhaps, but he had undoubtedly not been winning. There had been an abruptness in the manner of his leaving Sally at the Flower Garden which a perfect lover ought not to have shown. He had allowed his nerves to get the better of him, and now he desired to make amends. Hence a cheerfulness which he did not usually exhibit so early in the morning.

Sally was staring at him blankly. She had completely forgotten that he had said that he would come and take her for a drive this morning. She searched in her mind for words, and found none. And, as Mr. Carmyle was debating within himself whether to kiss her now or wait for a more suitable moment, embarrassment came upon them both like a fog, and the genial smile faded from his face as if the motive-power behind it had suddenly failed.

"I've—er—got the car outside, and. . ."

At this point speech failed Mr. Carmyle, for, even as he began the sentence, the door that led to the bathroom opened and Gerald Foster came out. Mr. Carmyle gaped at Gerald: Gerald gaped at Mr. Carmyle.

The application of cold water to the face and head is an excellent thing on the morning after an imprudent night, but as a tonic it only goes part of the way. In the case of Gerald Foster, which was an extremely serious and aggravated case, it had gone hardly any way at all. The person unknown who had been driving red-hot rivets into the base of Gerald Foster's skull ever since the moment of his awakening was still busily engaged on that task. He gazed at Mr. Carmyle wanly.

Bruce Carmyle drew in his breath with a sharp hiss, and stood rigid. His eyes, burning now with a grim light, flickered over Gerald's person and found nothing in it to entertain them. He saw a slouching figure in shirt-sleeves and the foundations of evening dress, a disgusting, degraded figure with pink eyes and a white face that needed a shave. And all the doubts that had ever come to vex Mr. Carmyle's mind since his first meeting with Sally became on the instant certainties. So Uncle Donald had been right after all! This was the sort of girl she was!

At his elbow the stout phantom of Uncle Donald puffed with satisfaction.

"I told you so!" it said.

Sally had not moved. The situation was beyond her. Just as if this had really been the dream it seemed, she felt incapable of speech or action.

"So. . ." said Mr. Carmyle, becoming articulate, and allowed an impressive aposiopesis to take the place of the rest of the speech. A cold fury had gripped him. He pointed at Gerald, began to speak, found that he was stuttering, and gulped back the words. In this supreme moment he was not going to have his dignity impaired by a stutter. He gulped and found a sentence which, while brief enough to insure against this disaster, was sufficiently long to express his meaning.

"Get out!" he said.

Gerald Foster had his dignity, too, and it seemed to him that the time had come to assert it. But he also had a most excruciating headache, and when he drew himself up haughtily to ask Mr. Carmyle what the devil he meant by it, a severe access of pain sent him huddling back immediately to a safer attitude. He clasped his forehead and groaned.

"Get out!"

For a moment Gerald hesitated. Then another sudden shooting spasm convinced him that no profit or pleasure was to be derived from a continuance of the argument, and he began to shamble slowly across to the door. Bruce Carmyle watched him go with twitching hands. There was a moment when the human man in him, somewhat atrophied from long disuse, stirred him almost to the point of assault; then dignity whispered more prudent counsel in his ear, and Gerald was past the danger-zone and out in the passage. Mr. Carmyle turned to face Sally, as King Arthur on a similar but less impressive occasion must have turned to deal with Guinevere.

"So. . ." he said again.

Sally was eyeing him steadily—considering the circumstances, Mr. Carmyle thought with not a little indignation, much too steadily.

"This," he said ponderously, "is very amusing."

He waited for her to speak, but she said nothing.

"I might have expected it," said Mr. Carmyle with a bitter laugh.

Sally forced herself from the lethargy which was gripping her.

"Would you like me to explain?" she said.

"There can be no explanation," said Mr. Carmyle coldly.

"Very well," said Sally.

There was a pause.

"Good-bye," said Bruce Carmyle.

"Good-bye," said Sally.

Mr. Carmyle walked to the door. There he stopped for an instant and glanced back at her. Sally had walked to the window and was looking out. For one swift instant something about her trim little figure and the gleam of her hair where the sunlight shone on it seemed to catch at Bruce Carmyle's heart, and he wavered. But the next moment he was strong again, and the door had closed behind him with a resolute bang.

Out in the street, climbing into his car, he looked up involuntarily to see if she was still there, but she had gone. As the car, gathering speed, hummed down the street. Sally was at the telephone listening to the sleepy voice of Ginger Kemp, which, as he became aware who it was that had woken him from his rest and what she had to say to him, magically lost its sleepiness and took on a note of riotous ecstasy.

Five minutes later, Ginger was splashing in his bath, singing discordantly.

XVIII

JOURNEY'S END

Darkness was beginning to gather slowly and with almost an apologetic air, as if it regretted the painful duty of putting an end to the perfect summer day. Over to the west beyond the trees there still lingered a faint afterglow, and a new moon shone like a silver sickle above the big barn. Sally came out of the house and bowed gravely three times for luck. She stood on the gravel, outside the porch, drinking in the sweet evening scents, and found life good.

The darkness, having shown a certain reluctance at the start, was now buckling down to make a quick and thorough job of it. The sky turned to a uniform dark blue, picked out with quiet stars. The cement of the state road which led to Patchogue, Babylon, and other important centres ceased to be a pale blur and became invisible. Lights appeared in the windows of the houses across the meadows. From the direction of the kennels there came a single sleepy bark, and the small white woolly dog which had scampered out at Sally's heels stopped short and uttered a challenging squeak.

The evening was so still that Ginger's footsteps, as he pounded along the road on his way back from the village, whither he had gone to buy provisions, evening papers, and wool for the sweater which Sally was knitting, were audible long before he turned in at the gate. Sally could not see him, but she looked in the direction of the sound and once again felt that pleasant, cosy thrill of happiness which had come to her every evening for the last year.

"Ginger," she called.

"What ho!"

The woolly dog, with another important squeak, scuttled down the drive to look into the matter, and was coldly greeted. Ginger, for all his love of dogs, had never been able to bring himself to regard Toto with affection. He had protested when Sally, a month before, finding Mrs. Meecher distraught on account of a dreadful lethargy which had seized her pet, had begged him to offer hospitality and country air to the invalid.

"It's wonderful what you've done for Toto, angel," said Sally, as he came up frigidly eluding that curious animal's leaps of welcome. "He's a different dog."

"Bit of luck for him," said Ginger.

"In all the years I was at Mrs. Meecher's I never knew him move at anything more rapid than a stately walk. Now he runs about all the time."

"The blighter had been overeating from birth," said Ginger. "That was all that was wrong with him. A little judicious dieting put him right. We'll be able," said Ginger brightening, "to ship him back next week."

"I shall quite miss him."

"I nearly missed him—this morning—with a shoe," said Ginger. "He was up on the kitchen table wolfing the bacon, and I took steps."

"My cave-man!" murmured Sally. "I always said you had a frightfully brutal streak in you. Ginger, what an evening!"

"Good Lord!" said Ginger suddenly, as they walked into the light of the open kitchen door.

"Now what?"

He stopped and eyed her intently.

"Do you know you're looking prettier than you were when I started down to the village!"

Sally gave his arm a little hug.

"Beloved!" she said. "Did you get the chops?"

Ginger froze in his tracks, horrified.

"Oh, my aunt! I clean forgot them!"

"Oh, Ginger, you are an old chump. Well, you'll have to go in for a little judicious dieting, like Toto."

"I say, I'm most awfully sorry. I got the wool."

"If you think I'm going to eat wool. . ."

"Isn't there anything in the house?"

"Vegetables and fruit."

"Fine! But, of course, if you want chops. . ."

"Not at all. I'm spiritual. Besides, people say that vegetables are good for the blood-pressure or something. Of course you forgot to get the mail, too?"

"Absolutely not! I was on to it like a knife. Two letters from fellows wanting Airedale puppies."

"No! Ginger, we are getting on!"

"Pretty bloated," agreed Ginger complacently. "Pretty bloated. We'll be able to get that two-seater if things go buzzing on like this. There was a letter for you. Here it is."

"It's from Fillmore," said Sally, examining the envelope as they went into the kitchen. "And about time, too. I haven't had a word from him for months."

She sat down and opened the letter. Ginger, heaving himself on to the table, wriggled into a position of comfort and started to read his evening paper. But after he had skimmed over the sporting page he lowered it and allowed his gaze to rest on Sally's bent head with a feeling of utter contentment.

Although a married man of nearly a year's standing, Ginger was still moving about a magic world in a state of dazed incredulity, unable fully to realize that such bliss could be. Ginger in his time had seen many things that looked good from a distance, but not one that had borne the test of a closer acquaintance—except this business of marriage.

Marriage, with Sally for a partner, seemed to be one of the very few things in the world in which there was no catch. His honest eyes glowed as he watched her. Sally broke into a little splutter of laughter.

"Ginger, look at this!"

He reached down and took the slip of paper which she held out to him. The following legend met his eye, printed in bold letters:

POPP'S

OUTSTANDING

SUCCULENT—APPETIZING—NUTRITIOUS.
(JUST SAY "POP!" A CHILD CAN DO IT.)

Ginger regarded this cipher with a puzzled frown.

"What is it?" he asked.

"It's Fillmore."

"How do you mean?"

Sally gurgled.

"Fillmore and Gladys have started a little restaurant in Pittsburg."

"A restaurant!" There was a shocked note in Ginger's voice. Although he knew that the managerial career of that modern Napoleon, his brother-in-law, had terminated in something of a smash, he had never quite lost his reverence for one whom he considered a bit of a master-mind. That Fillmore Nicholas, the Man of Destiny, should have descended to conducting a restaurant—and a little restaurant at that—struck him as almost indecent.

Sally, on the other hand—for sisters always seem to fail in proper reverence for the greatness of their brothers—was delighted.

"It's the most splendid idea," she said with enthusiasm. "It really does look as if Fillmore was going to amount to something at last. Apparently they started on quite a small scale, just making pork-pies. . ."

"Why Popp?" interrupted Ginger, ventilating a question which was perplexing him deeply.

"Just a trade name, silly. Gladys is a wonderful cook, you know, and she made the pies and Fillmore toddled round selling them. And they did so well that now they've started a regular restaurant, and that's a success, too. Listen to this." Sally gurgled again and turned over the letter. "Where is it? Oh yes! '. . . sound financial footing. In fact, our success has been so instantaneous that I have decided to launch out on a really big scale. It is Big Ideas that lead to Big Business. I am contemplating a vast extension of this venture of ours, and in a very short time I shall organize branches in New York, Chicago, Detroit, and all the big cities, each in charge of a manager and each offering as a special feature, in addition to the usual restaurant cuisine, these Popp's Outstanding Pork-pies of ours. That done, and having established all these branches as going concerns, I shall sail for England and introduce Popp's Pork-pies there. . .' Isn't he a little wonder!"

"Dashed brainy chap. Always said so."

"I must say I was rather uneasy when I read that. I've seen so many of Fillmore's Big Ideas. That's always the way with him. He gets something good and then goes and overdoes it and bursts. However, it's all right now that he's got Gladys to look after him. She has added a postscript. Just four words, but oh! how comforting to a sister's heart. 'Yes, I don't think!' is what she says, and I don't know when I've read anything more cheering. Thank heaven, she's got poor dear Fillmore well in hand."

"Pork-pies!" said Ginger, musingly, as the pangs of a healthy hunger began to assail his interior. "I wish he'd sent us one of the outstanding little chaps. I could do with it."

Sally got up and ruffled his red hair.

"Poor old Ginger! I knew you'd never be able to stick it. Come on, it's a lovely night, let's walk to the village and revel at the inn. We're going to be millionaires before we know where we are, so we can afford it."

THE END

A Note About the Author

Sir Pelham Grenville Wodehouse (1881–1975) was an English author. Though he was named after his godfather, the author was not a fan of his name and more commonly went by P.G. Wodehouse. Known for his comedic work, Wodehouse created reoccurring characters that became a beloved staple of his literature. Though most of his work was set in London, Wodehouse also spent a fair amount of time in the United States. Much of his work was converted into "American" versions, and he wrote a series of Broadway musicals that helped lead to the development of the American musical. P.G. Wodehouse's eclectic and prolific canon of work both in Europe and America developed him to be one of the most widely read humorists of the 20th century.

A Note from the Publisher

Spanning many genres, from non-fiction essays to literature classics to children's books and lyric poetry, Mint Edition books showcase the master works of our time in a modern new package. The text is freshly typeset, is clean and easy to read, and features a new note about the author in each volume. Many books also include exclusive new introductory material. Every book boasts a striking new cover, which makes it as appropriate for collecting as it is for gift giving. Mint Edition books are only printed when a reader orders them, so natural resources are not wasted. We're proud that our books are never manufactured in excess and exist only in the exact quantity they need to be read and enjoyed.

Discover more of your favorite classics with Bookfinity™.

- Track your reading with custom book lists.
- Get great book recommendations for your personalized Reader Type.
- Add reviews for your favorite books.
- AND MUCH MORE!

Visit **bookfinity.com** and take the fun Reader Type quiz to get started.

Enjoy our classic and modern companion pairings!